The Last Beach Night

book design and layout: SpiNDec, Port Saint Lucie, FL
cover design: Kris Haggblom

Printed in the United States of America.

Published by Poetic Justice Books
Port Saint Lucie, Florida
www.poeticjusticebooks.com

ISBN: 978-1-950433-15-5

10 9 8 7 6 5 4 3 2

Richard Pruitt
The Last Beach Night

Poetic Justice Books & Arts
Port Saint Lucie, Florida

To Donna
Without her encouragement, this novel would never have happened

For
Alex, Nick & Will

Thank you to ...
My colleagues at the Morningside Library
Writers Group, especially
Gene, Allan, Judith - with a double thank you to Kris.

The Last Beach Night

RICHARD PRUITT

CHAPTER ONE

The Umpqua River, Oregon, June 1954

The U.S. Coast Guard blocked his route into the Pacific. Frustrated, John Abernathy aimed his longboat up-river. He knew he couldn't outrun his pursuers. His outboard motor was already wide open. Full speed ahead.

He glanced back and saw a man with a rifle in the faster, Chris-Craft fishing charter. He turned his head from side to side, searching the shoreline. He spotted something on the west bank – a decaying dock with inlaid, concrete steps leading upward through the dense, Douglas fir forest . . . *leading to freedom. To Canada and his new woman, Debbie, who was waiting for him.*

Decision time: His confidence surged. Once on dry land he could outrun his pursuers! Give up the boat but steal a car and head north. Better yet, steal a big pick-up truck with a V8.

Abernathy rammed his boat into the shoreline and scrambled up the steps. The first bullet slammed into the bank inches from his head.

He continued up the steps. A second bullet thunked just under his right arm.

Douglas County Sheriff Henry Stark, cursed the rifle's sight, then realized it was aligned for a shorter man. He bent his knees, squinted over the rifle. Two rounds left.

Abernathy thought, maybe he should just stop and raise his hands, the man shooting must be a cop, what the hell, *two warning shots.* Maybe it was time to give up. There weren't any witnesses to his attack on the prissy bitch on the beach. *No live enemies.* What could they prove? The girl couldn't have seen his face. Dodd would tell no tales. The faggot, Tim, and the feisty almost-cousin could say he kidnapped them, but he could say it was a prank that went too far. Portman was his buddy now, a kindred spirit. The voice told him . . . *Surrender.*

He raised his hands, turned toward the man with the rifle and shouted, "Don't shoot. I give up!"

Five days earlier

The Siuslaw River crawls into the Pacific Ocean between ever-shifting, four-hundred-foot-high sand dunes near the town of Florence, Oregon. John Abernathy had been living with his mother in a houseboat three miles up the Siuslaw. John was a loner, although he did have one friend, Terry Dodd. Dodd owned a car and never disagreed with "Big John."

As a loner, John had a habit of talking to himself. "Time to move on," he told his image in the mirror above the bathroom sink in his mother's houseboat. He cocked his head, the way John Wayne did in his favorite movie, *Stagecoach*, and then continued buttoning his new shirt. He wished his widowed mother owned a full-length mirror so he could really check out how he looked.

It was the first time he'd worn the beige and green Pendleton he'd stolen from Florence Dry Goods & Clothiers. He figured if he'd worn the shirt in downtown Florence, the storeowner would see him and report the theft to the sheriff. A voice within his head, a voice only he could hear, had warned him not to wear the shirt in Florence. He always heeded the warnings of *the voice*.

Surely, the proprietor had missed the shirt and suspected John. But what proof did he have? *Today*, John thought, *being caught with the goods on him wasn't a worry*. He'd be long gone in Dodd's Plymouth.

John stuffed his remaining clothes and the 300 Savage deer rifle he'd inherited from his father into a large, dark-green duffle bag. He paused, stood still, then looked around the room. He had a feeling he'd forgotten something. He snapped his fingers. "My seaman's hat!"

He found it on the shelf in his closet, flipped it into the bag, zipped up his belongings and walked out the door. He made his way along the floating gangplank in front of the houseboats.

Ron Monroe was taking his chainsaw into the HomeLite dealer for servicing and drove by in his Chevy pick-up just as John reached the road. Ron stopped. It was better to offer Big John a lift than pass him by and risk a dose of Abernathy-wrath.

"Nice shirt," Ron called through the open window. "You're looking sharp, big guy."

Abernathy opened the passenger door. "Yeah, well, you look like shit."

Ron laughed, as if John had said something witty. "Where can I drop you?"

"Barbershop. Dodd's picking me up there."

Ron had noticed the duffel bag when John hefted it into the back of the pick-up. "Going outta town?"

"What's it to ya?"

Ron shrugged. "Nothing. Just making conversation."

To Ron's surprise, Abernathy gave him a straight answer. "No work in this piss-ant town. Me and Dodd are heading for Coos Bay. I'll find something there; maybe even do some boxing on the side. If I could find me the right manager, I could be a champion."

Ron nodded as if he agreed. Like everyone in Florence, he'd been delighted to hear the town's least favorite native son had been soundly thrashed by a black man in a boxing match in the Eugene Armory.

They drove in silence until Ron double-parked his pick-up in front of Red's Barbershop. "Here you go, Big John. Good luck in Coos Bay."

"Got a cigarette?" John demanded.

"Sure." Ron pointed to a pack of Camels on his dashboard. "Help yourself."

"Don't mind if I do." Abernathy grabbed the pack, slid out of the front seat and retrieved his belongings.

CHAPTER TWO

About the same time Big John was stepping into Red's Barber Shop in Florence, Jack Portman, a just-graduated senior from Reedsport, was asked to crew aboard a salmon fishing charter out of Winchester Bay. The bay is where the Umpqua River ends and the Pacific Ocean begins. It's located about twenty-five miles south of Florence, five miles south of Reedsport and twenty-five miles north of Coos Bay.

Jack didn't want the job. However, his mother, who owned and operated The Dock Tavern, insisted. "Harry's got himself a charter with that rich lawyer, McDonnell. I've told you about him. You don't say no to McDonnell. Twenty bucks now, twenty later and you don't have to split the tip with Harry. You'll be home in plenty of time for your Senior Beach Party. Do it for me, sweetie," she said as she stuffed the first Andrew Jackson into his shirt pocket and gave him a motherly peck on the cheek.

Captain Harry Norton's cabin cruiser was named *Greta* after Jack's mother. The captain, a devout bachelor, didn't entertain romantic notions about Greta Portman. His motivation was simple: The proprietor of The Dock Tavern was in a position to refer a lot of charter business. Harry wanted to stay at the top of Greta Portman's referral list.

With Jack as crew and McDonnell and his guest aboard, Harry steered *Greta* across a choppy Umpqua River bar and turned southwest into the endless Pacific. He cruised at twenty knots over to an area where he'd had action earlier in the week. Adjusting his speed to a slow troll, he swung the boat under a flock of gulls.

"This water looks real fishy," Harry shouted over the noise of his Mercury inboard. Jack flipped two lines overboard, each baited with a live pilchard. He then handed a rod to the big shot, McDonnell.

Jack said nothing. It was obvious McDonnell knew what he was doing.

Jack handed a second rod to the VIP's guest and instructed, "Forty-to-fifty yards and set the drag. Looks real fishy," he added, echoing his skipper.

Harry Norton knew his ocean. Within five minutes two fish hit, almost simultaneously. The salmon put up a good fight but were no match for the thirty-pound test line. Jack handled the net expertly and they boated two twelve-pound Cohoes. While the fishermen celebrated – shaking hands and slapping each other on the back – Jack slipped fresh pilchards onto the hooks and flipped them overboard. This time he let out the lines, set the drags and placed the butt-end of the poles into metal rod-holders.

Jack watched the VIP's guest open a pint of Jim Beam Whiskey, hold it skyward and then offer it to his host. The VIP waved it away. The guest slurped down four or five ounces.

McDonnell looked over at Jack and rolled his eyes as if to say, "We both know what happens next."

As the boat bounced and swayed over the up-and-down, up-and-down wave action, Jack and McDonnell watched the guest throw up his breakfast.

McDonnell, who wasn't the slightest bit sick, turned to Jack, "What the hell are we supposed to do, son? Go for our limit or let the poor bastard die?"

Jack couldn't help but smile at the words, "Let the poor bastard die." He bit the side of his cheek to stifle a laugh and said, "He won't get any better out here, sir."

McDonnell smiled, "No he won't." Then he took a closer look at Jack. "You wouldn't happen to be a senior in high school?"

"Yes, sir."

"Are you going to that crazy Beach Night? I understand why kids did that during the war. One last party before the government sends you to Europe or Asia to die – or if you were female – you got to do a *man's* job until the boys came marching home. But now? Your Beach Night, well, it makes no sense."

"Well, sir, yes, I'm going. Looking forward to it."

Pleasantly surprised by the young man's candor, McDonnell flashed a smile before saying, "Do me a favor?"

"Just ask, sir."

"Well, if you have the balls to approach the Coos Bay bonfire, live to tell about it and then come across my daughter, keep on walking. You're just the kind of good-looking kid she's going to fall for and I can be one mean son of a bitch when I have to be. Trust me, you don't want to mess with my daughter."

Jack stared back at the VIP in disbelief. A question flashed in his eyes: What the hell are you talking about? He didn't have to say it.

McDonnell held up his right hand, a gesture of peace. "I'm sorry, kiddo. Jack, is it? You're Greta's boy? She's a fine woman. You did nothing to deserve that. You don't even know my daughter. I'm just worrying out-loud, letting off steam. You'll understand when you're my age."

"Okay," Jack muttered.

McDonnell began shaking his head from side to side. His eyes found Jack's and he voiced the very next thought that popped into is mind: "Do you realize the total absurdity of our situation? Here we are smack in the middle of a school of salmon and instead of fishing, I'm being paranoid about my daughter while a state senator who came to the coast to ask for a favor is leaning over the railing retching green bile. Right now, the poor son of a bitch is probably wishing he could die."

McDonnell had shelled out almost two hundred bucks for an "All-Day" to accommodate the senator. Meanwhile, the most interesting person on board was a boy – a maybe smart, probably athletic, handsome boy – exactly the kind of male he worried would one day seduce his daughter. His goal was to choose the seducer.

McDonnell turned to Jack, "Probably ought to reel us in, son."

"Yes, sir."

Jack ripped the first rod from its holder and reeled it in fast. He took the second rod with the same intent, but as the pilchard came to the surface and bounced in the wake, a salmon at least twice as big as the first two took a swipe at it. Instinctively, Jack released the drag and let the bait go back to the fish. It struck and Jack set the hook, then glanced over his shoulder as he adjusted the drag and yelled at the VIP who'd warned him about a mythical daughter.

"You got yourself a Chinook, sir!"

The tall man grabbed the pole and started reeling. "Yeah, yeah, come to me, baby!" McDonnell shouted, relishing the action. It would be a twenty-minute fight. Sick senator or not, he was going to boat this 30 pound Chinook.

Maybe he owed the kid an apology. Maybe he shouldn't talk so much.

CHAPTER THREE

Two customers were waiting when Abernathy entered Red's barbershop. Clint Pender was next. Clint worked at the Chevron station on U.S.101 and was absorbed in a well-worn copy of the December 1953 Field & Stream Magazine. Les Fisher was second in line. He was the cook and half-owner of Anchor's Ahoy Café on River Street. When John walked in, Les was explaining the difference between frying ling cod and halibut filets.

"For ling cod we've been using beer batter but we never get fancy with the halibut – salt and pepper and a sprinkle of flour . . ."

Abernathy ended the discussion with a booming, "I'm next!"

No one argued. John was a quarter-of-an-inch shy of six-four and weighed a flat-bellied two-hundred-and-forty pounds. Big John paused to take a look into the large, wall-length barbershop mirror. He liked what he saw. The shirt looked "sharp," just as Ron Monroe said.

"What were you saying about ling cod?" Abernathy stared at Les. "Ling cod is a god-damn bottom fish. Is that the kind of shit you serve in that fly trap you call a restaurant?"

Abernathy tossed his duffle bag against the wall. "Ain't nobody going to ask where I'm going?"

"The fact you're going is music to my ears," Red mumbled, thinking Abernathy wouldn't dare do anything to him – not in broad daylight in front of two witnesses.

"Music to my ears?" Abernathy mimicked. He donned a menacing glare and moved it around the room – to Clint, to Les. He let go of the glare and cracked a wide-open smile.

"Well, kiss my ass and pass the whiskey, one person in this shit-hole town has the guts to talk back to me."

He shifted his eyes to Red. His wide-open smile twisted into a smirk. "I like you, Red. That's why I'm going to let you cut my hair and make me smell good. That will be my goodbye present to you, Red. When I'm famous you can brag to every son of a bitch who plops his worth-less ass in your barber chair that you cut John Abernathy's hair – an' it was such a privilege, you refused to take his money."

Abernathy stepped out of Red's Barbershop with a liberal sprinkling of Bay Rum masking his body odor. His only friend was waiting in a blue Plymouth.

"You better have bought beer," Abernathy said as he slid into the passenger seat and slammed the door behind him.

"Two six packs," Dodd said.

"Better be Lucky Lager, I don't drink that homo piss you plywood plant dorks call Olympia."

"Yeah, sure, John, I got Lucky."

* * *

Dodd followed US 101 south past Tahkenitch Lake, through Gardiner and over the Smith River Bridge. The Highway 38 Junction was now just ahead with an arrow pointing to Reedsport's business district.

"Let's go downtown for a look see," John said. "I fought in a smoker here once at the VFW Hall, big slow Okie. Knocked him on his fat ass in the first round. That VFW hall is somewhere downtown."

Dodd turned left, northeast, onto State Highway 38, which doubled as Reedsport's Main Street. The Ambassador, an eccentric, white-haired fellow wearing buckskins and English riding boots was standing on Main Street. He'd been to the post office, picked up a large package, put the package in the back of his pick-up, and then, for reasons of his own, parked his truck, got out and started into Barney's Outfitting Store, changed his mind, turned, stepped outside and launched into one of his soliloquies.

"Our Umpqua River isn't one of those wild, white water rivers like the Clackamas, Santiam and McKenzie that tumble out of the high Cascades. Those rivers may seem to have an exciting run, dancing down the mountains as they do, but I feel sorry for them. After all, if rivers could dream, they'd dream of one day meeting the ocean, face to face, like mortal souls in search of God. But none of those rivers find the ocean, they're all sucked up by the Willamette; one by one they turn into lazy water slouching north to the Columbia."

None of the townspeople stopped to listen. They looked straight at him as they passed; a few nodded hello. They were accustomed to him, just as they were accustomed to rain, fog, pot-holes in the streets and log trucks going too fast on narrow roads.

The Ambassador began walking up Main Street. As he wandered past the storefronts he switched to his favorite subject, *The Lost Tribe*. "A mountain lion was in full flight headed toward me," he announced, raising his arms as if to ward off an attack. "I was about to be dead when I heard the sing of an arrow and the big cat dropped like a chopped log at my feet. I looked up, and there was this tall, handsome Indian, dressed in buckskins just like the ones I'm proud to be wearing – and he was lowering his bow."

Sheriff Henry Stark was cruising Main Street when he saw The Ambassador shouting and waving his arms in front of the drug store. A broad shouldered ex-marine, Stark had earned a Silver Star and two Purple Hearts fighting in the Pacific. After WWII he found himself drawn to the tranquility of small towns. Shifting from second gear into low, he eased into an empty space along the curb. He shifted into neutral, got out and approached the older man.

"Afternoon, Mr. Ambassador, how you doing today?"

The Ambassador changed the subject. "Marcus Whitman and his do-gooder New York wife, Narcissa, a bitch if there ever was one, killed Chief Tomahas' family with measles. Tomahas exacted retribution with a tomahawk and Joe Meek, U.S. Marshall, hanged him for it. You're the sheriff. You tell me how justice was served?"

"Excuse me," the sheriff said, "but that was a long time ago and I didn't have much say in the matter."

The Ambassador wasn't listening. He'd fixed his eyes on the blue Plymouth passing by.

"There is evil among us," The Ambassador shouted. He pointed at Dodd's coupe. "I see evil. It is in our midst and searching for prey."

The Ambassador was a mild nuisance for Sheriff Stark, not a prophet. He didn't shift his eyes to the car the old man was pointing toward. Instead, he suggested, "Sir, might be a good time for you to head home – before the fog rolls in."

Dodd had spotted the sheriff's car. "Lower your beer," he said to Big John. "There's a cop over there."

Abernathy had been checking the other side of the street looking for the building where he'd knocked out the guy from Oklahoma. He turned, leaned out his window and said, "That cop is too busy harassing that old fart with the faggot boots to pay attention to us."

"What's the old guy yelling?" Dodd asked.

"Who the fuck cares?"

As Dodd passed the Shell station at the end of the downtown district, he peeked at his gas gauge. Less than a quarter tank. Way less. Alarmed, Dodd announced, "We need gas!"

At the 38/101 junction, Dodd turned south onto 101. A directional sign showed their eventual destination, Coos Bay, to be 31 miles away. An easy-to-access Texaco was straight ahead. Dodd pulled up to the pumps and switched off the engine. Skip Preston, a high school sophomore, dashed out. "Fill 'er up?" he asked.

Dodd rolled down his window. "Yeah. Regular."

Abernathy eased out of the car. "Where's your pisser?"

"Around back. It's open."

Skip took a second look at Abernathy and thought, *Gee, is he ever big.* Everyone knew it was Beach Night and he guessed Abernathy to be one of the football players from Coos Bay.

Skip blurted, "You play football for Coos Bay?" Reedsport kids were in awe of Coos Bay, a bigger town with a well-deserved reputation as a football and basketball powerhouse.

"Yeah, how'd you know?" John Abernathy said. The young attendant was impressed with the stranger's size and physique. John liked that.

"We don't grow football players as big as you around here," Skip answered, hoping to please the big fellow in the Pendleton shirt.

"You must be here for Senior Beach Night?" Skip offered.

"Oh yeah, little buddy, that's for fucking sure." Abernathy had heard about Beach Night but wasn't aware it was tonight. What a stroke of luck. He'd turned a few women's heads when he was boxing and he was looking especially sharp today with his haircut and new shirt.

"Be a lot of pretty gals out there tonight," Skip kept on talking. "Looking for action, huh? Wish I was a senior."

"If you was you could come along with us," Abernathy said, patting the teen on the shoulder. "I like you. Right off the bat I liked you."

Terry Dodd felt a quiver move up into is stomach. He'd never had a woman. He'd told Abernathy and his roommate in Florence he'd made it with Sally Crandall, a forty-year old divorced woman who'd worked the same shift at the plywood plant as Dodd, but that was a lie. He just didn't want to admit . . . he'd never done it.

"Yeah, Beach Night, that's why we're here," Big John told Skip. "But, if you can believe it," Abernathy pointed to Dodd, "my asshole buddy here couldn't find the right beach."

Skip was anxious to please. "Lighthouse Beach," he said like it was the answer to a quiz. "Head toward Coos Bay – just before Winchester Bay there's a turn-off, sign reads 'Lighthouse Beach / Parking'."

"Damn, we must have drove right by it," Abernathy said and headed for the restroom.

Abernathy pushed open the door labeled "MEN," unzipped and leaned into the urinal. The beer-powered urine erupted with such force he had to step back to avoid splatter. Finished, feeling better, he zipped up and paused at the sink, not to wash his hands, but to check his hair-cut in the mirror.

"Hi there," he said, "Name's John, I played football for Coos Bay . . ."

* * *

Captain Harry Norton steered under the screeching seagulls and into his slip in the Winchester Bay Marina. He cut the engine and Jack leaped onto the dock, secured the boat and jumped back on board. He took the three salmon from the fish-well and asked the customers if they'd like them cleaned.

"Better you than me," McDonnell responded. "There's a Willy's jeep parked one row over from your mom's tavern. My Coleman cooler is in the back." He tossed his keys toward Jack who deftly saved them from going into the water.

Fifteen minutes later, Jack stepped inside the saloon. Cigarette smoke was riding on the dim light, imitating the approaching fog. The jukebox was playing a Frankie Laine song. Jack liked the song. Unconsciously, he moved to its rhythm.

"Rose, Rose I love you with an aching heart;
Glory be your future, now we have to part . . ."

The Dock had about two-dozen customers. Greta wore khakis and a long sleeved white blouse. She winked at her son and nodded toward the booth with the VIP and state senator."

Jack walked over and placed the car keys on their table. "Your fish are cleaned and on ice. The Chinook weighed in at 31 pounds, two ounces. Nice fish."

"What do we owe you?" McDonnell asked.

"Captain Norton's charters are all-inclusive, sir. You don't owe me anything. We just want you to tell your friends what a good time you had in Winchester Bay." Jack's words were the stock speech everyone in town delivered.

McDonnell decided he liked Jack, daughter or no daughter. His day had been on the brink of nothingness, entertaining another stupid, useless politician – then the kid had handed him a rod with a 30-pound Chinook tail-dancing on the other end.

Greta made her way over to the booth.

"Let's see," Greta inserted, "Three salmon, cleaned, iced-down and carried to the car. The going rate for that is...

"Swede!" Greta called to a giant of a man standing at the end of the bar. "What's the going rate for cleaning and icing three salmon?"

Swede had a lion's mane for hair and a beard to match. He turned slowly and stared hard at the small man at the VIP's table. "Fifty bucks each!"

The state senator froze. He'd heard about places like this. His district was in the Willamette Valley. Word was that people on the coast didn't like state senators from the valley.

Swede belly-laughed and pointed at the VIP. "We got him!" Swede lifted his beer glass, "How are you, Mr. Mc-Donnell? Welcome back to Winchester Bay."

"Better than my friend here," James McDonnell grinned.

Everyone in the bar laughed and Greta put a friendly hand on the small man's shoulder.

She put her other hand on her Jack's shoulder. "As for tipping my boy here, do what you think is right. Mr. McDonnell already paid for the charter."

The state senator pulled out his wallet and thumbed through the bills. He showed McDonnell a twenty, received an "okay" nod and handed the "Andy" to Jack.

"Keep your wallet out my friend, you're buying drinks for the house," McDonnell ordered. "I'll have my martini, Greta, and a double ginger ale on the rocks for the honorable state senator from Lane County."

"Coming right up," Greta said. "I put the Beefeaters on ice five minutes after you booked the charter."

Swede wasn't a man to turn down a drink. He lifted his empty Lucky Lager stubby bottle toward McDonnell, and with his other hand, which he closed into a ham-sized fist, he pounded on the bar three times. "Three cheers for Mr. McDonnell."

The other customers, all locals, chimed in, "Hip, hip hooray!"

Even though McDonnell was one of those "rich bastards" from Lakeside, he was a straight-ahead guy who could kid around with the best of them and never failed to provide a round for whoever was lucky enough to be at The Dock when he happened by.

CHAPTER FOUR

Following the directions given by the gas station attendant, Big John Abernathy and his sidekick, Terry Dodd, found the road to Lighthouse Beach. They were early, five o'clock. Dodd was driving. When he reached the parking lot that served the lighthouse, Dodd stopped and shifted into neutral. His window was open so he could hear the roar of the ocean – but he couldn't see it. The Pacific was just beyond the lighthouse. The high dunes and a row of Douglas fir trees hid it from view.

"Christ, Dodd, don't park in here," Big John bellowed. "Take that service road." He pointed toward a one lane strip of concrete on the landward side of the tree line.

Dodd followed orders. The service road had been built for beach patrols during World War II. It connected the lighthouse to the north Winchester Bay jetty and then serpentined back to US 101.

"Keep going 'til I tell you to stop," Abernathy ordered. His window was also down and he took a deep breath of the ocean air. Just ahead a grove of Douglas fir poked out of a sand dune. "Stop!" Abernathy said. "This is fucking perfect. We'll park in the trees with the front of the car pointed east to the highway. If there's trouble, if cops show up, we'll be able to haul ass out of here with nobody ever seeing us."

Dodd didn't know what Abernathy was planning. He sensed it could be a night to remember.

"We looking for women?" Dodd asked, knowing the answer. He opened another beer. "I brought a blanket, it could come in handy."

Abernathy nodded approval, lit another of Ron's Camels and walked around the car for three or four minutes, thinking.

Dodd waited for his leader to speak.

"I heard 'bout Beach Night when I was working in the woods up in Mapleton," Abernathy began. "The different schools all have different bonfires." He licked his lips. "Since we ain't really seniors, we can't go down to a bonfire to meet girls, so we'd best to set up in the trees above the beach and just wait. Pretty soon, they'll start drifting around, the women, feeling horny you know. Some will come up into the trees to take a pee. Then, real friendly, we say 'Hi there, want to party?' If the gal isn't from Coos Bay, I'm going say I'm a Coos Bay football player like the kid at the gas station said that's what I looked like."

Dodd swallowed a mouthful of beer. "Sounds good, Big John, but what do we say I am? I want to be somebody, too. You could say I'm a baseball player. If you say it, they'll believe it."

"You got it little buddy."

"So what do I tell 'em? I mean, after that, after I say I'm a baseball player?" Dodd asked.

"Tell 'em you're getting ready to go to college on a scholarship"

"Which college?"

"I don't know, for Christ's sakes, which one do you root for?"

"Don't really care. Sometimes the Ducks; sometimes the Beavers. Depends on who's got the best team."

Abernathy shrugged. "Well, figure it out. You got 'til dark."

CHAPTER FIVE

Clutching his twenty-dollar tip, which made it a sixty-dollar day, Jack Portman headed for the interior stairwell, which was located between the MEN'S and WOMEN'S Restrooms. The steps ascended to the Portman's second floor apartment and also descended to a cellar-storage basement. When Jack's foot hit the first step, a German shepherd eased from behind the bar and started to follow. Jack spoke to the dog as if it were a person. "Sal! Stay with mom."

The dog cocked his head as if he understood and went back to his place behind the bar. Sal was short for Saloon Dog, a name Greta had bestowed and found amusing.

Jack dashed upstairs – heading straight for the shower. He stripped and waited for the hot water to make its way up from the heater in the cellar. When it finally arrived he scrubbed the fish smell from his hands with Lava soap before immersing himself under the spray.

Lighthouse Beach, he thought. Seniors from every school within eighty miles would be there – Coos Bay, North Bend, Reedsport and Florence for sure, maybe Waldport, Toledo and Bandon. He imagined himself by a bonfire talking to

Coos Bay football players. He remembered what the VIP had said . . ."If you have the balls . . ."

Hell, he knew plenty of Coos Bay lettermen from football and basketball. They'd voted him onto their All-Opponent Team. He'd be welcome at their bonfire. So, what would the old man's daughter be like? Skinny and weird like her father? No thanks.

In Jack's under-the-shower fantasy, Ellen, his ex girl-friend, walked by arm-in-arm with Pat Kelly a graduate from Coos Bay. Kelly was a little guy, but he was rich and a snappy dresser. In Jack's mind, Kelly was wearing saddle shoes and white cords. The night air was cool, so Kelly also had on a new, v-necked, light-blue Jansen sweater. While the hot water relaxed his shoulders, Jack visualized Ellen in a peasant style blouse showing some cleavage.

In this fantasy, Ellen stopped, looked at him and said, "Hi Jack, aren't you going to say hello?" She'd uttered those exact words when he'd accidentally crossed her path in the concession building at the drive-in movie.

Jack played the rest of the scene out as if he were rehearsing a part in the school play. "Oh. Hi, Ellen. Didn't see you. Hope you're having a good time."

His next emotion was anger, or was it frustration? He couldn't tell. Whatever it was, a surge of energy filled his upper body with a bolt of physical power. He feinted with his right and whipped a vicious left hook at the spot in the shower-spray where Kelly's head would be.

Jack exhaled and thought about what he'd just imag-ined. That wouldn't be right. Kelly was a little guy. You don't cold-cock a little guy. So they'd both fallen for the same girl? Couldn't fault Kelly for that. He breathed-in, deeply, and felt himself returning to normal. Forget about Ellen, he told himself. Better to think about the pretty girl in the Coos Bay Band and her amazing smile during the basketball game. Maybe she'd be at the Coos Bay bonfire?

CHAPTER SIX

Two of Jack's senior buddies picked him up in front of his mother's saloon a few minutes before six-thirty. Bobby Lacy was driving his 1946 Chevy coupe. The passenger, Larry Posey, was Bobby's antithesis. Bobby was a three-sport athlete, smallish, but quick and agile. Larry was an offensive tackle on the football team, big and slow. Larry's parents owned a dairy farm on Smith River and wanted him to go to Oregon State and major in agriculture. Larry wasn't keen on being a farmer. He and seven classmates had signed up for the army.

"You'll probably go to Germany," the recruiter told him, "and those German frauleins love big, strong American men."

Larry had two dates in high school: the Junior and Senior Proms. The prospect of being initiated into the wonderful world of women by German frauleins overpowered his parents' pleas. He'd signed the papers and was leaving for Camp Pendleton, California in June.

Bobby got out of the car, pulled the front seat forward and let Jack into the back.

Bobby, hyped by expectations, raised his right fist and yelled, "Beach Night!" He gunned the engine, spraying gravel behind him. Lighthouse Beach was two miles away.

"Slow down," Larry Posey instructed Bobby, "We don't need to get there early, we'll look like geeks."

"Be cool, Posey, Bobby Lacey never looks like a geek. Hey, Jackson," Bobby called into the back seat, "I heard bottles clink. You snitch a six pack from your mom's cooler?"

"That's for me to know and you to find out."

"Jesus," Bobby said, "you live in a tavern, if you can't get a six-pack, shit man, that's like living in a whorehouse and never getting laid."

"Kiss my ass," Jack fired back. He didn't like the whorehouse analogy and slammed a fist into the back of the driver's seat.

"Okay, okay" Bobby conceded, like a dog rolling over and showing its belly, "I was just kidding. Jeez. My brother bought me a six-pack and Pose paid for half. Sorry."

The apology was sincere. Jack was the alpha male.

The road into Lighthouse was a paved government road. Two lanes of blacktop led to the Lighthouse public parking lot.

It was dusk, the evening fog was moving in and the area had an eerie glow from car lights. Traffic was bumper-to-bumper.

Bobby rolled down his window, put his left arm outside, pumped his fist and shouted his war cry, "Beach Night!" He honked his horn. There was a spontaneous combustion of honks when other drivers followed suit.

Bobby parked the car and the three buddies divided their treasure: four Olympia beers each. Jack slipped his down the sleeves of his Letterman coat. His coat was black – with white leather sleeves. Stitched across the left breast, like medals, were sewn-on icons representing baseball, basketball and football. A big red R was sewn onto the right side. The R had three stripes, signifying the number of years he'd earned a Letter.

The threesome sauntered through the parking area past one-hundred-or-so milling-around seniors and their dates. Everybody seemed relaxed and friendly. They passed two guys leaning against a chopped, channeled, every-inch-customized, lacquered-black '49 Ford coupe. The two were of the super-cool set, hair cut short on top, with the sides swept back into ducktails. Their black trousers were meticulously tailored to blouse-out over the thighs, and then narrow over the knees – until becoming nearly skin-tight from the bottom of the calf muscles to one inch below the ankles. The combination of skintight fit and half-size cuffs made their white buck shoes appear two sizes larger. They also wore pink dress shirts, buttoned all the way to the top. The identical ensembles were capped off with black leather jackets, collars turned up.

As Bobby passed them, he raised his fist and whooped, "Beach Night!"

The two guys nodded. "Base," they said in unison. One year earlier, they would have said, "Basic," but whether for verbal economy or to keep pace with an evolution in super-cool phraseology, they had dropped the second syllable. "Base," as they employed it, could have any number of meanings depending on intonation. In this case it meant, "We're not looking for any trouble." To emphasize the point, the larger of the two tipped his beer toward the passing three-some. Posey wondered out loud, "Where are those guys from?"

Neither Jack nor Bobby cared, so Posey's question drifted away into the breeze. The three walked through a thick stand of fir trees, then over the sand dunes and down toward the beach.

Spread along the high tide mark – fifty yards apart – were nine bonfires. All nine fires were in full bloom, flames licking upwards, chasing smoke into the hovering fog. It was nearly dark. Jack slowed his pace and fixed his eyes on the horizon – to a faraway junction, west-by-west, where the ocean met the sky. The fast-sinking sun was balanced on the edge of infinity, diffused by the fog; it created a brilliant orange, gold and red glow. Jack marveled at the beauty of the sunset.

"Look at that!" He came to a full stop and pointed.

Bobby and Posey weren't interested.

Sunsets were an every day occurrence. Still, when Jack stopped, they stopped. They shuffled their feet while Jack scanned the horizon. This is Beach Night, an important night, Jack thought, a legendary night. Today we're all high school kids, tomorrow we'll either be working, getting ready to go to college or going into the military. Today's sunset deserves someone bearing witness to its passage.

"Which bonfire is ours?" Posey interrupted Jack's thoughts.

Bobby looked at Posey as if he were a lunatic.

"Ours? I want to check out Coos Bay, they have ten times as many good-looking women as any school on the coast. My brother came to Beach Night four years ago and said he could have danced with a Coos Bay cheerleader if he hadn't brought his girlfriend along."

Jack began walking toward the bonfire with the most silhouettes moving across the red glow. As the biggest, it had to be . . . Coos Bay.

The Reedsport interlopers strode boldly up to the flames, paused, glanced around, and tried to look as though they belonged.

"Portman!"

Jack heard his name. His eyes sought the source. A tall, athletic figure wearing a blue and silver Coos Bay Letterman coat was walking toward him. It was Kyle Smith. Jack and Kyle had been rivals in football and basketball. They had earned each other's respect. After each contest, they'd shaken hands and said, "Nice game."

Once again, Kyle Smith was holding out his hand. Jack took it. "Is this something?" Smith said gesturing to the scene around them.

Ignoring Bobby and Posey, Kyle put his arm around Jack's shoulder; the way schoolboys do on playgrounds. Kyle led Jack to where his friends were sitting.

Jack didn't intend to leave his two Reedsport buddies, it just happened.

There were six couples in Kyle's pack. They had multiple portable radios tuned to *Lucky Lager Dance Time*. Jack could hear Al Albert of the Four Aces groaning "*Twas just a garden in the rain.*"

He took a seat on a drift log. "Want a beer?" Kyle asked.

"Got one." Jack reached down his coat sleeve. "Could use a church key."

One of the girls tossed him a bottle opener. "You're cute," the girl said. "Kyle, why don't you introduce me to your cute friend?"

"Like you don't know who he is?" Kyle teased the girl. "Where you going to school, Portman?"

"Oregon," Jack answered.

"Got a ride?" a male voice asked from the shadows. He was referring to a Grant in Aid Athletic Scholarship.

"No," Jack shook his head. Jack hated to admit this – admit his team didn't play at the same level as Coos Bay, that his nine letters in three sports didn't count for much with college coaches – at least not with big time college coaches. Jack's lone scholarship offer had come from Linfield College. During the previous four years, six of Reedsport's better athletes had been recruited by Linfield, a mid-size, private college located in McMinnville about thirty miles South-west of Portland. Only one Reedsport player had been recruited by Oregon, an all-state fullback who clearly belonged at the highest level.

Jack and his mother had sat down with the numbers, they'd calculated that it would cost nearly as much to go to Linfield with a scholarship as it would to attend Oregon without one. Jack had set his sights on the University of Oregon in Eugene ever since Norm Van Brocklin led the Ducks to the Cotton Bowl in 1948. And now, Grant Bookman, Reedsport's great all-state fullback was there, assuring Jack a place in the fraternity where a picture of Van Brocklin, the Flying Dutchman, hung proudly on the wall above the fireplace mantle.

Jack decided to mention the offer from Linfield, just to let the group know he'd earned the right to wear a Letterman sweater to Beach Night. "Could have had a ride at Linfield, but I'd rather go to Oregon."

"I'm going to Oregon," a girl's voice chimed happily from the shadows. Jack squinted to see her face.

"How about you?" Jack asked Kyle.

"Maybe Cal in Berkeley. I'm not going to play ball, either. I just applied, but I think I'll get in. I've always wanted to go out of state."

Jack was impressed. He'd never considered a California school, never occurred to him. "That's great, Kyle," Jack said, meaning it. "Good luck."

The girl who'd said Jack was cute, not the girl who said she was going to Oregon, scooted away from the boy she'd been sitting next to and sat down on the log next to Jack. "Don't worry," she assured Jack, pointing to the boy she'd left, "We're just friends."

Jack could see her face in the fire's light. Was she the girl in the band? He decided she was. She was pretty, not quite cheerleader pretty but she had a great smile, which revealed the most perfect teeth he'd seen outside of a movie theatre. There was more to like. Her eyes were brimming with mischief, and sans band uniform, Jack noticed, there was an alluring bulge of breasts beneath her thick sweatshirt.

"I'm Jack," he said.

"I know. We've met. We were never introduced, but we've met. Do you remember?"

"Sure, I remember. You're the girl in the band."

"Kathy," she said, her heart pounding because he remembered. She leaned toward him and kissed him gently on the cheek. "I knew you'd remember." She took his beer, peeled the label from the bottle and counted the dots.

The number of dots on the back of an Olympia beer label was supposed to be a barometer of how well you'd fare with the opposite sex. One dot meant you'd strike out. Two meant you'd meet somebody. Three indicated a degree of success, and four meant you'd go all the way. Jack's label had two dots.

"Too bad," Kathy said, teasing him.

"I have more beer, more labels," Jack said with a grin.

He looked around. Standard rules of behavior were suspended for Beach Night. Kyle was locked in a long embrace with his girl, his hand under her sweatshirt. The guy sitting with Kathy had left the pack. The other couples were dancing to *How High The Moon*, a hit tune from Les Paul and Mary Ford.

Jack's eyes had adjusted to the light and it looked like over one hundred Coos Bay seniors were milling about around the bonfire. He looked for Bobby and Posey, but after being shunned, they had moved along in search of friendlier turf. He felt a twinge of guilt for abandoning them. Kathy's next question chased it out of his mind.

"You have a girlfriend you're supposed to meet tonight?" she asked, surprising both herself and Jack with her forwardness.

"No. Unless you want to volunteer."

"I thought I already had," she answered and moved closer to him. He put his arm around her and she scooted even closer. "Did you think I was terrible for staring at you during the basketball game?"

"No. I liked it. I had this funny feeling like I knew you."

"I know," she dropped her voice and closed her eyes.

He accepted the invitation to kiss her. Her mouth was open and wet and she tasted like Wrigley Spearmint gum. It was a delicious, two-sided kiss, and it got better and better as it progressed. He felt himself getting hard. They fell backward, off of the log and into the soft sand, she on top of him. "Do the girls in Reedsport kiss you like that?" she whispered when they came up for air.

When he looked up he realized there was a large, looming figure standing over them.

"Who are you?" the large, looming figure growled.

"He's okay. He's with me," Jack heard Kyle say.

The spell had been broken. Moments before, Jack had been alone with Kathy on a tropical island. Now they were part of an increasingly rambunctious crowd.

A group of ten males had started a ritual style dance around the fire. As they danced, they chanted, "...Beach Night... La-da-la-dah... Pirates... La-da-la-dah ...Beach Night..."

"Pirates" was a tribute to the Coos Bay High School mascot. When they chanted "Beach Night," they'd raise a fist. When they chorused "Pirates," they'd raise a beer.

The girl who was going to Oregon joined the line, kicking her knees higher than anyone else.

"Want a drink?" the large, looming figure asked Jack.

"Thanks, I'm good. Got a beer."

The figure leaned low and Jack recognized him. It was Number 78, Yablonski, Coos Bay's All-State tackle. "You want some vodka?" Yablonski asked, pulling a pint bottle out of his coat pocket.

Jack had tried vodka after a school dance and it made him sick. He didn't want it. He didn't want to get on the wrong side of Yablonski, either.

"You were Number 12," Yablonski said. "You're okay. Your team was shit, but you're okay. You were good enough to play for us. Take a shot." He held the bottle out. Jack took it, tipped it, allowing only a small amount into his mouth. "Ahhh," he faked satisfaction.

"Me, too," Kathy said, taking the bottle. She took a ladylike sip, coughed, wiped her mouth, and sat stunned for several seconds.

"It's awful, Yabo," she said. "Tastes like kerosene."

Yablonski found this hilarious. "Wouldn't know, Kathy. I never drunk no kerosene."

"Have a beer on me," Jack said, pulling an Oly out of his sleeve. Yablonski swilled the remaining four ounces of Vodka then bit the cap off the beer bottle and chug-a-lugged the contents.

"Vodka chased by Oly, sum-bitch, that's good!" Yablonski announced before belching. He hurled both empty bottles in the direction of the ocean and turned back to Jack.

"You're okay, Number 12." He lumbered away in the direction of the ocean.

"You alright?" Jack asked Kathy. Meeting Yablonski had erased his erection. For this, Jack was silently grateful.

"I think so." Kathy said, scrunching her face into a frown. The frown morphed into a smile. There were those teeth again. How could teeth be so perfect? How could teeth be so sexy? Jack was struck by the realization he really liked this girl.

"...Beach Night (Raise the beer)...La-da-la dah...
Pirates (Gulp the beer)...La-da-la-dah..."

The dancers circled back to Jack and Kathy's side of the bonfire. Kyle leaned over and spoke to Jack and Kathy. "We're going to take a walk," he said. "If anybody gives you a hard time, tell them you're with me – and Yabo. He likes you. Nobody messes with Yabo. We both voted for you on our all-opponent team, bet you didn't know that."

As Jack watched Kyle saunter away, arm around his girl, he felt a sense of danger. Senior Beach Night or not, he was in alien territory.

"...Beach Night...La-da-la-dah...
Pirates...La-da-la-dah..."

One of the boys tried to coax Kathy into the line. He acted as though he and Kathy might have dated. Pointing at Jack, the coaxer slurred, "Who's he? He's no Pirate."

"A friend of Kyle and Yabo!" Kathy shot back at him. She said it with a note of a warning, not as a shy explanation.

Jack knew he could handle the fellow with the slur, but there were so many of them. He didn't like the odds. As if she'd read his mind, Kathy squeezed Jack's hand, "Maybe we should take a walk, too."

Darkness filled everything outside the circle of fire. The fog rolled in and covered the moon and stars. It reduced the light from the bonfires to miniature orange glows. The lighthouse beacon was pointed far out to sea. From beach level, it was just a sliver of light that seemed to have no source. It was a shooting star; standing still.

The temperature had dropped to fifty-five degrees. The fog made it feel colder.

What now? Jack thought. He put his coat around Kathy's shoulders. They made their way over the sand dunes toward another orange glow. He didn't have a blanket. He didn't have a car. He had one beer left. But he had a girl, and there was something magical about the girl.

What was the word for something totally out of the ordinary? *Aberration*. That was it, Jack recalled. Beach Night was one day in your life that didn't count. An aberration. You got a pass, a one-night pass between high school and adulthood. Whatever happened didn't happen. Maybe a boy and girl could be in love for just one night?

Jack and Kathy stepped into the light of another bonfire. They quickly realized it was North Bend territory and moved off – aiming toward the next orange glow. Neither Jack nor Kathy recognized classmates at the next fire either. They passed a friendly couple and asked if they knew where the Reedsport bonfire was. They didn't. The couple said they were from North Bend, which was supposed to have three bonfires, but they couldn't find the one with their clique.

Jack took another look over the beach and counted more than a dozen bonfires. As he was counting, Kathy asked, "If I tell you something, promise not to laugh?"

They stopped walking. "Sure," Jack said, intrigued. "I won't laugh."

"I've wanted to meet you ever since I saw you play basketball. Remember when they called the foul against you and you just stood there and looked at the referee as if he'd lost his mind?"

Jack didn't remember. He never remembered what happened during the heat of battle, but he nodded as if he did. "I prayed I'd see you tonight," Kathy acknowledged, "and when you walked up to the bonfire, well, I asked Kyle to go get you. Do you think I'm silly?"

He wrapped both arms around her and pulled her close. "No, I'm glad. I thought about you, too. To tell the truth, I was hoping to meet you." He didn't mention he'd also thought about Ellen, his ex.

"We had to get together and tonight is the night," Kathy assured him, confident their meeting was preordained by a higher power. They kissed again. The kiss was nice, but the air was cold and it was awkward standing in the middle of a sand dune. They began trudging toward the parking lot, hoping to find a warm place, better yet, a warm, private place. They moved into the tree line near the parking area. That's when they saw flashing blue lights and three state police cars.

"Damn," Jack said, peeking at the parking lot action from behind a Douglas fir tree, "They have ten kids rounded up and they've put two into a patrol car."

"Hey!" It was a voice from behind another tree. "That you, Portman?"

"Yeah. Who's that?"

"Simmons. Stay there, I'll crawl over."

Tommy Simmons was a straight-A student who had always been too eager to please his schoolmates to become popular.

"Who's she?" Simmons asked, still on his knees.

"Her name is Kathy," Jack answered. "She's with me."

Tommy was both surprised and envious. Seeing a classmate with a pretty girl from another town made Tommy forget, momentarily, about the discord in the parking lot.

"Wow," Tommy stood up. He leaned close to Kathy to get a better look. "How did you meet a girl?"

"He's funny," Kathy said to Jack.

That sounded like a compliment to Simmons. Emboldened by two beers, he responded, "I can be very funny. Very clever, very entertaining."

"Never mind," Jack interrupted, "What's happening?"

Simmons recounted the events. "Jeez, well, the state cops showed up and at first just watched, not doing anything. Then, Remington – well, you know Georgie, he got a blanket and stood on top of one of the cop cars and started doing his imitation of William Holden in *Stalag 17*, you know, shouting 'Are you all good little Nazis'?

"Then George threw off the blanket and all he had on was his underwear, so the cops go bonkers and took off after him. He ran into the woods and the cops never did catch him, jeez, he must be freezing. Then everything started to settle down, the cops are ready to go, *but* somebody stole the rotor out of one of their cars, so the car is deader than a door nail, so everybody started laughing. That's when I decided to get out of there, so I ran over here and hid in the woods. It was scary, I kept hearing noises."

"There's nothing in these woods to be afraid of," Jack told him.

"What about the Lost Tribe?"

"That's a myth."

"Are you sure?" Kathy joked.

"Pretty sure," Jack smiled at her. "But right now, we need to figure a way out of here."

"We still have a beer," Kathy said cheerfully. "We could just sit here, drink our beer and wait for the police to leave."

The remaining beer was in the sleeve of Jack's coat, which Kathy was wearing. She reached down the sleeve and held up the prize.

"Ta-dah," she said.

"I can open it with my belt buckle," Simmons boasted, reaching for the beer. He took it, held it for a second and declared. "It's warm. I don't like warm beer, it tastes like dishwater."

"More like kerosene," Jack quipped.

Kathy smiled. She liked the fact Jack remembered what she'd said to Yablonski. She turned back to Tommy. Faking a stern voice, she ordered, "Open the beer."

Simmons wore a cowboy belt with an oversized buckle. True to his boast, he pried the cap off the bottle. He was rewarded for his effort by having the bottle foam-over on the front of his light blue, cotton trousers.

"Jeez," he exclaimed, dreading how raucously he'd be teased if other Reedsport seniors saw him.

"Have a little accident there?" Jack kidded. "Are you scared of the Indians or cops?"

"You know it's from the beer," Simmons retorted, falling for Jack's ruse.

"The beer, please." Kathy said.

Simmons handed it to her. She took a sip, swishing it around in her mouth before swallowing. "Lovely," she announced. Recalling how her father's sophisticated friends talked about wine, she ad-libbed, "The malt doesn't smother the crisp, hop-like tingle one enjoys so much in the better northwest brews. I'd say May 1954 is a very good month for Olympia beer."

Ceremoniously, she peeled the label off the bottle. She took out her book of matches, struck one, counted the dots and blew out the match. She smiled at Jack and held up four fingers. After carefully sliding the label into her back pocket, she handed the beer to Jack.

He took a swallow. "Very good. I often leave my beer in the kitchen sink to bring it to the proper temperature." Simmons didn't have a clue what was going on between the two of them. "Don't I get any?" he asked.

"Get any?" Kathy repeated. She started to giggle. She couldn't stop, she tried to quell the laughter by clenching her teeth, but all that did was make her sides and tummy hurt. She rolled on the ground as if she was having a fit.

She looked up at the startled Simmons and tried to explain her compulsive laughter. "You...said...'get-any'...

we have four dots," she managed to blurt before she was overcome by another surge of uncontrollable laughter.

Jack pulled Kathy to her feet. She was shaking. "We're out of here," he said.

CHAPTER SEVEN

They began running through the trees. They ran away from the bonfires, the parking lot and the blue lights. Simmons was plodding after them. They'd traveled about one hundred yards when Jack stopped to let Kathy catch her breath.

"I'm sorry for laughing at your friend," she panted.

"He's not my friend," Jack said, "But I thought you were great." He put an arm around her. "Talking about beer like it was wine was funny. Nobody I know would ever think of that."

"They didn't grow up around my father."

"Let's keep going," Jack said.

"Not until you kiss me again." She put her arms around him and tilted her face upwards. Their lips met and they melted into never-never land, thinking about four dots.

Simmons had been twenty yards behind them. He had stopped when they stopped. Winded, never an athlete and not used to drinking, he had fallen to his knees and vomited. Fearful he'd be left behind; he'd struggled to his feet.

"Portman, don't leave me," he pleaded. He closed to within ten yards. "I'm afraid by myself."

Jack and Kathy broke off their kiss. "Your little non-friend is calling," she said.

Jack hated the intrusion. What the hell was there to be afraid of?

"We can't just leave him," Kathy sighed.

Jack waved for Tommy to join them. "Let's go."

"Where we going?" Kathy asked. Wherever he wanted to take her was all right with her, she just wanted to know where *wherever* was.

"I live in Winchester Bay. If we follow the tree line, it shouldn't be much more than a mile from here."

Jack knew the saloon would be busy. His plan was to go up the outside stairs and get the car keys. He'd leave Simmons at the pay phone in front of the bait store and drive Kathy home. So what if he got in trouble with his mother? Beach Night was a once-in-a-lifetime phenomenon and Kathy was a once-in-a-lifetime opportunity.

"What will your parents think?" Kathy asked.

The next question was usually, "What does your father do?" When he was in grade school, he'd answer, "My father was killed during the war." It wasn't really a lie, the crane accident did happen during the war. If people wanted to presume his father was a war hero, so be it. But he'd outgrown that answer. He didn't like making up stories and having to remember what he'd said.

He'd learned to be blunt. "It's just my mom, my father is dead." Bluntness stopped interrogators cold. No one wanted details. It also made it clear his mother wasn't a divorcee. In the lower Umpqua valley, the Scarlet Letter wasn't A. It was D.

To Kathy's question, "What will your parents think?" Jack followed form, tacking on, "I'll get mom's car and drive you home."

Kathy said nothing. Being alone in a car with Jack appealed to her. Would he expect her to deliver on the four dots? She was a virgin. Could she just give that up because she'd been attracted to him when he played basketball? How many girls had he had sex with? He was too handsome not to have had sex. She was eighteen, a high school graduate. Other girls her age had sex. What would her father think? They started walking, holding hands. Jack set an easy pace, slowing occasionally to let Simmons catch up. He avoided the service road by following a well-worn hiking trail on the beach side of the tree line. He knew the trail crossed the north jetty. On the other side of the jetty there was a gravel pathway leading into Winchester Bay.

At first Jack mistook the strange sound as the screech of a sea bird, but sea birds were in their nests in the tall grass at night. Was it a bobcat? No. It was human. Female. Screaming..

"Listen! Is that a girl . . . screaming?" Kathy said, clutching Jack's arm.

"Stay here," Jack ordered. He raced in the direction of the scream. The only light came from fog-defused moonlight reflecting on the white sand. Jack could barely see – but the screaming was growing louder, so he must be getting closer. Without stopping he shouted, "Where are you? I'm coming!"

He climbed to the top of a large sand dune, looked down to the bottom, 200 feet away, and saw two shadow-like forms, a big one and a smaller one – they began moving away, then running. The screaming-sound lowered but continued at the base of the dune. Jack slid down the steep dune. The screaming subsided, turning into sobs. He moved forward and saw a young woman curled into a fetal position on a blanket, her peddle pushers had been torn away from her legs and as Jack approached, she pulled a corner of a blanket over her lower torso to cover herself. He recognized her. She was the girl who said she was going to Oregon.

Jack whispered. "I'm here to help you." She looked up and screamed again, although not as loud as before.

"Kathy!" Jack shouted in the direction from which he'd run. He cupped his hands, "Kathy!"

He heard her at the top of the dune. "I'm coming. I see you!"

Jack kept his distance from the frightened young woman. Kathy approached her. "It's okay, it's okay," Kathy soothed. "We're here to help you. Oh my God, Betty, is that you? Oh my God, what happened to you?"

Kathy took her battered classmate into her arms and began rocking her gently and stroking her hair. "It's okay, Betty, we're here. They're gone. You're safe. We'll take care of you."

Jack sat in the sand a short distance away and listened to Kathy comfort the young woman who had just been raped and beaten during this magical night.

This was supposed to be the night that didn't count, the night that never happened. If only it were true, Jack thought. If only it were true for the girl from Coos Bay named Betty. He remembered her dancing, joyfully kicking her knees higher than anyone in the impromptu Pirate dance.

He felt ashamed. He didn't know why he felt ashamed, but he couldn't help it. Ashamed because he was male and other males had done this. Ashamed because he was too busy scheming a four-dot evening to get here in time to save her. A few minutes earlier and he might have stopped it. Shame turned to anger. If he could catch them, he could beat them bloody and drag them into the ocean to drown. That's what they deserved, death. He should go after them now, but he couldn't abandon Kathy and Betty to fend for themselves on this black night adrift on a sand dune.

"Jack," Kathy called softly.

He crawled over to her.

"Jack, this is Betty, she was at our bonfire. I told her you're very nice and you're going to carry her to a safe place."

"We need to call the sheriff," Jack said, his instinct for violence giving way to logic. "We need to catch those bastards. Does she know who they are?"

"No. She left the bonfire to go up in the trees, to you know..."

Kathy didn't want to say, "to pee." She didn't want to say anything indelicate. "Go to the bathroom," she finished the sentence.

"They were waiting in the trees," Kathy continued, "and grabbed her, rolled her in this blanket and carried her out here where nobody could hear."

"We need to get her to my place and call the sheriff," Jack said.

"Don't. I don't want anyone to know," Betty pleaded through bruised lips, wiping blood away from her nose.

"Whatever you say, Betty." Kathy assured her. "But first, let's get you somewhere safe. We're going to Jack's house."

Jack was impressed by Kathy's calm. It seemed as though he'd known her longer than one night. He wanted to get to know her even better. How could he have been so lucky? How could Betty be so unlucky?

He picked Betty up, cradling her in his arms. She buried her face against his shoulder as he struggled through the deep sand. His thigh and calf muscles ached as he climbed the dunes. When he reached the trail he stopped to rest. He handled her carefully, as if she might break. He placed her on the ground, leaning her torso against a tree. When he stood up, Kathy hugged him. "You didn't think about the danger, you just ran to her rescue."

That's when Jack and Kathy became aware Simmons was missing.

"Where's your little non-friend?" Kathy asked.

"I don't know, but we can't worry about him. We have to take care of her . . ."

Simmons heard the screams and dropped to his knees. He heard Jack yelling, "I'm coming." A girl was in trouble and Jack was going to help. There was nothing he could do about it, Jack was the big jock, let him deal with it. There could be a fight and he'd never been in a fight. He began to crawl on his hands and knees through the trees, away from the screams and the ocean. He crawled through bushes and around tree trunks for fifty yards – and, what was that? His hand was touching pavement. He'd found the service road. Relieved, Tommy started to stand up, but just as he flexed his aching knees he heard the thumpity-thump of men running. He dove back into the woods and glued himself to a fallen log, not daring to look. If he could see them, they could see him. He heard heavy breathing as two men ran past him on the service road. The footfalls stopped. A man shouted. Tommy couldn't make out the words but knew the shouter was both angry and afraid. Abruptly, the shouting stopped and it was quiet again. A trunk lid or car door slammed. Another slam. An engine started. The car was driving away. Simmons counted to sixty ten times. It was safe now.

He crawled back to the pavement, stood, and began walking slowly toward the main parking lot. The front of his pants were wet again, but he didn't care. If he could get to the parking lot someone would give him a ride home. Why was the girl screaming? Why were the two guys running? What story should he tell? He couldn't admit he ran away. He could say he chased after the two guys thinking they'd caused the girl to scream. That would sound good. He'd say he tried to get the license number on their car but it was too dark. If he told the story right he might come out of Beach Night as a hero, not a coward.

CHAPTER EIGHT

"This is it," Jack said, standing in front of The Dock Tavern. He led Kathy around the side of the building to the outside stairway. His arms and legs ached. He was still carrying the raped girl named Betty. He looked at the stairway to his mother's apartment above the saloon. He was almost home. A surge of adrenaline launched Jack up the steps. At the top of the staircase, he asked Betty if she could stand for a few seconds. She was numb, in shock, but she managed to gasp a weak, "Yes." He leaned her against the side of the building, reached above the door and ran his fingers along the wood frame.

He handed the key to Kathy who opened the screen door and unlocked the French doors. Tenderly, Jack carried Betty to his mother's bedroom.

"Be back in a minute." He bounded down the inside stairway to the saloon.

It was a typical Saturday night. The bar was full and a shuffleboard tournament was underway. The jukebox was blaring:

You can throw a silver dollar down on the ground
and it will roll, roll, roll
because it's round, round, round. . .

The bartender, an ex-boxer who went by the nickname Champ, saw Jack and pointed toward a table in the far corner where Greta Portman was joking with three loggers. Jack dashed to her side. "Mom, I need you upstairs."

She didn't ask why. She left her tray on the table and followed her son. In the stairwell, he tried to explain. "The state police showed up, so we were taking the hiking trail home when we came on this girl...she's been beaten up... and...raped."

"Call Henry Stark," Greta ordered.

"She didn't want us to call the sheriff."

"That's crazy, honey. When a maniac rapes a girl you call the sheriff. Call Henry. Now!"

Greta entered her bedroom and she saw the girl curled up in the middle of the bed, thumb in her mouth. Greta's rigid posture sagged. She took a deep breath. "Oh, you poor baby, what you've been through."

Kathy had gone into Greta's bathroom for a towel and washcloth. She came back into the room.

"And who are you, dear?" Greta asked Kathy as she took the wet washcloth and began to gently wash Betty's face.

"Kathy McDonnell. Her name is Betty Wagner. We went to school together in Coos Bay. She's a nice girl."

Jack came back into the room. He couldn't believe it. McDonnell. The girl in the band's last name was McDonnell? He'd actually spent the evening with the daughter of the weird VIP who'd threatened he could be "a mean son of a bitch."

He heard his mother saying, "She's still a nice girl. This isn't her fault."

"Jack!" Greta raised her voice, "JACK!"

He managed to shift back into present time. "Yeah, mom, I'm here."

"Did you call the sheriff – we also need to call the doctor – and we need to call her parents."

"I called Sheriff Stark. He's on his way."

Sheriff Henry Stark was a chain smoker. Lucky Strikes were his cigarette of choice. He tapped each Lucky against the thumbnail on his left hand before lighting it with his Zippo. His Zippo was adorned with the US Marine Corps emblem.

Patiently, he lit another Lucky and squinted through the smoke at Jack and Kathy. They were sitting at the kitchen table in the Portman apartment. He was five minutes into his interview. "Think, Jack, think! You must have noticed something about those two."

"I told you, Sheriff, it was dark, they were like shadows on the sand. One shadow was big, the other small."

"Small. . .or smaller?" The sheriff pressed.

"I guess. . . smaller."

"Was the big one... tall-big, wide-big, or big-big?"

Jack wanted to help, but he was helpless to do so. He hadn't seen enough to offer a description. He slumped, frustrated because his powers of observation had failed him at a critical time. His mind turned back to the two guys with the customized Ford coupe that Bobby had spoken to in the parking area. It couldn't have been them; they were both of average size and build. He realized he hadn't paid attention to anyone. He'd gone to Beach Night looking for a girl and after he found Kathy everything else was peripheral. He felt Kathy's hand on his knee. It wasn't sexual. It was supportive. He reconsidered the sheriff's multiple-choice question.

"Big-big," he answered. "I got the impression one of them was a very big guy."

"Jack, I hate to go over and over this, but these details are important. I also respect the hell out of you for running in there, damn the torpedoes, full speed ahead, because let me tell you, the sick bastards that do these things just as often kill their victim as not. I think you might have saved Betty Wagner's life. I truly do. But if we don't catch them, they'll do it again."

Henry Stark ground out his cigarette. He ground it hard into the ashtray and kept grinding it long after the ember was extinguished. Then he smiled and turned to Kathy.

"I know you were behind Jack, I know you couldn't have seen them, but Betty talked to you. She's not talking to anyone now. She's trying to pretend it didn't happen. So you need to think back and tell me everything she said."

Kathy closed her eyes, trying to relive the moment. "I think she thought they'd come back because she was afraid of Jack until I told her he was with me. Then she said she'd 'just gone into the trees to' ... you know?"

The sheriff nodded, he knew why girls excused themselves and went into the trees. He pulled another cigarette out of his pack but he didn't start tapping it, he didn't want to distract Kathy.

Kathy opened her eyes and leaned forward. "She said there were two of them, one was 'powerful'...that was her word, and she said, 'The powerful one had a mask,' and said, 'If you scream, I'll kill you.' And he threw a blanket over her and carried her away."

Kathy paused, wishing she knew more. "Honestly, I didn't ask her much. I just wanted to calm her down so we could help her. I'm sorry."

Henry Stark resumed tapping his cigarette. "You have nothing to be sorry for, Kathy."

He placed the cigarette between his lips. "Out of curiosity, Kathy . . . Miss McDonnell, with the state police all over the place, why didn't you go to them for help?"

Jack and Kathy looked at each other and shrugged in unison. It hadn't occurred to them.

Jack finally answered for both, "I don't know, Sheriff. I guess we were running from them, not to them. And when we found Betty, it seemed like a better idea to bring her here."

The sheriff nodded, endorsing Jack's decision. "Tommy Simmons? What do you think happened to him?"

"The two guys were running away from the spot where we left Tommy," Jack answered, "The hiking trail isn't far from the service road. They might have had a car down there and circled back to it. Tommy might have gone down to the road, too, but he wouldn't have tried to take them on."

"So there's a chance he saw them?"

Kathy answered, "It was dark and he was afraid. He must have heard the screams. I think he would have hidden himself, the same as he did when the state police came."

"That makes sense," the sheriff nodded. "One last question: Do you recall seeing two young men who generally fit the description?"

Jack had already dismissed the two super-cool dudes, now he couldn't help but think of Posey and Bobby. Big and small – but they would never rape a girl. Besides, Posey couldn't move that fast. Whoever it was...was big and agile. He wondered about Yablonski, but that didn't make sense because everybody knew Yablonski. Betty would have known if it was Yablonski.

"No," Jack answered, "but the big guy moved quickly, you know, cat like. He was athletic, smooth and fluid, like someone who could play in the backfield, not just on the line."

The sheriff snuffed out his cigarette and pushed himself into standing position. "Jack, I need your help tomorrow. Be out front at six. I want to be on the crime scene at daybreak. By the way, don't talk to the newspapers, not even Harold. Don't talk to the state police either. If anybody asks, say you didn't see anything and you already gave your statement to the Douglas County Sheriff's office. Tell them to call me if they have any questions or information. You *did not* see anything. You helped the girl. Period. Got that?"

Kathy nodded yes. Jack said, "Yes, sir."

At that moment Kathy's father, James McDonnell, was driving to Winchester Bay in his Willys Jeep station wagon.

He'd picked the Jeep because it was the most eccentric vehicle he could buy without going to something exotic or impractical.

He'd taken on big lumber and won. He'd taken on the Longshoremen union and won. He'd defended the pinball, gambling kings of eastern Oregon and won. He'd invested in obscure tracts of timber during World War II. And won.

He was semi-retired and lived with his wife and daughter in a custom built home of glass and cedar in Lakeside, an exclusive community located north of Coos Bay. Lakeside residents sent their high school students to Coos Bay's Marshfield High School – which was rated highly for its academics as well as its athletic programs. In the 1950s, nearly forty-percent of Coos Bay's high school graduates attended college, compared to Florence and Reedsport's eleven-percent.

McDonnell's wife, Mary, sat in the passenger seat, leaning against the locked door; her arms folded across her chest. Her husband had received a phone call from a Douglas County sheriff saying their daughter needed a ride home from Winchester Bay. That if he and Mrs. McDonnell had heard about some arrests at Senior Beach Night, not to worry, Kathy wasn't involved. To the contrary, the sheriff assured James McDonnell, "Kathy helped rescue a classmate. She's safe and sound and can be found at The Dock." The sheriff added, "Upstairs. Not in the tavern."

For some reason, McDonnell was amused. His wife was not. He tried to pat her knee while he talked to her but she jerked away. "I'm telling you not to worry. Our Kathy can look after herself. Tonight, it seems, she looked out for someone else, too."

Best guess, he thought, a classmate got drunk and tried to swim in the ice cold Pacific. After three minutes, James surmised, he or she suffered from hypothermia. Kathy, being an excellent swimmer, helped in the rescue.

Mary McDonnell grimaced. "Did the sheriff say anything about Kyle? He must be with her. He promised me he'd take care of her."

"My dear Mary, Kyle takes care of Kyle."

When Kathy's parents arrived at The Dock, Mary took one look and announced, "I'm not going in there."

James knew she would say that. "Suit yourself," he sighed and released his long frame from the Jeep Wagon. He was wearing a custom tailored Oxford cloth dress shirt from Brooks Brothers and a pair of blue cords. He slouched his way into the bar, curious but not concerned.

Henry Stark's deputy and protégé, Cal Shinkle, was posted inside the door. Cal had been instructed to wait for Mr. McDonnell and usher him upstairs.

It was now after midnight, yet the tavern was going full-throttle. Word had spread. Elsie Brown, the telephone operator, reported Greta told the doctor, "It was a terrible, horrible crime." Elsie translated that as, "Murder or even worse and the sheriff has commandeered Greta Portman's apartment for his headquarters."

From a Winchester Bay resident's point of view, what better way to get the inside scoop than to go to the tavern, have a drink and keep your eyes and ears open?

Several of the patrons recognized McDonnell when he entered. The legendary lawyer's appearance fueled speculations: Were they holding the murderer upstairs? Had a wealthy parent called in the Clarence Darrow of the Oregon Coast to defend their accused teenager? Who could afford McDonnell? It would have to be one of those rich kids from Lakeside or Coos Bay.

James made his way up the interior stairs and found his daughter sitting at Greta Portman's kitchen table with of all people, the nice looking kid who'd handed him a fishing rod with a thirty-pound Chinook on the end of the line.

The sheriff gave McDonnell an abridged version of the evening's events. Understandably, the rape distressed McDonnell. It could have been Kathy – yet, ironically, she was safe and sound because she'd been in the company of the very young man he'd warned to stay clear of her.

James McDonnell had witnessed violence many times in many forms. He'd seen Longshoremen rampage against non-union dockworkers. He'd seen white thugs brutalize Asian Americans and set fire to their tiny restaurants and hole-in-the-wall laundries. He'd seen loggers duel with axes. In his youth, growing up in Oregon's Willamette Valley, he'd seen Anglo-Americans overturn the farm wagons of German-Americans during World War I, then stone the German immigrants as they tried to salvage their harvest of beans, prunes, peaches and beets.

But those acts were inspired by twisted reason and driven by ignorance. Rape was different. To McDonnell, a rapist was a non-human, a primeval brute that stalked its prey in darkness and administered brutal violence out of an inner-greed to prove itself something it would never be: a man. For McDonnell, there could be no redemption for rapists. They should be captured, killed without ceremony and dumped on the garbage heap. No funeral, no burial, no acknowledgement that they were ever part of humankind. The anger welled inside him, although no one in the apartment witnessed it. He commanded his scorn for the perpetrators to subside and walked over to the parents of the victim. They were sitting in Greta's living room, listening to the doctor Greta had summoned.

The Wagners owned and operated a Shell service station on the busy strip of coast highway between North Bend and Coos Bay. Mr. Wagner was dressed in his brown uniform. His name, Art, was embroidered in red thread over the left breast pocket. Mrs. Wagner wore a simple black skirt and white blouse.

The distressed couple sat quietly as the doctor advised, "I think it would be a good idea to take her to Coos Bay Memorial hospital, at least for one night. I've called and they're expecting her. She's in shock, and I'm worried she has a concussion. There's also risk of infection. I've given her penicillin. Let's play it safe, err on the side of caution.

"There, there," the doctor handed his handkerchief to Mrs. Wagner, who had resumed crying.

McDonnell tapped Art Wagner on the shoulder and handed him a card. "If there's anything I can do, call me. Anything. No fee. I mean that."

McDonnell collected his daughter, thanked Greta Portman for her hospitality and shook hands with Henry Stark.

"If there's anything I can do to help, call me. I mean that."
He handed Henry a card.

In the stairwell, he took his daughter by the elbow.
"How did you come to be with Jack Portman?"

"He's a friend of Kyle..."

"Never mind," the father waved off the explanation.
"You're safe, that's all that matters."

Father and daughter reached the bottom of the stairwell. "I'd rather not try to explain all of this to mother,"
Kathy said. "Can I just get into the backseat and pretend
to fall asleep?"

"Sounds reasonable. If she asks about your new friend,
Jack, stick with your 'friend of Kyle' story. She likes Kyle
because he's going to college in California and his mother
kisses her butt."

They opened the door at the bottom of the interior
stairs and stepped into the tavern. A reporter in a crumpled
gray suit jumped out from the crowd.

"Harold Gilbert, *Umpqua Valley Journal*, Mr. McDonnell,
can you shed some light on what happened here tonight?"

"First, it didn't happen here. It happened over on the
dunes under the watchful eye of the Oregon State Police.

"Second, neither my daughter nor I are involved in any
way. Third? Well, hell, Harold. No comment. It's past my
bedtime and I'm going home."

CHAPTER NINE

The main street of Winchester Bay bustled with activity at sun-up on Sunday morning. Fishermen, commercial and sport, clogged the parking lots, sidewalks and the public boat ramp. They were all in a hurry – to get breakfast, to get on the boat – to get out on the water and hook the biggest Chinook salmon in the Pacific Ocean.

Jack was waiting in front of his mother's tavern at 6:00 a.m. A sliver of light was beginning to appear against the tree line that topped the low-slung mountains to the east. The air was thick with fog and laden with the salty scent of the bay.

He saw the sheriff's car approach and stepped to the edge of the wooden sidewalk. Henry leaned across his seat and unlocked the passenger-side door.

"Think you can find the exact spot?" the sheriff asked as he sipped coffee from his thermos cup.

"Yeah, think so. The blanket should still be there. Drive over to the North Jetty and we'll walk from there."

The sheriff kept talking. He wanted the kid to like him. More importantly, he wanted the kid's mother to like him. Being on the good side of Jack wouldn't hurt his cause.

"Those damn dunes are spooky," the sheriff chatted away, "The way the sand shifts, doubt if we'll find anything but we have to look. Want some coffee? Clean, empty cup under the seat."

Jack took a bye on the coffee.

"About your buddy, Tommy Simmons," the sheriff continued, "he got home safe and sound."

"He's not my buddy," Jack corrected.

The sheriff smiled, "Anyway, he told my deputy he heard the victim scream, then chased two guys down to the service road. Said he tried to get the license but it was too dark. He also said he heard them arguing or fighting before they drove away."

"I don't think Tommy would have chased them," Jack said.

"I don't either. I think he stumbled onto the service road, heard them coming and ducked for cover. Can't fault him for that. He's probably telling the truth about hearing them arguing and that could turn out to be something."

"How's that?"

"Well, the 'powerful' one did the rape. So, I might be able to get the other one to testify against him."

"Yeah," Jack said, impressed. The sheriff's conjecture stirred Jack's curiosity. "What else do you think, I mean – so far?"

"I think Betty happened to be the unlucky victim. They were waiting in the trees for a female. Soon as they got one they hauled her toward the beach like a couple of wolves with a fresh-killed fawn. They'd parked on that service road for a quick getaway. I'm guessing the smaller guy had second thoughts. That's why I need to find him."

Jack tossed out a rhetorical question. "What if you can't find him?"

The sheriff shrugged and maneuvered his souped-up, V-8 Chrysler as close to the jetty as he could without getting stuck in the sand. Once parked, they stepped outside to wait for more daylight. The sheriff took out his Lucky Strikes.

"Awful habit," he confessed to his young companion.

The morning light crawled slowly down the coastal mountains toward the white sands. The sheriff smoked his cigarette, field-stripped it and took a last swallow from his thermos cup.

"It's light enough," Jack said, "I can find it."

Jack led the sheriff along the jetty to the spot that intersected the hiking trail. He took the trail until he recognized the tree he'd leaned Betty against. "This is where we came out."

He looked across the dunes through the morning mist and down to the shoreline. White ribbons of foam danced along the slate gray water. The waves stretched toward land, exhausted themselves on the beach and retreated back toward the deep. Small white birds darted along the foam-line searching for morsels of crab, clam and tiny sea creatures. Jack stared at the surf and thought about Kathy.

Was that strange or not? The way her father had warned him earlier – as if he'd had a premonition. And there she was at the bonfire, the girl in the band. The way they had kissed. The way they had worked together to save Betty

Wagner. The way her hand felt when she reassured him under the table.

Thinking about Kathy, he almost forgot what he was here for. He forced his mind back to the task at hand.

"Down there, maybe a football field away," he pointed into the dunes, "at the bottom of that biggest dune."

He trudged up one dune, down another and up another. Every day the dunes looked the same, but every day they were slightly different. The incessant, ever-shifting sand had erased the tracks from the night before.

"There." Jack pointed at a half buried, brown army blanket.

The sheriff made his way down the dune and examined the blanket. "Nothing here," he said, "Except poor Betty's blood. So, all we got is a standard issue army blanket. Must be millions of these floating around."

Using the blanket as the center of his search area, the sheriff began to walk in ever-widening circles. He moved slowly, kicking the sand gently with the toe of his boot, literally trying to dig up evidence.

Fifteen minutes later the sheriff's persistence paid off. He spotted a piece of blue cloth protruding from the sand. Reaching down, he removed a blue knit, stocking-style seaman's hat. Two eyeholes had been crudely torn in the knit fabric. "Poor man's ski mask," Henry said, holding it up for Jack to see.

"High school kids from Florence wear those," Jack offered. "They call themselves the Siuslaw Sailors. Last year they wore white Navy caps to all the games. Year before it was blue seaman hats like that one."

The sheriff inspected it. Betty had told Kathy the rapist had a mask. "It's stretched out," the sheriff noted. "Big man, big head." It was a crude disguise, Henry thought, but clever. He turned the hat inside out. Jack walked over to take a closer look. He pointed, "Lot of loose hair in there."

"Maybe he just had a hair cut?" Henry surmised.

"Yeah," Jack agreed, recalling loose hairs in his baseball cap after getting a haircut.

"Well, Jack, you've been a big help. We're looking for a big powerful guy traveling with a little guy. The big one may be from Florence, has close-cut blonde hair and went to the barber-shop yesterday. I think I'll take a drive up to Florence."

The sheriff picked up the blanket and began walking back to the car. Jack fell in step. "Season before last, my junior year," Jack said, "Florence had a big fullback, not real fast, but he moved good. When he got up a head of steam he was hard to bring down."

"Remember his name?"

"Abernathy, number 13. He had a nickname, *Nasty*. Only played one year. Don't know the color of his hair."

"Anything else?"

"His teammates didn't like him."

"What makes you say that?"

"They didn't block for him. The way they treated him in the huddle. The way they said his nickname. You can tell, but he was good. Powerful."

The sheriff lifted an eyebrow, "Powerful? Sounds familiar."

The two reached the car and the sheriff lit another cigarette. He slipped behind the steering wheel but left the door open while he smoked.

"If anybody asks, like if *The Coos Bay Times* or old Harold Gilbert comes snooping around, we didn't find anything out here this morning."

"Okay," Jack agreed.

"Want to know why?"

Jack took a guess. "Because the longer they think no one is looking for them, the easier they are to find?"

Henry cracked a grin. "You catch on fast." He then field-stripped his cigarette, closed the door and started the engine. "What flusters me," he said, as he backed the car onto the roadway, "is this shouldn't have happened. If the state troopers had been on the ball, they would have spread out and just made their presence known. Patrolled the perimeter up by the trees but let you and the other seniors have your damned beach party. I think some fool politician just got a hair up his ass to clamp down on teenage age drinking, forgetting he did the same damn thing when he was eighteen. I say, 'Old enough to die on a beach in the South Pacific, old enough to drink one or two beers here'." The sheriff sighed. "We have a bunch of harmless kids sitting in the Coos Bay jail for drinking a few beers and that rapist is running loose."

* * *

In 1954 – if you drove down Main Street in Reedsport toward the river, you'd pass the movie theatre on the right and Barney's Outfitting on the left.

Turn left at Barney's, go two blocks and you'd come to the Horse Shoe Café. It was one of the two spots in Reedsport where the high school kids hung out. The other hangout was the drive-in cafe at the junction of U.S. Highway 101 and State Highway 38.

The Horse Shoe Café also had adult customers, probably because it was the only place downtown where you could get coffee, sodas, chicken fried steaks, hamburgers, a different blue-plate special every day and a variety of sandwiches and deserts. The name, Horse Shoe, was descriptive of the interior layout. The diner-style red formica counter was shaped like a giant horse-shoe.

For whatever reason, the high schoolers took the stools and booths to the left; the adults took the stools and booths to the right. A young (Class of '52), shapely blonde with a beehive hairdo served the high schoolers; a matronly, (Class of '39) blonde with a beehive hairdo waited on the adults.

The two-restaurants-in-one concept was a practical arrangement for the town and the times. By noon on Sunday, the Horse Shoe was crowded. High schoolers gathered there before the matinee movie to swap stories about Beach Night; adults were having after church coffee and pie. Unlike much of America during the same era, churchgoers were a minority on the Oregon coast, but between the Baptists and Methodists who attended the 11:00 a.m. services, there were enough of them to fill every stool and booth on the right hand side of the cafe.

On the student side, Tommy Simmons found himself in the unfamiliar circumstance of being the center of attention. He was seated in one of the booths (having ordered a Green River soda and French fries with gravy). A shapely cheerleader, Janet Preston, Skip's big sister, was sitting next to Tommy. Her leg and arm were actually touching him. The fact it was a four-person booth with six people crammed inside didn't register with Tommy. Janet was touching him.

"You were with Jack Portman last night?" Janet asked, seeming in awe. "That's too much, too much. So, why was the sheriff looking for you, Tommy?" she cooed.

"Did you see the guys who did it?" Jerry Johnson interrupted, cutting to the chase.

"I'm not supposed to talk about it," Tommy answered, intoning self-importance.

"You can tell us," Janet urged.

As she said this, it seemed, at least it seemed to Tommy, that she pressed even closer. The side of her fanny was touching the side of his.

Green River was a fountain drink served in a Coke glass with ice cubes and a straw. Tommy leaned over and put his lips around the top of the straw and sucked an ounce of the sweet, green, bubbly liquid into his mouth.

It appeared like he was considering whether or not to share his insider information. In point of fact, he was fine-tuning his story. If the story were good enough, maybe they'd ask him to sit with them at the one o'clock movie. Maybe he'd get to sit next to Janet; after all, she'd broken up with Louie Matson and was acting as though she liked him, Tommy Simmons, hero of Beach Night. Why else would she have elected to take the seat next to him, start a conversation and press against him?

"Jeez," Tommy began, "I went to Beach Night, went to the big Coos Bay bonfire, had a couple of beers – and I ended up with this girl, Kathy something. Never got her last name. We weren't real interested in last names if you know what I mean . . ."

"Yeah, I'll bet," Johnson confronted Tommy. "I talked to Bobby Lacey, and Bobby said Jack, Posey and him went to the Coos Bay bonfire. Bobby didn't say anything about you being there. Bobby might show up here any minute, let's ask him if you were at the Coos Bay bonfire."

"Shush," Janet said to Jerry Johnson, winking and putting her index finger against her lips.

Tommy took this as his invitation to continue, "Kathy and I were headed for her car, looking for a little privacy, if you know what I mean, but when we got near the parking lot, the cops were all over the place."

Tommy took another sip from his Green River and picked up one of his soggy French fries.

Jerry Johnson was slightly jealous of the attention Janet was giving Tommy. "Yeah, the cops were there! Like we don't know the cops were there?"

"That's when I spotted Portman," Tommy responded to Jerry Johnson's challenge. "I knew Portman lived in Winchester Bay, so I said, 'Hey, Jack, do you know a way outta here?' I didn't want the cops to get Kathy, and jeez, to tell you the truth, I didn't look forward to spending a night in jail." Tommy thought the part about spending the night in jail was a good touch. He took another sip.

"So the three of us headed down the trail, and jeez, we were almost to the North Jetty when I heard this screaming, like a girl in trouble. Then I saw some guys running. I yelled at Portman, 'You and Kathy help the girl,' and I took after the two guys."

"Like, what were you going to do if you caught 'em?" Johnson sneered.

"Let him finish," Janet urged Jerry, placing her hand on Tommy's wrist.

She leaned into Tommy, her breast touching his upper arm. She coaxed, "Did you see them, Tommy? Who was it? Nobody from here was it?"

"It was dark, can't say for certain." He was blushing. Janet's breast was touching his arm. Did he dare move? If he moved, would she think he was getting fresh? But then she was the one who leaned against him. What signal was she trying to send? Be cool, Tommy told himself.

"I've already said more than I should." He moved his arm slightly, as if he was trying to get a better grip on his glass. Janet didn't leap back. Tommy took this as a good sign.

"Okay, jeez," Tommy said, "I'll tell you this much. They weren't from around here. You guys going to the movie?"

The booth emptied. "Maybe." Janet said. "Maybe we'll see you there."

The younger of the two Horse Shoe waitresses had overheard just enough . . .

"Sounds like Tommy Simmons saw the rats who did it."

Rumors began falling on the town of Reedsport like a hard rain.

"There wasn't a rape," Alma Price, one of the church-goers, reported, "A prostitute came down from Portland, built her own bonfire and was taking on all comers, $25 per. One of the kids wouldn't pay so she screamed and yelled rape."

Ben Thatcher, a sawmill worker who had once been busted by a state trooper for driving under the influence, used the incident to say, "The state police made the whole thing up to justify their raid."

Two loggers having a beer at Carl's Tavern & Billiard Parlor acted like they knew what they were talking about when they claimed, "A girl broke up with her boyfriend, had too much to drink and went berserk, accusing her ex of raping her, and he wasn't even there."

The Ambassador insisted, "It wasn't the Indians..."

Deputy Sheriff, Cal Shinkle, made one thing clear. "Jack Portman saved the girl's life."

The younger waitress at the Horse Shoe stuck to her story. "I know what I heard with my own two ears: Tommy Simmons saw the bastards who did it, excuse my French."

CHAPTER TEN

If someone happened to be in Reedsport during the 1950s and turned left at the Horse Shoe Café, he or she would find themselves on a gravel road flanked by wooden sidewalks. On the left hand side of the street was a furniture store. A handsome sign over the doorway proudly announced:

Grafton & Daughter

Fine Furniture & Music Store

Mr. Glenn Grafton, a widower, kept to himself, although when he did interact with people, including customers, he seldom passed up an opportunity to be rude, or at the very least, conspicuously unpleasant.

The owner of the Horse Shoe Café hated to see Glenn Grafton walk in the door, claiming Glenn was bad for business. "Rosie is a great gal, but Glenn is bad news in capital letters. Nobody in town will sit next to him at the counter. Busiest time of my day and he takes three stools out of commission."

Glenn's personality was in sharp contrast to his younger brother, Wayne, who owned the only grocery store in the affluent community of Lakeside, where James McDonnell and other "rich folks" lived. The two brothers hadn't spoken since the death of Glenn's wife in 1950.

In Glenn Grafton's defense, he was a first rate carpenter and handcrafted many of the finer pieces in his store. The store survived because of the quality of its goods and the genial, pleasant service provided by Glenn Grafton's daughter, Rosie, a plump, thirty-three-year old, eternally cheerful woman who had the bright idea to open a music and record department in a corner of the furniture store. This had turned out to be a boon for the store's cash flow.

She also had a crush on the sheriff. Her record business was flourishing. Her romance with the sheriff was not.

Down the street on the right was the weekly newspaper. It was contained in a white frame building badly in need of paint. The name of the newspaper, *Umpqua Valley Journal*, was printed on the front window in the same Olde English typeface as the masthead.

Below the name, in smaller type, was the newspaper's slogan:

Covers the Lower Umpqua Valley Like the Morning Mist.

Beneath the slogan, the two proprietors were listed:

Karl Schmidt, Majority Owner & Master Printer.

Harold Gilbert, Editor & Publisher.

The front office, Mr. Gilbert's dominion, occupied a small part of the long narrow building. There was a counter, and behind it, a roll-top desk with a battered Underwood typewriter. The expansive backroom contained the linotype machine, drawers of type, work tables and the printing press. The backroom was empty on Sunday as Mr. Schmidt was a member of a tiny band of Lutherans and took his minister's decree to "Rest on Sunday" seriously.

Most of the paper's revenue came from the printing operation. However, the ads, which local merchants felt obliged to run, were the difference between break-even and profitability.

On this particular Sunday afternoon, Mr. Gilbert was sitting at his roll-top desk nursing a cup of what he called half-and-half: Half-coffee, half-whiskey. He wore the same frayed, crumpled suit, shirt and tie as the night before when he'd confronted James McDonnell at The Dock.

Harold was in his late forties but appeared older. His hair was receding and streaked with gray. His complexion was sallow and he had dark circles under his eyes from too many years of half-and-half. On this day he faced his typewriter in a serious mood. This was the biggest story he'd had since a cougar attacked the Cochran girl on a farm up Smith River.

Mrs. Cochran saved her little girl by taking after the animal with a hoe, chasing it back into the hills. Mr. Cochran and two neighbors rounded up two bloodhounds and an Airedale and tracked the cougar into a stand of old growth Hemlock and Doug fir. After they treed it, the father of the little girl killed it with a single bullet from his Winchester 30-30 carbine.

Harold took a picture of the father, mother and little girl standing behind the dead cougar. It ran on the front page with the story of the mother's courage and the father's ultimate revenge.

Harold sensed that the rape on Beach Night was an even bigger story. Although it posed a dilemma: His weekly paper didn't come out until Thursday. Today's news was the rape.

Thursday's news could be the capture. Harold pondered. What angle should he take?

He thought about his "interview" with the lawyer, McDonnell, the night before.

What was it McDonnell said? It was something about the state police. He began typing:

STATE POLICE ARREST TEENS FOR ROTOR THEFT, RAPISTS ESCAPE.

Good, he thought – accurate, newsy, but with a clever, cynical edge. Problem: If they caught the rapists during the week it would be irrelevant.

He started thinking about the rumors flying around. Harold hadn't been able to talk directly with the sheriff, but he reckoned the deputy, Cal Shinkle, had given him the straight scoop. "Girl was beaten and raped. Name and address withheld," which is the procedure in rape cases. No eyewitnesses. Two high school seniors, Jack Portman and an unnamed girl from Coos Bay High, found the victim on the beach and called the sheriff." Speculation pointed to the lawyer's daughter, Kathy McDonnell, as the unnamed girl, yet Cal would neither confirm nor deny her identity. Regardless, the rescuers reportedly saw two men fleeing the scene, identities unknown. Tommy Simmons had been in the immediate area and confirmed the part about "two men running from the scene."

Damn little to work with. Still, he had until Wednesday afternoon. By then he'd have more facts. Harold wheeled his swiveled, roller chair across his small office to the cabinet under the counter and refilled his coffee cup. This time he left out the coffee. Why not? he thought. He didn't have to answer to a wife any more.

CHAPTER ELEVEN

Two things troubled Sheriff Henry Stark as he drove north on 101 toward Florence: One, Betty Wagner may not be the rapist's first victim; Two, rapists almost always worked alone.

According to Jack Portman's sketchy description, the big, powerful guy had to be a loner, yet in Betty Wagner's case he had an accomplice, a smaller guy. Piecing it together, the powerful one was the rapist. The little guy happened to be along; someone Abernathy dominated through intimidation. So, *if* he could get the sidekick alone, he could offer an army enlistment in lieu of prison. Good strategy, Henry thought. The smaller guy was probably afraid of Abernathy and was looking for a way out. For good reason, Henry thought, rape is first cousin to murder.

When Henry passed Tahkenitch Lake he slowed and pulled into the small resort. He hoped he might learn something from the resort owner, George Budge. Tahkenitch Lake Resort consisted of a row of twelve cabins, bait and tackle shop, boat dock, dockside café and boat launch. Mr. Budge also rented a fleet of small skiffs equipped with five horsepower Johnson outboard motors.

The lake was a popular fishing spot, offering planted rainbow trout, native cutthroats, largemouth bass, perch, blue gill, crappie and from June through September, salmon. Henry saw Tim Budge, George's son, working on the dock. He liked Tim, another member of Reedsport's Class of '54. Tall, blond, baby-faced with sparkling blue eyes, Tim was easy to like. Tim drove a Kaiser Henry J, one of America's first compact cars. His parents bought the car on Tim's sixteenth birthday so their son wouldn't have to ride on the school bus with "the little kids." The petite car was lime green and Tim painted the word "Intelligencia" on both car doors. Henry had worried about Tim when he first got the car. Tim seemed mature and sensible in school and around the resort. However, a reckless streak emerged when he slipped behind the wheel. Stark had caught Tim speeding over the bridge from Reedsport to Gardiner. He pulled Tim from his car and dragged him over to the bridge railing. "If you want to kill yourself, Timmy, jump off the bridge, that way you won't take anyone with you."

This got Tim's attention.

The sheriff released him. "It isn't worth it, Timmy. Wherever you're going, it'll be there five or ten minutes later. If I catch you speeding again, well, hell, I'll throw you in jail and take away your license. How do you like them apples? Now get out of here."

He didn't give Tim a ticket, and so far, a full year later, Tim had a light foot on the gas pedal, at least on Henry Stark's roads. Tim waved at Henry Stark. The sheriff was one adult he respected.

Stark entered the café. The breakfast rush was over and George Budge was doing the dishes. Henry had informed Mr. Budge about the altercation on the bridge. Mr. Budge had thanked him.

Henry placed his thermos on the counter. "Got any fresh coffee?"

"Got some stale coffee. Same price and you won't have to wait."

Henry laughed. He tried to think of a clever rejoinder, but couldn't.

"I'll make some fresh, if you're paying," Budge said with a sly grin. He was a fifty-year-old version of his son. The hair was gray, but all the lights were turned on behind his eyes.

The reference to paying was a running joke. Henry Stark always insisted on paying.

"Hear you had a little trouble last night?" George Budge, past master of understatement, volunteered. He started the process of brewing a pot of coffee, waiting for a response.

"You could say that. I see Tim escaped the drag net. How'd he manage that?"

"He didn't go."

"Thought all the seniors were going."

"Well, Henry, I knew the state police would be out in force. There was talk up and down 101 that the state cops wanted this to be the last Beach Night."

Henry hadn't heard this. He nodded.

Mr. Budge continued, "I also know my son. If there was trouble he'd be in the thick of it. If not starting it, egging it on. So, I reached into my wallet and said, 'Tim, this is a picture of Benjamin Franklin, one of our nation's most revered founding fathers. You can have Ben Frank-lin's portrait to do with as you please on one condition, you stay home tonight and help me get the boats ready for tomorrow.' Mind you, I never said, 'You can't go to Beach Night.' I think my son made a good decision. But you didn't come up here to check on Tim?"

"No. Sorry to say a girl was raped last night. I was wondering if you've heard about any other such incidents, maybe around Florence?"

"Incidents?" Mr. Budge repeated. "That's a mild word for rape." He stared at the coffee pot and took a deep breath. "What the hell gets into people, Henry?" He was working himself around to answering the sheriff's question.

The coffee was nearly ready so George Budge took Henry Stark's thermos into the kitchen and rinsed it. When he came back to the counter, fresh coffee was dripping into the lower pot.

"Last spring, there was some talk," Budge said as he filled the thermos. "A couple of car-loads of college kids drove down from Eugene for a picnic at Cleowox. You know how that lake sits there right in the dunes? Nice sandy beach. Water's warmer than in the bigger lakes. College kids love it."

"So?"

"It's only a story, Henry, not the gospel. Story is one of the girls took a dare to swim all the way across. She gets out on the other side, she's tired, so she starts taking the trail back and somebody jumped her."

"Who told you?"

"Fella who owns the store by Siltcoos Lake – only place to buy beer between Gardiner and Florence. He overheard the college kids talking. Didn't have any details. If he did, he would've told me. Loves to talk. He could give The Ambassador a good run."

"I know him," Henry said. "He'd sell beer to an eighth-grader on a bicycle. How much for the coffee?"

"Five cups, fifty cents. With your civil servant discount, you can have it for half price. Cash, no credit."

The sheriff reached into his pants pocket. "Damn, your prices are killing me. I pay more for coffee than gasoline."

"If you'd rather drink gasoline, Tim can fix you up outside."

Henry Stark met with his fellow Sheriff, Buck Kincaid. After an exchange of niceties, Henry asked if there had been any rapes in the Florence area during the past year.

Buck frowned; displeased that a colleague would think such a vile act could occur in his town. "Not that I recall, Henry, and I believe rape is the sort of thing that would stick in my mind."

"Had to ask," Henry said. He took a chair and down-loaded the information he'd gathered, concluding, "I'd like to talk to the big guy named Abernathy. I'd also like to find any 'little guy' he may run around with and question him separately."

Sheriff Kincaid scratched his head with three fingers, which seemed to jar his memory.

"Come to think of it, Abernathy does have a buddy. Terry Dodd. Not a bad kid, worked the night shift at the plywood plant 'till they shut-down that shift, so he could be anywhere."

"Call the barber, ask if Abernathy was in for a haircut yesterday."

Sheriff Kincaid picked up the phone and waited for the town operator to respond. "He'll be fishing," he predicted. "Martha, this is Buck, look up Red Peterson's home number and ring it for me, darling."

Buck Kincaid was a pleasant looking man in his late forties. He kept himself in decent physical condition, save for the over-sized stomach betraying his love of fried chicken and apple pie. Henry watched Buck handle the phone call, admiring his counterpart's congeniality and knowledge of his townspeople.

"Shirley, this is Buck Kincaid, is Red around the house or has he gone fishing again?"

Pause.

"That's what I thought."

Pause.

"Heavens no, he's not in any kind of trouble, my dear. I just want to ask him a question about one of his customers, John Abernathy."

Long pause.

"You tell Red to call me next time something like that happens. That's what you pay me for – and thanks, Shirley, this helps."

Buck placed the phone back on the receiver. "He got a haircut Saturday morning. Jumped in front of two of Red's customers and then stiffed him for the bill."

Kincaid rose from behind his desk and walked over to a bookcase. He pulled the 1952-53 Siuslaw Sailors yearbook from the shelf and handed it to Henry. "Nasty is nineteen or twenty, looks older. Flunked a couple of grades, never finished high school but he did play football one year. Both his and Dodd's pictures will be in there."

Buck picked up his car keys and strapped the revolver around his ample waist. "I've got nothing better to do, Henry. Let's go over to Abernathy's place and have a little chit-chat with him."

As the two sheriffs drove down to the Siuslaw River and turned east, inland, Buck told Henry what he knew about John Abernathy. "His nickname is Nasty. Started out as Abernasty and got shortened down. You don't get a nickname like Nasty without earning it one way or another."

Henry nodded, encouraging Buck to continue.

"His old man was a timber topper, good at his work but meaner than a rabid skunk. He beat his wife. He beat his kid. One day he flipped his strap over the top of the spur tree and came tumbling down like the Giant in Jack and the Beanstalk. He was probably drunk at the time. Killed him deader than a stone."

"What about the mother?"

"Don't know much about the mother other than it makes your eyes water to look at her. She works as a cleaning woman in those new condos along the beach north of town. I cut Big John some slack, figuring he'd had a rough go, but he was always in fights. Finally, they kicked him out of school. He got a job setting chokers for

U.S. Plywood up the road in Mapleton and I heard he was a good worker. Then he decided to be a boxer. Fought in the smokers up and down the coast, did pretty good, I'm told, until he got a real fight in the Armory in Eugene and had his clock cleaned by a Negro from California. Nobody likes him, that's for sure. One store-owner swears he stole a Pendleton shirt, but hell, he didn't see him steal it. Can't arrest him for that. Truth is, Nasty hasn't made any trouble for me, so I let well enough alone."

Buck stopped the car in a pullover along the Siuslaw River. It was a wide spot in the river. A row of houseboats bobbed on the water below the road. Houseboats were the trailer parks of coastal towns in the 1950s.

"Nasty has been staying with his mother the last few months." Sheriff Buck Kincaid pointed, "She lives in the one with the pink trim."

The two lawmen made their way down the rickety wooden staircase and onto the cat-walk. The houseboats were all the same size – one-story with six hundred square feet of living space inside. The houseboats and catwalk were kept afloat by logs and empty oil drums.

Kincaid knocked on the door of Number 16. A woman opened it. She was taller than average, about five feet, ten inches. Tall or not, she was bent and gnarled like an oak tree left standing after a forest fire.

"Looking for your son, Mrs. Abernathy. He home?" Sheriff Kincaid asked in a polite, kindly manner.

"He didn't do nuthing!" She spit the words at them.

"I need to talk to him."

"Well, he ain't here. He left Friday, or it might have been yesterday. Him and his friend went down to Coos Bay to get work; God knows there ain't no work around here. They shut down the second shifts at the mills and what jobs they got don't pay spit."

"Did he give you an address or phone number where we could reach him?" Sheriff Kincaid asked.

"I ain't got no phone. Why would he give me a phone number?"

"Mind if I come in and have a look?" Kincaid asked.

"Yeah, damn right I mind, but that won't stop you. Stick a badge on a monkey's chest and he thinks he's King Kong."

Kincaid ignored the insult and removed his hat as he entered the houseboat.

Stark waited for five minutes.

Kincaid stepped back outside. The woman slammed the door shut behind him.

"Nice talking to you, Mrs. Abernasty," Kincaid cracked, then reported to Henry,

"He isn't there, most of his clothes are gone. Good bet he owns a deer rifle and it wasn't there either. Let's check on Dodd."

Terry Dodd had been sharing a one-bedroom walk-up in a rundown, wood-framed apartment building near the harbor. One of his two roommates was home. The roommate was nursing a beer and listening to a Hank Williams song on the radio. He turned his radio off and invited the two sheriffs to sit down at the table in the small dining nook. He said Terry Dodd had packed a suitcase Saturday morning and left town.

"Terry didn't say where he was going and I didn't ask. If you're interested, Dodd drives a blue, '48 Plymouth coupe." The roommate added, "I've stayed clear of Terry since he started hanging out with Nasty."

"You ever hang out with Nasty?" Kincaid asked.

"He's bad news," the young man shook his head. "He'd say something that was supposed to be funny, then he'd punch you on the shoulder, like guys do, you know, but he'd hit you hard, real hard, then stare you down, you know, daring you to say something."

"What did he say that was supposed to be funny?" Henry Stark questioned.

"It was usually something about women. Dirty talk, you know . . . "

"Don't know," Henry said. "Give me an example."

"Like a woman would walk by and Nasty would say, 'I bet she'd like to fuck all three of us if one of us would go ask her. Dodd, go ask her.' Then he'd laugh, and punch me on the shoulder like he was kidding. But he left bruises on my shoulder." The young man rubbed his shoulder, recalling the pain.

"Did Terry ever go ask?" Stark asked.

"Naw, Terry's not a bad guy. He's just scared shitless of Nasty, that's all. I told him he should stop hanging out with him but he didn't know how to get out of it. You know, afraid of what Nasty might do? Nasty doesn't have a car and expects Terry to drive him everywhere. I figured maybe that's what Terry was doing Saturday, you know, leaving town? Like maybe he was trying to shake free of Nasty."

"When Terry left town," Buck Kincaid probed, "Did he say whether Nasty was or wasn't going with him?"

"No, he didn't say one way or the other. He just squared it with me for the rent and left."

"You wouldn't happen to know the plate number of his Plymouth coupe?" Buck asked.

The young man brightened, "Yeah, I'm good with numbers – license plates, addresses, phone numbers. I see 'em once and they stick in my head, you know. Terry's plate is P852-42. Easy for me to remember because I graduated in 52 and 42 is exactly ten numbers less."

"Good man," Buck said, patting the young man on the back. "If you get into any trouble, you call me. You just earned yourself a favor."

When they drove away from the apartment, Buck spoke first. "Looks like you might be right about Abernathy. I'll find the other roommates and see what they know. Howsoever, we sure as hell got enough to put out an all-points on Dodd's Plymouth."

"We sure do," Henry Stark agreed.

Buck Kincaid took one hand off of the steering wheel so he could point to himself, "It appears like, at least to this old hoss, we're looking in the wrong town. Nasty's lovely momma said he was going to Coos Bay. Winchester Bay is on the way. So they're driving along, see all the cars gathering for Beach Night and Nasty says to Terry, 'Let's just stop here for awhile and rape somebody.'"

CHAPTER TWELVE

Greta closed The Dock Tavern on Sundays and Mondays. Sunday was a concession to the local clergy. "So they can't blame me for their pitiful attendance." Monday was a concession to herself, "I need two days out of the week when the only person I wait on is my son."

By the time Jack returned from showing the sheriff the 'crime scene,' she'd finished vacuuming the apartment, changing the bed linens and dusting the frames around her art collection. She heard her son come up the outside stairs and open the door into the apartment. She quick-timed it to the kitchen.

"Find anything on the beach?"

Jack had stepped into the kitchen, uncapped a quart of milk and was about to down it. He took it away from his mouth and answered his mother's question. "No. I didn't see zilch but the sheriff did. He's pretty sharp. Has a suspect. He's driving up to Florence to check it out."

Hearing a positive remark about the sheriff pleased Greta. "Well then – I suppose we're making progress."

"Hope so," Jack answered before downing half the milk and heading for the shower.

She'd wanted to ask another question but Jack had already closed the bathroom door.

"Did you like the Sheriff?" she asked the empty space. He heard her. *Was something going on between his mother and the sheriff?* He stripped and stepped into the shower, thinking – *Better the sheriff than one of those wimpy assholes that ogled and tried to flirt with her in the tavern.*

He let the warm water wash over him, opting not to pursue the subject any further.

When Jack had showered, put on clean Levis and a fresh, white tee shirt, he asked if he he might "borrow" the car.

"'Borrow' the car? What do you have in mind?" Greta asked.

"Nothing in particular. Maybe up with Tim, Bobby or some of the guys."

She cast a dour look at him and said, "I thought you might go to Lakeside and see that Kathy. I liked her."

"Yeah, sure. Her old man would welcome me with open arms, I'm sure, the arms being a Colt 45."

"Don't be silly," she said, now casting a stern look at her son. "James McDonnell is one of the most decent men in all of Oregon. And I'm sure he's grateful to you now."

She looked over at her son. His clean white tee shirt accentuated his tan. She changed the subject. "You're a great looking kid! I should say 'young man.' Girls ever whistle at you?"

He laughed and shook his head. "Forget the car for now, I'll go down to the docks. I'll take Sal with me." Jack made a kissing noise with his mouth and the dog sprang to its feet like a Jack-In-The-Box.

The screen door banged closed behind them. Greta lit a cigarette, first of the five-a-day she allowed herself, and watched the smoke curl toward the ceiling. The smoke had a hypnotic effect. She drifted back in time. Her father, Gustavo Kuhn, was born near Worms, Germany in 1879. His parents were peasant farmers subject to the whim of an aristocratic landowner. Gus mastered the craft of butchering, saved his money and escaped to America. His dream was to own property, a right denied his class in 19th Century Prussia. Bertha, Greta's mother, was the second daughter of the gamekeeper on a large estate near Wismar in Northern Germany. The gamekeeper had one son and three daughters. He trained the son to succeed him – yet he feared for the fate of his daughters. Men in the district favored fair skinned, golden haired, ample-bosomed frauleins with an aptitude for servitude. His slender brunettes were taller than most men, and to complicate matters, independent minded.

The gamekeeper hatched a plan. He would poach in the forest he'd sworn to protect. With bootlegged grouse, venison and boar, he paid for his oldest daughter's passage to America. In turn, she earned the fare for the second sister, Bertha. Bertha was Greta's mother.

Gus and Berti, first names now Americanized, met in the Germantown section of Chicago in 1901. They married six months later, paid the third sister's boat passage and set out for a faraway land called Oregon. Eventually, the Kuhns purchased property along the Sandy River, forty-five miles west of Portland. They opened a restaurant and general store, had two children, survived the depression, and although they never became wealthy, they prospered. Gus and Berti retired and moved into a comfortable cottage with a view of the Sandy River. The son, Gus, Jr., took over the restaurant and transformed it into a popular roadhouse for skiers' and sightseers visiting Mt. Hood.

Greta, born in 1914, began working at the restaurant when she was thirteen. Business perked up considerably in the mid 1930s when President Franklin Delano Roosevelt ordered the Work Projects Administration to build Timberline Lodge at the base of Oregon's tallest and most beautiful peak, Mt. Hood.

The WPA workers came down from the mountain on payday, earnest young men with hope in their eyes. The first time she placed a cup of coffee in front of John Portman, she knew he was the man for her. Greta wiped a tear from her eye and endorsed her lovely memory with a smile.

A knock on the side door broke Greta's spell. She dabbed her eyes with the corner of her apron and went to the door.

"Hi, Mrs. Portman," Kathy said cheerfully. "Sorry to bother you but I was wondering if Jack was home."

Greta thought, *Well, well, well... Jack could wait a few days but you couldn't.* Had Kathy set her cap for her Jack, just as she, two decades ago, had plucked his daddy out of the herd of earnest young men working to find their dignity on a faraway mountain?

* * *

Jack sat on a sawed-off piling overlooking the marina. Absentmindedly, he ran his hand over the thick fur on Sal's back. The dog relished the attention and pressed against his master's leg. A flock of mudhens, also called coots, were bobbing on the water directly in front of them. A skiff cut through the flock and the birds flapped their wings and began running along the surface. They traveled twenty-five yards, never airborne, and dropped back onto the water. Sal barked at the flurry of activity and Jack stood. "Let's go," he said. They took the steps down to the wooden walkway that ran between the moorings. A dozen kids, age six to low-teens, were fishing for tomcod and bullheads. Jack stopped to watch. One of the boys looked up.

"Does your dog bite?"

"Not unless you give him a reason."

"Can I pet him?"

"Sure." Jack allowed.

Tentatively, the boy reached out and ran his hand over Sal's back. "Is he a police dog?" the boy asked.

Jack considered saying, 'No, he's a saloon dog,' but knew it would go over the boy's head. Instead, he explained, "Some people call them police dogs, but the actual name is German Shepherd."

"That's interesting," the boy said. He withdrew his hand and stuffed it into his pocket.

"What's your name?" Jack asked.

"Edward. You're Jack Portman, everybody knows who you are. I saw you play football once, you dropped a pass in the end zone."

Instinctively, Jack defended himself. "We won the game anyway."

Of all the good plays he'd made, he thought, why would this kid remember the one time he'd dropped a sure touchdown. As he thought about it, it struck him as funny. He chuckled his way into a wide grin.

"You play ball, Eddie?"

"I want to. I'm good at baseball. If I get big like you, I'll try out for football."

Jack reached out and rubbed Eddie's head. "Good, remember to watch the ball all the way into your hands."

"I will," Eddie promised.

Jack moved farther down the walkway. A charter captain was washing down his boat. "Any luck?" Jack asked.

"Salmon were nowhere to be found. Went six hours yesterday without a strike. Had a group from Corvallis, it was one of their birthdays, and they kept saying, 'C'mon, skip, get us a birthday present.' So, I said to myself, 'Forget the salmon.' I rigged for lingcod; we went down to the bottom and it was boom, boom, boom. I'll tell you true, Jack, they took some fish home."

The man went back to cleaning his boat. Jack decided not to tell him that Captain Harry Norton had found a school of Coho mixed with Chinook yesterday and would have limited if one of the customers hadn't gotten seasick. Then he thought, my God, was that only yesterday? He'd lived a year since yesterday.

Continuing along the walkway, he came to a power yacht, sixty-feet long, and wondered what it cost. The name on the stern was *Mary Anne, San Francisco*.

Jack tried to picture the owner. He'd be tall and handsome. His black hair would be streaked with gray. He was an adventurer from San Francisco who had fallen in love with a beautiful woman named Mary Anne. Ann with an e, meaning she was high born – from a wealthy family, maybe from Boston. In his mind's eye the man looked like Clark Gable and the woman was a dead ringer for Grace Kelly.

"Why are they here?" Jack asked Sal. "With all the ports of call in the world, why Winchester Bay? Are they hiding here? Running from the law?"

Jack felt a tap on his shoulder. "Penny for your thoughts," Kathy purred.

Jack turned and soaked in the glow of her eager eyes. He was immediately happy, although, he hoped, she hadn't heard him talking to his dog.

He took a moment to answer. "I was going to call you but I thought I should wait a couple of days."

"I couldn't wait. I had to see you."

They looked into each other's eyes. Sal worked his way between them and made a moan-like sound, sensing something unusual happening to his master.

"I had to see you," she repeated. "I don't have much time, I told my mother I was going to the store. But we have to see each other again. Can you come to our house next weekend? Sunday for sure, maybe even before Sunday? Just say yes."

"Yes."

She pressed a piece of paper into his hand. "This is the number for my phone in my room. It's unlisted. Call me."

She leaned against him, lifted her mouth and closed her eyes. Their lips met. It was a lovely kiss, soft, but with hot breath and deep yearning. They broke it off, knowing it was not the time or place to pursue the promise of the kiss.

"I've never done anything like this before," she said, proud of herself for having the gumption to come and see him. She'd never felt such longing and intensity for a boy before. She had jumped to the conclusion she had fallen in love.

She turned and ran back toward dry land and the parking lot. He watched her run. He adored the way she ran, like a girl, from the knees down.

"Kathy came by," Greta said when she heard the screen door slam shut. "Did she track you down?"

"She sure did," Jack answered cheerfully.

"Nice girl. I like her," Greta volunteered.

"I do too."

He fell silent.

"That's all you have to say? 'I do too.'"

"She asked me to her house next Sunday, or maybe before. We didn't decide exactly when."

"You going?"

"Sure, definitely. I want to go. I want to see her. I'll need the car."

"If you're going to Lakeside, you will," Greta agreed, turning away so he wouldn't see she was clenching her teeth to keep from laughing.

CHAPTER THIRTEEN

Sheriff Henry Stark returned to his office in downtown Reedsport a few minutes past six. He had the *Siuslaw Sailors Yearbook* under his arm and he was debating whether to call Karl Schmidt at home. He'd decided to print Wanted Posters and distribute them up and down the coast. One little problem: it was Sunday. It had been a long day and he was tired. It might be best to see Karl in the morning. Karl arrived at the newspaper/print shop promptly at six-thirty every morning. You could set your watch by him.

Deputy Cal Shinkle had manned the fort while Henry was in Florence. He'd left a note: "Nothing happened that won't wait till tomorrow except that district judge in Roseburg, Robert Stoval, called. Twice!!!!!"

Henry had dealt with Judge Stoval before. The less the judge knew about his business the better Henry liked it. The judge was a politician with the power of the robe. What was it other law enforcement practitioners said about Stoval? "He has very long toes. Walk carefully around him." He lived in Roseburg, the county seat. Henry dialed O for the local operator and Elsie picked up. She worked double shifts because, in her words, "There's just nothing else I'd prefer to do." He gave her the number and listened as the phone rang, once, twice.

A throaty, actor-quality voice answered, "Good evening."

"Good evening to you, Judge Stoval, this is Sheriff Stark in Reedsport returning your call."

"Yes, Henry, isn't it?"

"Yes sir."

"Henry, I'm sorry for intruding on your Sunday, please apologize to your wife . . ."

Henry thought, I don't have a wife and you should know I don't have a wife, but okay, you're the judge.

"Henry," Stoval droned, "I'm told we've had a rather nasty incident down there. Nasty situation."

Henry liked the irony of the judge's choice of words. *Nasty situation*? Indeed it was.

"Yes, your honor, a nasty situation. A high school senior from Coos Bay was beaten and raped on Lighthouse Beach near Winchester Bay."

"I understand this took place under the very nose of the state police?"

"Well, your honor," Henry offered, "the state police were in the area, true, but..."

"There are some issues here, Henry," the judge interrupted, "Delicate issues. I'm not going to ask you to evaluate the performance of our state police, but on the other hand, I don't want to whitewash culpability, if there was any, and I'm not implying there was. Do you understand what I'm saying?"

Henry didn't understand – but he indicated he did. "Yes, your honor."

"Conduct a vigorous investigation – if you encounter difficulties, need a warrant or more manpower, whatever, I want you to call me or the Douglas County Prosecutor. Do you have his number?"

"Yes, sir."

"Have you made any progress?"

"We have two suspects. We have an all-points out." Henry took a deep breath. He remembered being warned by the Reedsport Justice of the Peace: "Stoval might throw something tricky at you one day. He has friends in high places and likes to scratch their backs."

Carefully, Henry continued, "I believe we're on the right track but if there is a problem it's good to know I have someone higher up to turn to."

"Good." There was a long pause. "Good," the judge repeated. "Good night, Harvey."

He hung up.

Henry took out his pack of cigarettes, discovered it was empty and wadded it up. Expertly, he side-armed the crushed pack across the room into a brown waste paper basket. *Harvey?*

Henry went over to the file cabinet where he kept a carton and armed himself with a fresh pack. He thumped a Lucky against his thumbnail. Someone with influence had asked the judge to call – to build a fire under the investigation? Who would do that? Who had a stake in this? The victim's father who lived in Coos County wouldn't call a Douglas county judge in Roseburg. Besides, Henry surmised, Judge Stoval wouldn't care a rat's ass about the daughter of a gas station operator in Coos County.

James McDonnell? Why would he meddle in this, his daughter had come to no harm.

Henry placed the cigarette between his lips. Damn the judge! Girl gets raped and the politicians start scheming about how they can turn tragedy into personal gain. With Harry Truman out of office, Henry reckoned, the politicians would soon be running the country. Ike was a fine man, hell, a great man, but lately, it seemed Ike was more interested in golf than what was going on in Congress. And that curly haired Quaker, what was his name? Nixon? He was next in line.

Take care of the crime, he reminded himself. That's what you're paid to do. Stop working yourself up about things you can't control.

He flicked his lighter. Was it too easy? Had he rushed to judgment? Had he rationalized small clues and circumstances into an open and shut case? He moved the flame to the cigarette and inhaled. The small clues added up. If Abernathy and Dodd were innocent, they'd have alibis. Someone would have seen them someplace else. That would be the end of it. No one was being railroaded.

He exhaled. His mouth felt dry and sour from all the tobacco. He admonished himself. He needed to stop smoking.

Too bad The Dock was closed on Sunday, he thought. It would be nice to see Greta. She was one helluva woman. Cool under fire. Damn, she'd handled the mess last night beautifully. Did a great job raising her kid, too. But Jack would soon be off to college. Maybe, Henry, old boy, you have a chance?

A knock on the door ended Henry Stark's wishful meander. A chirpy woman's voice called out, "Henry! Henry? I know you're in there, I saw your car." It was Rosie Grafton.

She was holding a glass dome with an apple pie inside. The pie looked delicious, Rosie didn't.

"God in heaven," Henry asked himself, intending no sacrilege, "Why did I ever sleep with her?" Every time he saw her he asked himself the same question and came up with the same answer: It was the stupidest thing he'd ever done in his life.

"I was just driving by and saw your car," Rosie chirped. "Thought you might be hungry after a long day chasing down evil people."

He hated her voice too. *Why can't I ask her to go away and leave me alone?* He answered himself: *Because you are a civil servant and have a responsibility to be civil to all you serve. You're the one who screwed up. You felt sorry for her because she lives with the sorriest, grumpiest man in Reedsport. After five invitations, you consented to dinner in your home. She brought chicken and dumplings and smooth-as-silk Canadian whiskey. She offered herself for dessert. You felt sorry for her and you also let yourself get a wee bit drunk – but that's no excuse.*

Henry had known women who had done the same thing for men. In the United States Marines it was called A Mercy Fuck. "Suck it up, Henry," he ordered himself. "Be nice. Pay your penance."

Referring to the pie, Henry finally responded to his unwelcome guest. "That's really thoughtful of you, Rosie."

Given an opening, she pressed on, "You know, there's a musical at the movie house, Judy Garland. I'll treat."

"Sounds great but I've been up since five this morning and I have another big day tomorrow. I'm going home and hit the rack."

"Well," Rosie waggled her sizable hips, "Like some company?"

It wasn't a question. It was a request.

"I wouldn't be good company, Rosie. I'm really beat. But I thank you for the pie."

He didn't want the pie either but he bit his lip. If he told her, as he wished he could, "Please, get the hell out of here and take your damn pie with you," it would be cruel and he was not a cruel man. He terminated the conversation by saying, softly, "Thanks for stopping by." He didn't make the mistake of adding, "Some other time." He was careful not to offer Rosie any encouragement.

He'd leave the pie in the office with a note, "This pie is courtesy of Rosie Grafton. Help yourself." Cal and the secretary could eat it, offer a piece to anybody who came by. Then he'd get Cal to return the glass dome.

CHAPTER FOURTEEN

If you were driving by the Lakeside exit on U.S. Highway 101 in 1954, you'd see Grafton's Grocery store and not much else. So, unless you were in a mood for a six-pack and a bag of potato chips, you'd probably just zoom past. Even if you were low on gas you wouldn't stop. Grafton's didn't have a gas pump.

The exit, a gravel road, didn't turn toward the ocean. Why follow a road that didn't lead to the beach? If you thought about it at all, you'd figure the road to Lakeside would dump you in front of a few rows of shabby, weather-worn wooden houses with rusted cars sitting on blocks in weed-only yards – just like the other clumps of houses you'd seen along the non-beach side of the highway.

However, if a whim insisted you turn east on that non-descript road, you'd drive down one sand-dune size hill and up another and lo and behold, the road would widen. Widen and morph into an elegant four-lane, blacktopped boulevard lined with rhododendrons and magnificent Sitka spruce. Behind the spruce and rhododendrons, you'd note, the terrain sloped gently toward a large lake. Along the lakeshore you'd see custom built homes. Many of which, size-wise, could pass for a resort.

Mary McDonnell took enormous pride in her Lakeside home. It was – in her mind, her greatest achievement – with the single exception of giving birth to a daughter and thereby meeting her obligation to provide an heir for her husband.

She confided to friends, "My home is my statement. It showcases my soul."

For inspiration, Mary studied copies of *Sunset Magazine*. She especially liked the coastal homes near San Francisco, admiring their understatement and simplicity of design. She became an advocate of the architect J. Pennywell Jones who opined, "Architecture serves mankind best when it unites us with nature – and ourselves."

Jones kept his buildings low, "So as not to obstruct the sky." He used glass to "Invite the outdoors inside." He recommended natural wood siding, preferably redwood or cedar and had disdain for painted exterior wood or "Manufactured wood with disgusting battens and other pretentious linear distractions."

The defining moment of Mary McDonnell's life was when she met the incomparable J. Pennywell Jones and retained his services to design what she first positioned as, "My villa."

"My dear, if you lived in Tuscany, I would build you a villa. But for you, I will create the ultimate Lakeside Manor. My unique concept will flatter your gentle artistic soul, and at once, defend you from the ferocity of coastal storms."

Mary McDonnell spent so much time with the architect that people in Coos Bay and Lakeside suggested she might be having an affair. Perhaps she was having *An Affair of the Mind*. Most certainly, it was not a traditional affair. Anyone who knew Mr. Jones' sexual preferences could and would have verified the purity inherent in Mary's relationship with her architect.

It was an enchanting time for Mary. The resulting structure was, in Pennywell's words, "Aesthetically functional and functionally aesthetic." Mary liked this description so much she often used it herself.

Kathy McDonnell steered her black MG sports car between two giant Sitka Spruce and down the sloping drive to a five-car garage.

From street level the house looked smaller than the garage. Kathy parked her car and skipped down two flights of redwood steps. She walked past the main entrance and entered the McDonnell lakeside manor through a sliding glass door. She said hello to Mrs. Ordway, who hardly looked up. Mrs. Ordway was busy preparing dinner for the McDonnells and their Sunday guests. Kathy had expected her mother to be in the kitchen, supervising, but she wasn't. Kathy wasn't disappointed. Her mother might have asked why she'd taken over an hour to run a twenty-minute errand. Kathy had planned to say, "I was the only one in the store and you know how Wayne Grafton likes to talk."

Kathy looked out the window and saw her father in his favorite lounge chair on the boat dock. The boat dock was thirty-seven feet below the house. James McDonnell had a fishing line in the water and appeared to be reading. She guessed her mother was seated at her vanity in her bedroom suite, brushing her hair or experimenting with cosmetics. Kathy didn't like to interrupt her mother when she was at her vanity because it always prompted a requiem on the unfairness of age and the loss of beauty.

Kathy considered going down the stairs to the dock and talking to her father but he looked content. She decided not to disturb him. She had formulated a plan.

Every Sunday, her parents hosted a dinner party. It was mandatory for Kathy to attend. This was part of her father's agenda to make her comfortable with adults and expose her to a variety of people and ideas. To balance his command-appearance edict, Kathy had been encouraged to invite her own friends to these gatherings.

Her father might object to her dating Jack Portman under present circumstances, which would mean she'd have to resort to lies and subterfuge. But once her father got to know Jack he would surely see he was a young man of quality, because, after all, her father took pride in being one of the world's foremost judges of character.

Confident she could make everything work out perfectly – Kathy went into her bedroom to dress for Sunday dinner. She chose to wear the black cocktail dress her mother bought at I. Magnin in San Francisco. She liked it because it made her look less like an eighteen-year old girl and more like an eighteen-year woman. Her parents needed to get used to the idea she was an adult.

As she searched her lingerie drawer for her black bra, she came across a newspaper clipping. The headline read PIRATES CRUSH BRAVES. She hadn't saved it as a reminder of the Coos Bay basketball team's romp over the outgunned visitors from Reedsport. She saved it because one of the players in the photo was Jack Portman.

As first clarinet in the high school band, she had attended all home games. The basketball floor had proved to be a giant display case for young males. Via the mysterious stimulus that stirs a young woman's heart, she had developed a crush on Jack Portman. She'd also noted that Jack and Kyle Smith were respectfully friendly toward each other. That observation had proved useful on Beach Night.

Kathy picked up the clipping, smiled at it and slipped it back into the drawer. Carefully, she covered it with several silk panties. This prompted her to remember something. She retrieved the pants she'd worn Saturday night from her dirty clothes hamper and took the Olympia beer label from the back pocket. She positioned the label under her clean undergarments and closed the drawer. Her eyes fluttered as she remembered their first kiss.

Her instincts had been right, she thought, she and Jack belonged together even if he did live above a beer hall. He was going to college and she could help him be anything he wanted to be. She sat down at her vanity. *I am attractive*, she thought. *A catch!*

Kathy smiled at herself in the mirror, paying special attention to her perfect teeth. It was worth it, she thought. The braces, the twice a year visits to the orthodontist in Los Angeles. It was all worth it. As her father had said, "Sometimes nature needs a nudge in the right direction.

"Take my beard," he'd confided. "As a rule, I abhor facial hair, but I have no chin. Without the beard I look weak and undistinguished. I trim it every day. I sculpt it, actually. No one notices the hair on my chin is an inch longer than the beard along my jawbone."

Down on the boat dock, James McDonnell was re-reading a volume from Carl Sandburg's trilogy on Abraham Lincoln. James ranked George Washington as America's greatest man but rated Theodore Roosevelt and Lincoln as the greatest presidents. He had a special affinity for Lincoln. It was after studying photos of Lincoln, pre- and post- Lincoln's beard, that James had grown his own.

On this Sunday, Sandburg's narrative was unable to hold James's attention. His mind preferred recent events. Impatiently, he watched the red and white bobber on his fishing line dip below the surface, reappear and dip again. Bluegill, he guessed, and decided to let it steal his bait. "Don't swallow the hook," he suggested, aloud, talking to the bluegill.

The bobber ceased its bobbing and returned to the surface. Good, he thought, I can fish without being bothered by the damn fish.

Art Wagner, the rape victim's father, had called him. Wagner asked if he should withdraw the charges made against the unidentified assailant – to protect his daughter's anonymity.

McDonnell recommended against this, volunteering to represent Betty Wagner's legal interests without charge. He assured Art Wagner that he would personally appear at any court proceedings as the Wagner family's legal representative. He assured his new pro bono client the court would be sensitive to the victim's identity.

"If we withdraw charges now," McDonnell counseled, "They will call off the hunt."

Then, purposefully, McDonnell, hit below the belt. "When this rapist strikes again, what are you going to say to the father of his next victim?"

McDonnell had questioned himself, "Why get involved in this situation?" He answered himself – with a hint of self-serving sarcasm: "It's one of the advantages of being rich, you can pick and choose what you do."

The purity of his logic made him smile. But the smile was dislodged by a reoccurring thought. It could have been Kathy. The thought made him shudder. What if she'd been the one to wander away from the safety of the pack and step into those woods? His anger flared – but it wasn't as intense as the previous night. Anger is useful, but only when it's managed, he reminded himself. Anger's greatest virtue was that it strengthened resolve.

How could he help Betty Wagner? He'd read about an association in Salem, Oregon's State Capitol. A group of rape victims had banded together to help heal one another. He didn't recall the group's name but the answer to most questions was seldom more than three phone calls away. He'd start by calling the publisher of the *Salem Statesman* newspaper. He made a mental note: *Call Statesman on Monday*.

A Cooper's hawk caught his eye. Most people would call it (and its look-alike, the Northern Goshawk) a Chicken Hawk, but James McDonnell knew its real name. He could easily distinguish it from the Goshawk by its longer, rounded tail and larger head. The bird he was watching was a male with an impressive thirty-five-inch wingspan. It was soaring in a circle, hungry, searching . . . sure enough, the Cooper's hawk dipped and dove, disappearing into the trees. The descent was breathtaking. The bird shot out of the sky like an arrow, straight down. James counted *one, two, three, four, five*. The hawk reappeared, a chipmunk clutched in its beak. The bird landed on the limb of a Douglas fir tree, gulped the little rodent down and then took to the wing again. It resumed circling in search of more prey.

James wondered, *Is last night's rapist doing the same?*

CHAPTER FIFTEEN

In the 1950s – if you were driving north from Reedsport on U.S.101, then over the Smith River Bridge, you'd end up in Gardiner. Gardiner boasted a large plywood plant and pulp mill. People with the good jobs at the plant and mill lived in Reedsport, making Gardiner the reverse of a bedroom community.

Equidistant from the plant and the mill's parking lots was the Teddy Bear Tavern. Because everybody who worked or lived in Gardiner knew everybody else, it was next to impossible to be served at the Teddy Bear unless you could prove you were twenty-one. Even the big stranger with the short-cropped blond hair and stubble of beard had to show ID.

"No problem," the stranger said. He plucked an Oregon Drivers License and Social Security card from his wallet and laid them on the bar. Because he had two pieces of ID, the bartender barely glanced at the photo on the license. When squeezed down to fit inside a one-inch square, the mug shot of one broad-faced, blond Caucasian looks pretty much like another. The ID said the stranger was Jake Sloan from Newport.

Putting his ID back in his wallet, Abernathy ordered a Lucky Lager beer. He was alone now. Dodd had yelled, whined and cried about the girl and Abernathy had to shut him up. Couldn't trust him. Dodd hadn't even wanted any of her, so, by John's way of thinking, it was a good bet Dodd was queer.

John had been exhilarated by the experience. Her screaming heightened his moment of supreme conquest and ecstasy. When he exploded into her, he'd felt like king of the world. *These women who twitch their asses, stick out their tits and flaunt the pleasure-zone between their legs, then act like they are too good for John Abernathy, a real man who knows the truth about them, these women – well, he'd shown two of them who the fucking boss was.* Soon, he thought, it would be time to show another.

He sipped his beer and struck up a conversation with the fellow sitting one bar stool over. "Quiet around here," Abernathy ventured.

"It's Sunday, man, and this is Gardiner, man. Loudest sound you hear around here is the noon whistle and it ain't noon."

Abernathy laughed, wanting to seem like a congenial sort of guy.

The man at the bar was nicknamed Punk because he made his living in the woods as a whistle punk. Whistle punking was an essential job requiring keen vision and constant vigil. The whistle punk sat in an elevated position and watched over the logging operation. Each crew-member in the outfit had his own signal: one short blast; two short blasts; one short/one long; et cetera. When the whistle punk spotted potential danger he blasted a warning. Many a logger owed his life to the alertness of a whistle punk.

"Just passing through?" Punk asked.

"Heard there might be work at the pulp mill."

"Wouldn't know," Punk said.

As a logger, Punk was indifferent to jobs in the plants and mills. To him, Abernathy looked like a logger. Otherwise, he wouldn't have engaged him in conversation.

"Work in the woods?" Punk asked.

Abernathy was wearing loose-fitting Wrangler jeans and a red flannel shirt. Logger clothes. He was slightly miffed to think he'd have to dispose of his new Pendleton shirt, but what else could he do? It would shrink if he washed it. And he reckoned, it would be stupid to take it to a dry cleaner and ask, "Can you get these blood stains out?"

"I've set choker, second-loaded," Abernathy answered; listing the two jobs he'd held during his logger days.

"There's a gypo outfit up Dean's Creek might be looking."

Gypo was short for gypsy, which in turn was a euphemism for portable. Gypo outfits contracted to cut smaller stands of second growth timber. They logged it, milled it, trucked it and moved on to another stand of second growth.

A friend of Punk's came in and called for a Lucky Lager, the brand of choice for most loggers.

"Hear what happened last night at Lighthouse beach?" Punk's friend yelled.

"You mean Beach Night?" Punk yelled back. "Hell, I don't know what doesn't happen on Beach Night. Shit, man, the year I went," Punk stood, raised his beer above his head, "There were a lot fewer virgins at the Horse Shoe Café on Sunday than there'd been on Saturday."

"Yeah!" Punk's friend shouted over the tavern noise. The jukebox was blasting *Detour*, a song by Kate Starr.

"Yeah, but Saturday," Punk's pal yelled, "There was a rape and the cops are out for blood!"

"Rape?" Abernathy said feigning both disgust and surprise. He stared at the bartender.

The two men exchanged disapproving head-shakes.

Big John took his beer and walked over to Punk's friend. "You're not shitting us," Abernathy said, putting his hand on the young man's shoulder.

"No, hell no, some gal got raped. State police were buzzing around that beach like flies at an outdoor crapper while somebody grabbed a woman, carried her down the beach and had his way with her. The girl was from Coos Bay. They're looking for two guys. A big one and a little one. I'm not sure, but one of the Reedsport seniors might have had a look at them. Said he heard the girl screaming and chased after them."

"Big one and little one? That's all they know?" John Abernathy, alias Jake Sloan, asked.

"That's what I heard. They're not looking around here. Sheriff Stark drove up to Florence."

Abernathy maintained his composure. *Big guy and a little guy? Good thing he wasn't traveling with a little guy anymore. Could anyone have seen him and Dodd together?* John asked himself. *Think. The kid at the Texaco and the crazy old man with the faggot boots could put him in Reedsport – but not at the beach. No one had chased them. That part was bullshit. The guy at the top of the dune might have gotten a glimpse – enough to say "big and little." But no one had seen his face. Why would the sheriff go to Florence? The hat? It had twisted around and he'd pulled it off to see the guy at the top of the dune. The hat could point to Florence but hundreds of people wore those hats. He'd snatched his off the head of a wise-ass sitting in front of him in the movie house.*

John thought back. He would have driven to Coos Bay on Saturday night after his conquest but as luck would have it – when he pulled up to the stop sign on 101 – two state police cars passed him going south toward Coos Bay. The voice in his head whispered, *Go North.* He'd nodded in agreement and he turned north, back toward Reedsport. Maybe he should have dragged Dodd's corpse into the trees right where he killed him, he thought. Then he wouldn't have the body in the trunk. No. That would have been stupid, he told himself. The cops would find the corpse at the edge of the dunes and nail him dead to rights – for car theft and murder.

He asked the bartender for another beer and ordered himself to act natural. All he needed to do was get rid of the body and the car.

Punk and his logger pal went to the shuffleboard table. It was easy to see Punk was a master of the game. Abernathy watched and sipped his beer. He would wait for it to get dark before venturing out again. He waved off the opportunity to challenge Punk at shuffleboard.

"You're too good for me. Hell, little buddy, I'll buy you both a beer right now and save you the trouble of beating me."

Jake Sloan would be remembered by the patrons of the Teddy Bear as a big, soft-spoken, polite fellow who was looking for work.

CHAPTER SIXTEEN

Ellen Reilly screamed at her mother for the first time in her life. "You don't understand me! You don't even try." She ran upstairs to her room.

Eleanor looked at her husband, rolled her eyes to display her consternation and said, "All I did was ask if she and Pat had plans tonight."

The rebellious Ellen slammed the door to her room, sat down on her pink bedspread, picked up the stuffed panda bear resting on her pillow, clutched it close to her cheek and cried.

This should be the happiest time of her life. Yet she was miserable. She had wanted to go to Beach Night but Pat said he'd been to Beach Night the year before and said it was just an excuse for high school kids to drink beer and act stupid. Besides, his father had warned him that the state cops would be crawling all over the place. So, he'd taken Ellen to a drive-in movie. The feature was a western with Howard Duff. Although she despised westerns, she pretended to be interested to keep Pat at bay. She wished she hadn't surrendered her virginity to him. It hadn't been a pleasant experience. His kisses were too hard and his tongue darted in and out like a frog's. He had grabbed her breast and pushed it around like it was a sponge that he was using to wash his car.

Ellen had a B+ average, typed ninety-two words a minute, best in the entire school, and wanted to go to business or secretarial school – but her mother wanted her to marry Pat Kelly.

Eleanor had arranged the first date, lobbying that Pat was from a fine family in Coos Bay and his father, Arthur Kelly, wanted his son to settle down with a nice girl and get serious about the family business.

Ellen regretted not battling her mother from the start. It was so . . . so old world. . . an arranged marriage like they used to do in Europe and still did in the Middle East, India and China. It was like being sold into slavery. Her mother said she would learn to love him. To that, Ellen now wished she'd said, *HA! You try kissing someone for the rest of your life whose lips feel like they're sewn against his teeth.*

Ellen's father was no help. He said, "You can work in my office while you get to know Pat better. You don't need to learn shorthand to work for me. And I'll buy you a car."

Why had her parents placed so much emphasis on her grades? Why did they demand she get A's and B's? Why bother studying your way onto the Honor Roll if all you're going to do is move to Coos Bay and have babies?

When she was a little girl, she'd been close to her father. Since she started high school, their conversations seldom went beyond, "How was school today?"

"Fine."

"Good. What has your mother planned for dinner?"

Whenever she tried to talk to him, he deferred to her mother. Her parents were hopeless. It was clear they didn't care about her. Her role in life was to marry someone who could help her father's business and enhance her mother's social ambitions. To think – she'd almost fallen into their selfish trap. The one boy she liked, they hated. Well, her father hadn't hated Jack, but he didn't stick-up for him either.

"Oh, Jack," she said to her panda.

His kisses had been soft and sensual. He never tried to force his tongue into her mouth. Jack's hands were tender and shy. She'd let Pat "do it" to her, why not Jack? She wondered if she'd ever feel sexually aroused again. Why had she said yes to Pat and no to Jack? The time she'd come so close with Jack was amazing – a miracle. What a feeling. She didn't have to go "all the way" to go all the way. With Pat it had been degrading and, well, her word, yucky. She promised herself she would never see Pat Kelly again.

Her friend, Olive, had grilled Janet Preston for all the gossip about Beach Night. Olive said, "Janet went on and on about how Jack and a girl from Coos Bay rescued another girl.

"Janet also said her brother, Skip, might have seen the rapist earlier in the day."

Olive reported, "Janet said Skip said the guy was a monster. If he was the rapist, Portman was really gutsy to rush in and save the girl from Coos Bay."

Ellen asked herself, what was Jack doing with a girl from Coos Bay? Jack was cute – beyond cute, Ellen thought.

Half the girls in school had a crush on him and he didn't even know it.

When she'd walked down the school corridors with Jack, every girl wished they could trade places with her. Little wonder a girl from Coos Bay went after him. He was "The bravest of the Reedsport Braves."

The emotion of her senior year surged through her. She remembered the pep rally in the gym before the Homecoming Football Game with Toledo.

The head football coach was standing on the stage; the band was playing the fight song. The coach shouted over the noise, "And our captain, our bravest of the Braves, our warrior who doesn't know the meaning of the word quit, Jaaaaccck Portman!"

Everyone who wasn't already standing leapt to their feet and applauded. The trumpets blared and the drums banged as he walked across the stage and waved his shy wave. As she watched him and saw her peers cheer him, she remembered the worst moment of her life. She remembered giving back his ring after the baseball game because her mother said Jack was a worthless nobody from Winchester Bay whose low life mother operated a tavern.

As Ellen sat on her bed, the pep rally flashed through her mind. She remembered hating the other kids for applauding Jack in such a brassy, brazen, extreme and shameless manner, and for chanting JACK! JACK! JACK! BRAVES! BRAVES! BRAVES!

Instead of feeling pride, she had squirmed with jealousy. "The Bravest of the Braves?" She hadn't seen that side of him. He didn't pursue her after she broke up with him. He didn't call. He did nothing. What kind of "warrior" would let his girl go without a fight?

What did the football coach mean when he called Jack a warrior? Ellen remembered the story football players told about Jack when he was a sophomore. It had to do with Eldridge Olsen, a senior, a huge senior – a two hundred and forty-three pound lineman to be exact. Jack was smaller then, still less than six feet and only one hundred and sixty pounds, but Jack had been named a starter on defense. Eldridge had decided Jack needed to be initiated into "the club." There was precedent for this. Two years earlier, seniors had initiated Eldridge when he'd made varsity. So, as Bobby Lacey and other players told it, one Wednesday afternoon after practice, Eldridge got a jar of Red Hot from the training room and he called to Jack, "Okay, Portman, you're a starter now. We have an initiation ceremony when you make first string. I have the honor of administrating it. I'm going to give you a dose of Red Hot right up your ass and you're going to stand there and take it like a true Reedsport Brave."

Jack didn't say a word. He charged across the locker room and with a flying block, slammed Eldridge Olsen over the bench and into the lockers.

When the dazed Eldridge Olsen looked up from the floor, Jack was standing over him, holding the jar. "You looking for this?" dropped the jar onto Eldridge's oversized belly, picked up the overturned bench and walked back to his own locker.

Jack's burst across the locker room had been so un-expected, so fierce, so final that a full minute ticked by before anyone in the locker room moved. Then several of Eldridge's friends considered taking up the humiliated lineman's cause.

At that point, the great Grant Bookman raised his hand in the international "stop" sign.

No one dared go against the All-Star fullback. The look on Grant's face signaled the consequences. He whispered, "You take on Jack and you deal with me."

Bookman then jumped up on the bench and shouted at his teammates. "Did you see that? That's the way we play this game. A true Reedsport Brave doesn't take shit from anybody.

"Remember that on Friday when Coquille comes to our house. We're going to hit them so hard they'll be lucky if they can limp onto their bus to drag their sorry asses home."

The players cheered and began chanting, "Beat Coquille! Beat Coquille! Beat Coquille!"

The coaches had been in their office and witnessed the scene through their glass window. They loved it. That Friday, two days later, Reedsport pounded Coquille, fifty-two-to-zip. The team's star and captain, Grant Bookman, gave the game ball to a sophomore and future captain, Jack Portman.

The incident became part of the school's mythology, not quite on the lofty plane as Grant Bookman's 85-yard touchdown run against Coos Bay, but among Jack's own classmates, not too far below it.

Ellen was aware Jack didn't get into fights. Other boys got into fights, but Jack didn't. They left Jack alone. When the boys were horsing around, doing the silly roughhouse stuff, the show-off stuff they always seemed to do in front of girls, even then, they didn't punch Jack on the shoulder or try to push him the way boys pushed each other, testing . . . Was it because they liked him so much or because they were afraid of him?

When the coach asked Grant Bookman why he'd taken such a liking to Jack, he shrugged his broad shoulders, smiled his broad smile and answered, "He never backs down, he just keeps coming. It's hard to explain, there's just something about Portman I like."

Ellen Reilly decided that she should have been with Jack at Beach Night. She would have helped save the girl and all the kids would have called her today and asked what happened – and she would have told them, "Oh, you know my Jack, he's always been the bravest of the Braves."

Pat Kelly wouldn't rush in and save anyone, Ellen knew that much. If someone tried to rape her, Pat Kelly would run away and later shun her as damaged goods. Not Jack. Jack would rush in and bowl them over just as he'd done with Eldridge. As she thought about Jack she became aroused. Her fingers in her private place weren't the same as Jack's. No use even trying, but it was good to feel that way again. The tears stopped and she went over to her vanity. She was prettier than her mother had ever been. Her mother must be jealous. Why else would her mother try to make her settle for Pat Kelly? It wasn't fair.

Ellen knew her father would let her take his Cadillac. He wouldn't discuss anything serious with her but he would lend her his car. Ellen decided to call Olive. They could have a girl's night out. She'd wear the white cashmere sweater that showed off her figure. Ellen stared at herself in the mirror. She unbuttoned her blouse and let it slide off her shoulders onto the floor. She put her hands under her bra and hoisted her breasts, exaggerating the cleavage. Yes. She and Olive would go to the drive-in café and maybe the drive-in movie. She slipped into the sweater, turned left, then right. She approved. Maybe she'd just happen to run into Jack. It was Sunday. Jack would probably be with Bobby or Tim. Should she flirt with Bobby or Tim and make Jack jealous? Bobby wouldn't know how to handle a flirt. Tim might. Ellen went downstairs and called Olive. After she hung up she tracked down her father. "Daddy," she cooed, as if there hadn't been a scene with her mother thirty minutes earlier, "Can I use your caddy tonight? I promise to be careful."

CHAPTER SEVENTEEN

Jack drove his mother's two-tone green, Chevrolet Deluxe Coupe into Reedsport. He had planned to meet-up with Tim at the drive-in café and . . . "They'd do something . . ."

He saw Tim's Henry J in the parking lot and tucked the Chevy into the spot next to it. The drive-in was stuffed with high school kids. The volume-cranked jukebox was blaring an up-beat, popular tune sung by Teresa Brewer.

"Got along without you before I met you, going to
get along without you now; going to find some-body
twice as cute, 'cause you didn't love me anyhow."

Jack spotted Tim in a back booth and made his way through the crowd. Two sophomore girls nearly swooned as he walked by. One summoned the courage to say, "Hi Jack Portman, do you remember me?"

"Hey, Carol"

As he passed, she spun back toward a booth full of sophomores to gloat. The dreamy Jack Portman knew her name. Teresa Brewer continued belting her hit tune.

"You took my money and you took my time; ran around all the time with every gal in town. Boom-boom, boom-boom, going to get along without you now."

Tim was wearing a navy blue crew neck sweater and pleated khaki trousers, which he called "Suntans." Tim already had the college look down pat.

Jack wore his usual Levis and a gray, loose-fitting sweatshirt. The waitress, a former cheerleader from the class of '52, made her way over to them.

She teased them, "What can I do for you two hunks tonight?"

Jack ordered a cheeseburger and French fries.

"You sure that's all you want?" The waitress flirted. "Not everything is on the menu, you know."

It went over Jack's head. Not Tim's. He tried to compete for her attention via sophistication. "I'll have a gimlet, very dry, straight up. But if you don't have Rose's lime juice, forget it and bring me a cherry coke."

"Very funny," the waitress dismissed him. She turned back to Jack, "You want a Coke, Jack? I won't put it on your check."

"Thanks, that would be great."

"I think she likes you," Tim said when the waitress left.

"No. She has to be nice to everyone. My mom does the same thing."

"Five bucks says she'd say *yes* if you asked her out. I hear she puts out for Bookman, bet she'd do the same for his protégé."

"Protégé?" Jack smiled at Tim's choice of words. "I can't ask her out anyway. After last night, well, I'm sort of going with someone."

Ellen and Olive cruised the drive-in and saw Tim's car. The Portman Chevy was next to it. The girls parked Mr. Reilly's caddy and went inside.

Ellen took a deep breath and marched straight back to Jack's booth. She sat down next to him. "Hi, Portman."

Tim made room for Olive on his side of the booth. When the other juniors heard she was with Tim, Ellen and Jack on Sunday night, her stock would definitely go up, she thought.

Tim wasn't one to pass up an opportunity. He smiled at Ellen and said, expansively, "Please join us. Jack was just telling me about his new girlfriend." Tim stood, pretending to look over the crowd, "Where's the illustrious, wealthy, man-about-town from Coos Bay, Pat Kelly? He meeting you here?"

Ellen was not backing down. "You're not funny, Tim Budge," she snapped.

Three days earlier, Jack would have been elated if Ellen had sat beside him. Now, he didn't know how he felt. Should he say something cutting like, "Does your mother know you're here?" He resisted the temptation.

The waitress returned with the order. "Hope you two aren't getting back together," she quipped. "You girls want something?"

"No." Ellen was brusque, hoping to chase away the good-looking waitress.

Jack turned to face Ellen. "So, Ellen, Olive, what's going on?"

"Just driving around," Olive answered, smiling at Tim.

Ellen turned toward Jack. "How about you? You really have a new girlfriend?"

"I don't think that's any of your business."

Ellen countered in a jaunty, devil-may-care voice, trying not to sound as desperate as she felt. "Well, Jack Portman, maybe we should go out one more time, you know, for old time's sake?"

"How about a party?" Tim suggested. Olive was looking good. During the past year the boys had stopped teasing her – that is, they'd stopped calling her "Olive Oil." She was no longer skinny and flat-chested.

An idea slipped into Tim's head. "There's a summer house on the lake. The owner lives in Eugene. He asked me to check on it from time to time so I have a key."

Ellen seized the moment. "Sounds like fun."

"Sounds crazy to me," Jack said. "We can't just take over somebody's house."

"Why not?" Tim countered. "They'll never know. It's like the tree falling in the forest. Besides, what else is there to do? Sit here? Go to a movie? We're only young once."

"I don't know," Olive said slowly, thinking it sounded exciting, but... The question she wanted to ask was, "What will Tim expect from me?" Ellen's intentions were obvious to Olive.

"Oh come on, Olive!" Ellen reprimanded her friend, "You're such a chicken, such a baby."

Ellen had gotten on this roller coaster. She didn't know where it was going but she was determined to hang on until the end of the ride.

"Live fast, die young and have a good looking corpse," Tim offered, reciting a line from the Bogart movie, *Knock on Any Door.*

Jack wanted to go but pride intervened. Ellen had rejected him. A taste of her own medicine would do her good. She shouldn't be able to snap her fingers and have him come running. What kind of man would let a woman get away with that? And there was Kathy.

"You guys go ahead," Jack said. "I told my mother I wouldn't be late." He'd told his mother no such thing but he figured he needed an excuse.

"Your mother?" Tim confronted him. "We graduated last week, remember? The robes, the diploma, the speeches about being adults with a responsibility to make our own decisions – remember? C'mon, Jack, let's live a little before they come up with another Korea and send us off to some bleak, forgotten land to have our asses shot off."

Tim's face was flushed. The speech about being sent to another Korea was sincere. Tim had an inner-desperation to live his life before someone or something took it from him. Tim's passion almost changed Jack's mind. He teetered but didn't fall. Ellen needed to be taught a lesson. And there was Kathy.

"Tim, you're going to do what you're going to do. I'm going to eat my cheeseburger and go home." To emphasize his point, Jack picked up the ketchup and plopped the thick red condiment onto his fries.

Ellen hadn't seen the impassioned, fatalist side of Tim. She liked it. But she was convinced she loved Jack. How could she reach Jack, stir him to remember how much he'd cared for her? She could make him jealous. It was worth a try. Ellen gathered her poise. "Sounds like fun, Tim. At least it's something different. I'll go with you."

Ellen fascinated Tim but there was the code of honor. Ellen had been Jack's girl. Jack was his friend. Jack had listened when he'd vented, "Why are we alive right now? At this precise moment in time? On this obscure little spot on a mere speck of a planet?"

Was the answer – so he and Ellen would get together? Ellen was ready to go with him to an empty cabin. It had to be fate. But he had to honor the code.

"That okay with you, Jack? If Ellen and I go?"

Jack held up his left hand and wagged his ring finger, calling attention to his Letterman ring. "She's not wearing this anymore, Tim. If you two want to go, go. I'll drop Olive off on my way home."

CHAPTER EIGHTEEN

Abernathy drove Dodd's Plymouth back over the bridge to Reedsport. He passed the drive-in café and thought about pulling into one of the slots and checking out the girls. *Keep going,* a voice told him. *If the cops are looking for Dodd's Plymouth, the drive-in will be the first place they'll check. You have work to do, Big John.*

He followed 101 south toward Winchester Bay. His eyes scoured the side of the road for a place to turn off the highway. Just past the high school, he spotted a private road that turned west. He figured it would lead to the ocean or the Umpqua tidal basin. There was a wooden gate across the entry held closed by a chain The chain was secured by padlock. However, the padlock wasn't locked. John opened the gate, drove inside, shifted the car into neutral and walked back and closed the gate. When he did this, he made sure the open padlock was in exactly the same link on the chain.

Abernathy had chanced upon the private road to Barney's (of Barney's Outfitting Store) twenty-five acre tidewater ranch. Calling it a ranch was somewhat of a reach, but Mr. Barney was originally from Oklahoma and preferred the word "ranch" to farm.

Mr. Barney kept three Angus steers on the ranch along with two gelded quarter horses, two brood mares and a foal sired by a friend's Tennessee Walker stallion. He also had a barn with a new tin roof. The barn was wired for electricity.

Abernathy opened the double barn doors and drove the car inside. He left the headlights on until he found the light switch. He judged it to be good place to spend the night. Better than last night when he'd slept in the car, hiding in plain sight, parked in the lot provided for Gardiner plywood plant workers.

Abernathy lifted Dodd's body out of the trunk and dropped it onto the dirt floor with a thump. The corpse landed on its side, stiff from rigor mortise and bent into a grotesque posture from hours in the trunk. Abernathy looked at his victim and felt a shiver of remorse. Damn it to hell, anyway. Why did Dodd have to start yelling at him? He didn't mean to kill him, it just happened. He grabbed him around the neck to shut him up, and without thinking, broke his neck.

He bent over the body and began going through the pockets. There were two twenty-dollar bills in Dodd's wallet. He found three rumpled dollar bills and some change in one of Dodd's front pant pockets. Discovering pocket money reminded him that Dodd had talked about putting "emergency money" in his shoes. John removed Dodd's well worn, black loafers and found another twenty-dollar bill.

Then he remembered Dodd's wristwatch: An Omega with a stainless steel stretch band. Dodd had cherished it because it was a high school graduation gift from his grandmother.

Abernathy slipped the watch off the corpse, commenting, "You won't be needing this any more, little buddy."

Finally, he searched the dead man's suitcase and found nothing but clothing. It was all too small to be of any use to Big John. Yet with Dodd's sixty-plus dollars added to his forty, he was in pretty good shape.

He was hungry. He looked around the barn and saw a shelf stacked with canned goods. Directly below the shelf was a weathered, oak table with a hot plate and iron skillet. He checked the canned goods. Tuna fish, Spam, baked beans. He opened the drawer in the oak table and found a can opener and a Phillips screwdriver. He took the screwdriver out first, held it by the blade and hurled it, like a knife, trying to stick it in the barn wall. It bounced with a bang off of the fir planks. He considered retrieving it and trying again. "Naw", he said out loud. "Time to eat."

Heating the beans was too much trouble so he gorged himself with two cans of cold Spam and two cans of Star-Kist tuna. He felt better. But Dodd was beginning to stink. He complained to the dead body. "Wha'd you do? Shit your pants?"

To minimize the odor he stuffed his late friend into the front seat of the Plymouth, rolled up the windows and closed the door.

During the last year, 1953, when John had killed Jake Sloan, it had been on purpose. He'd thrown the body over his shoulder and carried it to the sawdust burner at Mapleton Lumber Mill. Nobody ever missed Sloan. Everyone figured he'd drifted into Mapleton, got a job, picked up a paycheck and moved along. Abernathy believed Sloan got what he deserved. John had asked Sloan to buy him a six-pack. Sloan laughed and said, "I don't like you, Nasty. Why should I buy a loser like you a six-pack?"

Sloan was three years older and the same size as Abernathy. He didn't fear him. "You know what I hear?" Sloan taunted. "I hear they don't call you Nasty because you're so tough. I hear they call you Nasty because you smell like a shithouse. Fact is, Nasty, I saved your life today. Want to know how?"

Nasty was the perfect foil. "Oh-Yeah! How?"

"I killed a shit-eating dog."

Sloan laughed. He loved it when men fell for that joke. Still laughing, he squeezed into the cab of a pick-up with two other men from the logging crew and headed toward the Mapleton Tavern. Abernathy didn't have a comeback for the "shit-eating dog" insult. Later, after he thought about it, he decided he should have responded, "Yeah! Well, I saw that dog. He ran past me looking for you!" If he'd said that, he thought, he, not Sloan would have had the last word. As it was, he was left standing by the road with no beer, no companions and nothing to do. Fury boiled inside him.

Abernathy and Sloan were bunking at the same place, the Evergreen Cabins, which catered to itinerant loggers and truckers. Sloan's cabin door was unlocked. John went inside and waited.

At two in the morning Sloan opened his door, half drunk, trying to remember if the bed was on the right hand side of the room or the left.

The last words Sloan heard before the axe handle hit him square between the eyes were, "You're the one who smells like a shithouse."

But that was then, this was now, Abernathy thought.

He ran back through his inventory of information. *Big guy and little guy. Sheriff went to Florence. Bastards in Florence would love to pin it on him. Dodd's car was the easiest way to find him.*

Why not leave Dodd and the car in the barn? He hadn't seen any houses. The barn was here for the livestock. Could be weeks before anyone came by. Days were all he needed. Abernathy found a pair of cloth work gloves, pulled them on and went about the task of wiping down everything he had touched in the car and barn. He'd seen enough Robert Mitchum and Dick Powell movies to know about fingerprints.

When finished, he stuffed his bloody shirt into Dodd's gym bag for disposal in the morning. He then assembled his deer rifle, laid down on the hay and fell asleep.

CHAPTER NINETEEN

James McDonnell often invited guests for long week-ends. Sunday supper was the centerpiece. Guests included the political elite, successful businessmen, writers, artists and other "Unusual Suspects," as James McDonnell liked to describe them, his twist on the famous line from *Casablanca*.

On this last Sunday in May 1954, James did not have a stellar guest list. "A pair of regulars," he explained to his wife. "I'll do my salmon."

"My salmon" was a recipe James concocted through years of trial and error. He wrapped the smaller of the two salmon he'd caught the day before in aluminum foil and cooked it over a fire fueled by barbecue briquettes and cedar chips on his outdoor grill. At a certain point (depending on the size of the salmon and the state of the fire) he unwrapped the salmon and seasoned the cavity with lemon, butter, salt, black pepper, cooking sherry, white wine and slices of red onions. He covered the barbecue with a wet bed sheet and steamed the salmon until the last of a series of probes with his extra long barbecue fork signaled perfection.

Nate Clark was, indeed, a regular. If James McDonnell had a best friend, it was Nate. Nate was a medium-sized man in his early fifties. Fair skinned, freckled and slightly overweight, he looked like an accountant or pharmacist. His looks were misleading. He was a highly successful writer of Western novels and short stories.

Originally from Nebraska, Nate had gone to New York with the intention of becoming another Fitzgerald, Faulkner or, at the very least, John O'Hara, but his serious work was rejected and rejected and rejected.

Resilient almost to a fault, he didn't give up. One day he read an article in *Writer's Digest* touting the market for Western short stories. He decided to give it a go. He went to the library, read Owen Wister's classic, *The Virginian*, for background and banged out a story.

Two weeks later he received a check for $75.00 and a hand written note from the editor requesting more submissions.

Since his first success, he'd written more Western short stories than he could remember, published twenty-five Western paperback novels and sold options to Hollywood for five of his novels. One had been produced, *Canyon's Edge*, starring Randolph Scott. Nate had gone to see the movie and critiqued, "I recognized the plot, I've used it a dozen times, but I'm reasonably certain it wasn't the plot for *Canyon's Edge*."

Nate was now in the midst of what he called "My most serious project." He was enraptured with the story-telling power of the new medium of television (at least new to the west coast). In 1954 the Oregon coast was one of the few areas where TV reception was unavailable.

Nate was planning a nine-part dramatization of the opening of the American West with the working title, *Beyond the Great Divide*. Arriving early (as always) for dinner, Nate joined his host on the deck. "Still trying to make salmon edible?"

"Trying and succeeding brilliantly," McDonnell jabbed back, happy to see his friend. "How's your epic?"

Nate ducked the question. "I was hoping for rack of lamb." He stepped closer to the grill. "If I'd known we were having fish again, I would have stayed home and boiled hot dogs."

"Stuck, huh?" McDonnell diagnosed.

"I wanted to do one full episode on Meriwether Lewis and another on William Clark, but you can't separate them."

"You'll figure it out," McDonnell assured him. "Why don't you pour us a Scotch? It'll dull your taste buds and sharpen your creative thinking."

"Excellent idea." Nate headed for the bar.

For Kathy, the dinner conversation was stimulating. Nate talked about the John Fremont episode in his proposed TV series. According to Nate, Fremont was a charming scoundrel from Charleston, South Carolina who courted and married Jessie Benton, the daughter of a powerful senator, Thomas Hart Benton. As a leading advocate of Manifest Destiny, Benton sent his flamboyant son-in-law to survey the Oregon Trail in 1841.

"On the one hand, Benton was hoping Fremont would catch an arrow," Nate Clark professed. "On the other, he wanted Freemont to romanticize the west to spur expansion."

"What happened to Jessie?" Kathy asked.

Nate paused to sip his Scotch whiskey, "Come to think of it, Kathy, that's the story I should write. Jessie was the one who made John Fremont famous. She turned his mundane journals into dazzling, flowing prose. Her write-ups made him a celebrity and inspired his auspicious nickname, The Great Pathfinder.

"When his glory years were over," Nate continued, "After he was stripped of his command by President Lincoln and lost all his money through ill-advised investments, the loyal and loving Jessie Benton Fremont supported her husband in a Manhattan apartment by writing magazine articles and paperback books."

"Sounds like you'll have a stimulating hour on Fremont," James McDonnell encouraged his friend.

Confident her phone would ring, Kathy excused herself and went to her room. Jack must feel like she felt, therefore, he would have to call. As she paced, she thought about Jessie Benton Fremont. She admired Jessie for standing up to her powerful father and marrying the man she loved. Kathy understood Jessie's devotion to the dashing young man from Charleston. When you love someone, you stand by him. You love him forever, through good times and bad. She pictured Jessie in a dimly lit apartment, candles flickering, quill in hand, supporting her once famous, now disgraced husband. In Kathy's vision, Jessie was smiling.

Her phone finally rang. "Hello," she answered with a smile in her voice.

"Kathy?"

"Yes. I knew it was you, Jack. I missed you from the moment I left you. What are you doing?"

"Nothing much. Went out for a while, but all I did was think about you, so I came home."

"I know," she sighed.

* * *

Jack had crewed on the fishing boat, *Greta*, on Saturday because Captain Harry Norton's regular deck hand had called in sick.

That had led to Jack's first encounter with James McDonnell, Kathy's rich and famous father.

Captain Harry Norton suspected his regular deck hand was more likely a victim of a hangover than a flu bug. So, the captain, who ranked reliability above tenure, had offered Jack full-time employment for the summer season, starting the following Monday. Jack agreed to "think about it."

However, on *this* Monday, only two days since the fateful Beach Night, Jack was "officially" on vacation. With no school and no work, he was looking forward to just fooling around for an entire week.

He awakened at seven, tried to go back to sleep, yet a strange dream lingered in his mind. He pulled on a pair of jeans, slipped on a tee shirt and went into the kitchen. In the dream he was playing tennis with Kathy as his partner. This struck Jack as illogical as he'd only played tennis a few times. But in the dream, it was a serious match with a championship at stake. He and Kathy were winning when his shoelaces became untied. Between serves, he tried to tie the laces, but they turned into thick strands of frayed rope and he couldn't make a knot. He sprinted off the court and begged spectators to loan him their laces but no one would help. Instead, they stole his shoes. He heard an announcer calling the play by play. Kathy was losing because she didn't have a partner. Shoeless, there was nothing Jack could do to help her. What did this dream mean?

He'd dreamed about Ellen many times. Those dreams were mostly sexual fantasies. He knew what they meant.

Greta was sitting at the kitchen table sipping a cup of coffee. "Morning, handsome, I'm driving into Coos Bay to do some shopping. Be nice to have company."

He heard her but he didn't hear her. He was trying to decipher the dream. He poured a cup of coffee and sat across from his mother. "Do you believe in dreams?"

Greta fast-shuffled her priorities to accommodate her son's mood. "Dreams?" She repeated the word as if she was a contestant in a spelling bee. "I believe dreams are nothing more, or less, than a hodge-podge of what you're thinking about when you go to bed. When you sleep you lose your common sense. Your thoughts get scrambled around like a bunch of candy wrappers blowing in the wind. Sometimes I wake in the middle of a dream and it seems as real as life itself. Presto-change-o, a few seconds later, poof, it's gone, evaporated like morning dew. To tell the truth, honey, I don't think much about dreams. I also make a point of never worrying about them." Before continuing what she considered bartender mumbo-jumbo, she reached across the table and patted her son's hand.

"I don't think they're premonitions, or warnings, or anything like that."

"That's really interesting," he said, spooning sugar into his coffee. "I've had that happen too, you know, where a dream seems real, then it skips out of my mind and I try to remember it – but can't.

"So," Jack said to his mother, "It's your Monday off, what are you going to do?"

She wound herself back three minutes and started the conversation from scratch. "I'm going to Coos Bay. Like to keep me company?"

"Business?"

"A little business, a little shopping"

Jack didn't enjoy shopping. On the other hand, he didn't have any plans.

"What kind of shopping?"

"Oh, I thought I'd look at new cars, maybe some speedboats, then mosey through a sporting goods store."

"Seriously?"

"Seriously, I have an appointment with my liquor wholesaler, then I thought we could buy you a new sport coat at that classy men's store in downtown Coos Bay. Then. . . "

She sipped her coffee, calculating . . .

"Then we can have lunch at the hoity-toity restaurant with the male waiters, the one over-looking the yacht club. Maybe I dreamed about being waited on by a man last night?"

Her joke sailed over his head. "You don't have to buy me a new sport coat. My blue blazer still fits."

"Sure it does, assuming you want to show-off your wristwatch. Your arms are too long. Besides, I have a sneaking suspicion you're going to need one that fits – if you're going to date the McDonnell girl."

"Next Sunday," he said. "We have a date. But that's a long time away. I'd like to see her before. I called her last night."

"That why you came home so early last night? To call her?"

"There wasn't much going on."

"I see," Greta said, rising from the table. "Get dressed. You're driving."

CHAPTER TWENTY

Abernathy heard a noise. It came from the front of the barn. He took the safety off of his rifle and crept around to the side door.

The intruders were a brood mare and her April foal looking for hay.

"You're a cute little rascal," Abernathy said, taking a step toward the foal.

Nature had programmed the foal to run from unexpected objects or movement, so it bounced away from him on long, gawky legs. The mare followed, keeping herself between the strange man and her baby.

"Fuck you!" Abernathy yelled after the mare.

The sun was up. Time to leave. He packed, shouldered his duffel bag, grabbed the late Terry Dodd's gym bag and closed the barn door behind him. When he passed a small, spring-fed pond, he stopped, added rocks to the the gym bag, which was stuffed with Dodd's belongings and the blood spattered Pendleton shirt. He then zipped the bag half-way and tossed it as far as he could toward the center of the pond. When it hit the water, six mallards took flight from behind a cover of cattails. He lifted an imaginary shotgun to his shoulder, took aim and said, "Bam, Bam, Bam."

He calculated he would have dropped all three drakes.

The bag was still floating on the water. He pointed his imaginary shotgun, shouted, "Sink damnit!"

He repeated "Bam!" That did the trick. The bag tilted, dipped, gurgled and sank to the bottom.

Abernathy reached the gate, dropped the duffel bag containing his real gun on the other side and climbed over. Workday traffic was streaming up and down 101: logging trucks, cars, pick-ups, and the small yellow busses called crummies that transported logging crews to and from work.

Go south, a voice inside Abernathy's head advised. *Hitch a ride to Coos Bay or North Bend. From there, you can catch a bus to Eureka or Crescent City in Northern California.*

He'd heard Georgia-Pacific had a Redwood operation near Crescent City in a small town named Samoa. That would be a good place to go. Days from now, maybe weeks, when they found Dodd, they would start looking for John Abernathy from Florence. Lots of luck, he thought. He was Jake Sloan from Newport. He would let his beard grow and shave his head like the wrestlers he'd seen on the posters in the Armory in Eugene.

He might become a wrestler, he thought, become rich, buy a yellow Lincoln convertible and have red-haired women in tight dresses with big tits clamoring over the ropes trying to touch him. But that would have to be later, after he worked a few months in Samoa.

He was hungry. He remembered seeing a café just before crossing a bridge. Trucks stopped at cafés; be a good place to get a ride. He'd use the big-friendly-guy-looking-for-work routine that had gone over at the Teddy Bear last night. No reason it wouldn't work today. Nobody would guess he was a great warrior on his way to becoming a famous wrestler. A phrase raced through his mind: *Never leave a live enemy.*

He smiled. "Good motto for a great warrior," he said out loud.

He'd conquered the college girl at Cleowox Lake. She had been asking for it, no, begging for it, by having half her tits exposed above her wet bathing suit and by breathing hard, which made her breasts pump up and down, up and down – so more and more of her breasts showed.

If that wasn't "begging for it" – what was? Ditto for the twitchy-assed girl Saturday night, squatting to pee behind a tree like nobody should watch, when she wanted men to watch. He had conquered her, too. The screaming was the best part. Her fear. Next time he would kill her, whoever she might be. He would spurt his manhood inside her and when she stopped screaming he would kill her with his bare hands. No witnesses. No live enemies.

He paused across from Reedsport High School. It was the last week of school – except for the seniors who had been dismissed into the world. It was a few minutes before eight in the morning according to Abernathy's newly acquired Omega wristwatch. The five-minute bell stopped ringing and there was a last minute rush into the school. He wondered if the girl he had his way with

Saturday night had gone to Reedsport. He watched until the tardy bell rang. The bees were safe in the hive. But, the voice within his head warned him, *Hanging out by the school in hopes of catching another girl was not smart.* He resumed walking north on 101 toward the restaurant he'd spotted the night before. In another town a high school could be prime hunting grounds, he thought, but once he became a famous wrestler, maybe he wouldn't need to hunt girls, they'd hunt him. Maybe he'd meet a nice girl like the actress, Debbie Reynolds, in *Singing in the Rain*, and settle down.

The area adjacent to Reedsport high school was called The Flat. The Flat stretched two miles – from the school to the bridge over Scofield Creek. The nicest homes in Reedsport were located on the western side of 101. This area was referred to as the *ta-mat-toe* side of The Flat. Homes on the eastern side of the highway were more modest, the *tomato* side.

He considered veering off into the *ta-mat-toe* side. Have fun with a woman, kill her – never leave a live enemy – take her money and steal her car. Again, not smart, he thought, especially in broad daylight. Stick to the plan. Eat. Hitch a ride. Disappear.

Abernathy walked briskly until he came to the bridge over Scofield Creek. He stopped halfway across, leaned over the sturdy iron railing and stared down. His eyes were drawn to the row of ten houseboats moored along the wide, slow-moving creek. One of the houseboats was abandoned; half of it was listing in the water. It had a **For Sale** sign on it, but it was an old sign. John could tell the sign was old because the bright red ink had faded to pale pink.

Abernathy wondered why people would abandon a perfectly good houseboat. He reckoned a couple of barrels would raise the sunken section out of the water. The wood would dry in a week. He could patch the floor, lay down a few sheets of plywood and the place would be good as new.

The vacant, partially sunken houseboat that captured his attention had been the home of Washington Armstrong and family. The Armstrong clan was among the last of the Umpqua tribe of Native American Indians. Two years before, every member of the nearly extinct tribe received a check for $30,000 from the Bureau of Indian Affairs. There were five members of the Washington Armstrong family: Washington, his wife, Nina, their two sons, Jackson and Lincoln, and their daughter, Martha. The total had come to 150,000 US dollars. Washington also had a brother, Adams. Adams was, the government recorded, "single, no children." He received "one share," $30,000.

Within a week of striking it rich, Washington Armstrong and family moved out of their houseboat and into a four-bedroom home in downtown Reedsport.

Even though Washington bargain-priced the houseboat at five hundred dollars, no one bought it. The locals didn't want the stigma of living in a place "that wasn't good enough for an Indian."

Abernathy was unaware of the houseboat's history, so its vacancy puzzled him. House-boats didn't sit empty on the Siuslaw, he thought. As he surveyed the floating neighborhood, his thoughts turned to his childhood and his mother. His feelings toward her were confused. He knew he should love her but he didn't. She should have protected him, he thought. She'd watched his father beat him. She just stood there and watched and if his father wanted whisky afterwards, she would walk to the Green Front Liquor Store and buy it for him.

And he had heard their bed at night – *squeak-squeak... squeak-squeak... squeak-squeak* – it seemed to last an eternity. Then there would be a few minutes of silence followed by the sound of the toilet flushing. A few more minutes of silence and his father's snoring would begin – growing louder and louder, ripping through the house – *snort, oink, snort, oink, snort, oink.*

He was fourteen when his mother told him his father was dead. He was stunned. His terrifying, invincible father no longer existed? He didn't feel sadness; he felt relieved. No more beatings. No more squeaking bed.

"How?" he'd asked his mother.

"Fell," she answered, offering no detail. "There's a little insurance, the house is paid for and I can get a job. We'll be okay." She didn't appear to be sad, either.

Abernathy had a recurring dream: he was in the playground of the elementary school. There was a pretty girl on the swing. She was blond with blue eyes and she smiled at him, jumped off the swing and walked away. She took a few steps and turned, looked back at him, smiled again, showing her white teeth while she mouthed the words, "Catch me if you can," just like the *Gingerbread Man* said in the story his first grade teacher had read to the class.

Like the Gingerbread Man, she "ran and ran as fast as she can" and John Abernathy ran after her. Just as he was close to catching her, she turned around and it wasn't the pretty little girl. She was still a little girl, but she had his mother's old face with yellow teeth. Then, the girl-mother image rematerialized into a likeness of the Northwest's legendary Big Foot. It was gigantic and apelike – with the angry face of his father. The Big Foot/father image began chasing Abernathy. As he ran away from the monster, Abernathy realized he was, himself, naked, and he was grown-up and running through a sawmill. All the men were laughing at him. He wanted to stop and fight the laughing men but knew if he slowed down the monster would overtake him. He raced to a high cliff; the Siuslaw River was below him.

As the monster reached for him with six inch claws on huge, hairy fingers, John climbed over a railing and jumped. He always awakened in the middle of the jump, sailing through the air, delighted that he could fly.

The voice inside Abernathy's head interrupted his remembrance. *Move on, Big John*, it commanded. He spotted the cafe on the other side of the bridge, just as he'd remembered. He hoisted his duffle bag and aimed himself toward it.

The Y-Café was so-named because it was located at a Y junction. If you were headed north, as John was, the left fork of the Y represented U.S.101. It by-passed downtown Reedsport, taking a direct route to Gardiner, Florence, Yachats, Waldport, Newport and points north. The other fork in the Y was the old highway. It veered northeast into downtown Reedsport, branched off at the end of town and led to Eugene and the Willamette Valley.

CHAPTER TWENTY-ONE

Harold Gilbert was having a cup of coffee at the Y Café with the man who owned the tire retread shop on 101. Harold was trying to sell the retread man a half-page ad in the weekly newspaper.

"By advertising twelve times you get my special rate," Harold explained, showing him a rate card. "See," Harold pointed at the numbers, "It works out that you get one ad free."

"Oh, hell, Hal," the retread man gave in, "Go ahead and sign me up, but I want a new ad with a different special every week."

They both noticed the big logger when he passed their booth. Abernathy smiled respectfully and took a seat at the counter.

"Now that I'm a customer," retread man said, "Tell me what you know about Beach Night? I heard a girl got herself raped."

"Wouldn't say she 'got herself' raped," Harold replied. "Like she had a choice in the matter. But some slime grabbed her. And you know, did her the dirty deed. Hurt her bad."

"I hope we catch the slime and lynch 'em by the balls," retread man said, slamming his fist on the table as an exclamation point.

"I will tell you two things," Harold disclosed. "There was no eye witness but Sheriff Stark has a suspect."

"No eye witness? What about the Simmons kid?"

"Well," Harold said in an almost-whisper, "The deputy, Cal, told me the kid made the whole thing up to impress a girl."

"No shit," retread man shook his head in disgust, "These kids have it too damn easy. Half of 'em got cars and they all want these brand new Goodyear tires with the extra-wide, white walls. I can put four tires on a car for what they pay for one new white wall."

"That'd be a good ad," Hal said. "Big headline 'FOUR LIKE-NEW TIRES FOR WHAT YOU'D PAY FOR ONE NEW WHITE WALL.' I'll work that up for you and show it to you. You might've hit on something." Harold headed out the door.

Retread-man, joined two fellow 101 businessmen and filled them in on the latest gossip. "Simmons kid didn't see anything," he told his cronies, "Made the whole thing up to impress a girl."

Abernathy overheard Harold and retread man. He stayed calm and smiled when he ordered a breakfast of pancakes, eggs, ham and toast.

He'd been right, he thought. No one had seen him. Yet why had the local sheriff gone to Florence? As for those two old farts referring to him, a proven warrior – as

Slime? Their last sight on earth might just be a two-by-four between their droopy eyes. Not now, but someday.

Driving back to the newspaper, Harold considered stopping at Grafton & Daughter. Their store was only a block from his office. Rosie was always an easy sale but if old man Grafton was there in his usual sour mood, well, he'd need at least a shot or two to deal with the damn fool. He pulled his car over next to a vacant lot and reached under the driver's seat for a fifth of whiskey he'd stored there. He took a couple of slugs and decided the Graftons could wait. He'd walk over there at lunchtime while the mean-spirited bastard, Glenn Grafton, was at the Horse Shoe Café, yeah, that's what he'd do. Time it so he only had to deal with Rosie. The walk over would do him good. Right now, he'd just close his eyes for a minute or two. Then he'd scoot back to his office and see what Karl was up to.

It was a few minutes past ten when Harold arrived at the newspaper. The sheriff's car was parked in front. While Harold had been snoozing, his partner had been printing Sheriff Henry Stark's wanted posters. Schultz had done a remarkable job. He'd used the two pictures from the *Siuslaw Sailor Year Book* as clip art to print a quantity of 500, 8-1/2 by 11-inch wanted posters.

"You're a genius, Karl," Henry praised the proud printer. The posters were sitting on the counter, ink still wet. As Harold walked by them – in route to his desk – he did a double take.

"This one right here," he said, tapping Abernathy's likeness, "I swear he looks like the big logger I saw having breakfast at the Y."

"You sure?" Henry said, spinning around.

"Pretty sure. Fellow at the Y was a tad older, had a stubble, needed a shave. Dressed like a logger . . ."

Harold squinted, "But the eyes, cheekbones – I'd bet a fifth of Wild Turkey it's the same man."

"How long ago?" Henry asked anxiously.

Harold checked his wrist watch. "Maybe an hour."

Henry grabbed a stack of posters and rushed out the door. Over his shoulder he ordered Harold or Karl to call his deputy, Cal Shinkle. "Have Cal meet me at the Y, pronto."

Henry was furious with himself. If he'd called Karl last night, and printed the posters last night, they would have been distributed up and down Highway 101 . . . last night!

If he'd just done that, like he thought about doing – before returning the call to the judge, before dealing with Rosie and her damn pie – if he'd just followed his instincts as a sheriff, he might have this bastard in jail!

"If, if, if – shit, shit, shit," he repeated as he turned on his siren and sped toward the Y.

* * *

Frenchy Montand was Reedsport's lath-and-plaster man, "An artist," his customers said.

"There's real time and Frenchy time," Mr. Barney of Barney's Outfitting professed. "But if you want it done right, you'll wait for Frenchy and be thankful you did."

Frenchy's passion was fishing. Not just any kind of fishing. He specialized in the wily steelhead and finicky, sea-run, cutthroat trout called bluebacks. Lately, he'd added striper bass to his list of prey.

Striper bass were a recent phenomena along the Oregon coast. The species, native to the Atlantic Ocean, had been planted in San Francisco Bay in the 1940s. Without fishing pressure or formidable natural enemies, their numbers multiplied and their range expanded north along the California coast to the Oregon coast. Frenchy caught his first striper by accident in 1952 while casting a silver Flatfish lure for spring bluebacks under the Smith River Bridge.

He now had two prime striper fishing holes. One was beneath the railroad trestle over the Smith River outside of Gardiner; the other was Barney Point on the edge of Barney's tidewater ranch.

Frenchy scorned boats, believing they gave fishermen an unfair advantage. He would either wade or cast from the bank. He had permission from Mr. Barney to access the point. In return for fishing privileges, Frenchy would stop at the barn and put hay out for the horses. Prime fishing time for stripers on the point was one hour before and/or after high tide. High tide on Monday morning was eleven fifty-seven. At ten-thirty, Frenchy parked his pickup in front of the barn. Barney's pinto gelding saw the truck coming and was waiting in front of the barn door when Frenchy braked to a stop.

The pinto was skittish, sniffing the air and kicking his back legs. Something wasn't right. Frenchy didn't catch the scent until he opened the barn door. It was unmistakable.

He looked into the window of the car. The ghastly, twisted body of Terry Dodd greeted him. Two rats had managed to gnaw their way through the floorboard and fixed their gaze on Frenchy with possessive belligerency. They had been feasting on the eyes and nose and resented the intruder. Frenchy had a strong stomach but not that strong. He went outside and retched. He got back into his pick-up and headed for the nearest telephone. There would not be any striper fishing today.

* * *

Sitting in the Y-Café, John's confidence gave way to uneasiness. Wariness. People all around him were talking about a "Terrible crime."

"Slime."

"A big guy and little guy."

As the only "big guy" in the Y, John began to feel conspicuous. He had second thoughts about the way he'd dealt with Dodd and the Plymouth. He should have done a slicker job of hiding the body and car.

Ron Monroe, Red and the wimps at the barbershop – all of them knew he and Dodd left Florence together. But that was when he was John Abernathy, Nasty reminded himself.

A log truck driver with a load of second growth Douglas fir took the stool next to him. Being the friendly sort, he asked John, "How you doing?"

"Could be better. My car broke down and I need to get to Coos Bay."

"I'm hauling a load of second growth to the stud mill in Hauser. You're welcome to ride that far with me. Bound to be somebody from the mill going into Coos Bay."

The two men downed their breakfasts and "Jake Sloan" accepted the truck driver's offer. He figured, anything was better than standing on 101 with his thumb out. He'd be on a truck heading south. Cops wouldn't be looking for him in a log truck. Cops would be looking for him in a blue Plymouth.

CHAPTER TWENTY-TWO

As the log truck passed the entrance to Lighthouse Beach, John felt a surge of pride over his accomplishment. His confidence returned.

"Hear they had a shit-pot full of trouble at that beach Saturday night," John ventured to the log truck driver.

"Oh, yeah?" the driver said, disinterested, putting a pinch of Copenhagen under his lip. "I don't pay much attention to what goes on around here, I just drive my damn truck. Every time I get a few dollars ahead the son of bitch breaks down. Shoulda stayed in the army. You ever in the army?"

"No," Jake Sloan said.

"I was in Korea, Yalu River, we had them gooks on the run, coulda chased 'em all the way to Peking, but the politicians took over."

Jake/John tried again. "I was at the Teddy Bear Tavern last night and the bartender heard one of those rich high school girls was raped back there."

"Oh, yeah?" the truck driver responded. "Well, sometimes they say they're raped and they ain't exactly raped if you know what I mean."

"I know what you mean." John-alias-Jake said, leaning over and nudging the driver with a friendly elbow. The driver's comment made John think about his dead buddy. Too bad Dodd hadn't seen it the same as this truck driver. He wouldn't have had to shut him up, and come to think of it, if Dodd hadn't screwed up, they'd probably both be job hunting in Coos Bay.

When they passed the Lakeside entrance the truck driver motioned his thumb out the window.

"You talk about rich girls, that's where the real rich ones live."

"Back there?" Jake Sloan looked, straining to see. He would have missed the Lakeside entrance altogether if the driver hadn't called his attention to it.

"Oh, yeah! All the doctors and lawyers and fat cat timbermen live back there on Tenmiles Lake. I'd like to get rich just so I could live there, piss off my boat dock and throw my beer cans in the water to let 'em know what I think of 'em. There weren't nobody from Lakeside at the Yalu River when them chinks come after us."

"You kill any of them?" Jake Sloan asked.

The driver rolled down his window and spat out his snuff. His mood changed – from cocky rebel to pensive. He didn't like the question.

"I shot into 'em, but I never thought of it as killing. It was like the shooting gallery at the carnival, you shoot; the duck goes down and pops right back up. I don't like to think of it as killing, more like protecting yourself and your buddies. I don't like shooting anymore, don't even own a deer rifle."

This struck Jake Sloan as cowardly. He'd started to like the guy, even respect him, now he turns out to be a coward.

They reached Hauser and the truck driver pulled into the mill yard. He braked his truck and told his rider, "There's the office if you want to ask about a ride. Just tell them you're with me, Randy Morgan. I got to go down to the pond and get these logs scaled."

* * *

Henry met his deputy at the Y-Café and the two of them began asking questions. The waitress, Tammy Burns, was the most helpful. "The guy on the poster left with a log truck driver," she reported. "I heard him say he was going to Hauser."

"Hauser?" Henry repeated, shaking his head. Abernathy was in another county and at least an hour ahead of him. He would have time to hitch a second ride. But there was a thin chance he'd think he was home free and hang out around the mill.

Hauser was out of Henry's jurisdiction, but he could fudge his way around that detail with the "law of hot pursuit." Judge Stovall would back him up. What if he did catch him? There was a minor problem called "evidence."

What do I charge him with? Having a bad reputation? Without a witness, he didn't have a case; he could only push him hard with the circumstantial evidence and try to wrench a confession out of him. Or get Dodd to turn. But they'd obviously split up. Where was Dodd?

Abernathy had hitched a ride. Where was the car? Had Dodd stopped the car to let Abernathy out, to take a leak or run into a store, and then gunned the engine and escaped? Henry scolded himself and said out loud, "You're wasting time."

"There's a phone call for the sheriff," the dishwasher called out.

Henry sprinted to the wall phone in the kitchen.

"You better get over to Barney's tidewater place," Elsie told him. "Frenchy says he saw a dead man inside a car in the horse barn."

"He say what kind of car?"

"Blue Plymouth, didn't say the year."

"That's close enough," the sheriff sighed. He lit a cigarette and motioned to his deputy. "All hell just broke loose, Cal. Looks like Abernathy might have killed the other suspect. Frenchy found a body and a blue Plymouth in the barn over at Barney's tidewater place."

"What do you want me to do?" Cal asked. "Just tell me."

"First, call the Coos County Sheriff and have him meet me at the stud mill in Hauser. Then call the state troopers. Tell them what happened."

"You sure you want me to call the troopers? After what they did Saturday night?"

"Jesus H Christ, Cal, yes!" Henry almost lost his temper. He took a deep drag from his Lucky. "Sorry," Henry apologized. "No reason to bite your head off, I'm the one who screwed up. But we need everyone with a badge on this one. We have a killer on the loose."

"Yes, sir, I understand. That was dumb of me."

Henry held his hand up to cut off further discussion. "Don't worry about it. One more thing," Henry instructed, "After you notify everybody, hustle over to the barn and cordon it off. Don't let any one in there who isn't part of the investigation."

"That it?"

"Not quite. Call Judge Stoval in Roseburg, give him an update – and do the same with that lawyer, James McDonnell, in Lakeside."

Five miles from Hauser, Henry switched off his siren. Luck, like a pendulum, might swing his way. No point in warning Abernathy he was coming.

But he was too late. Randy Morgan was still there and recognized the picture on the poster. "That's him alright, but he gave me a different name, Sloan. Said his first name was Jake. I sent him to the office over there."

Randy pointed at the office even though it was in plain sight. "I sat next to him at that Y Café back in Reedsport. He told me his car broke down and he needed to get to Coos Bay."

No one in the office had seen Abernathy. No one in the entire mill had seen him.

The old timer who operated the Red & White Grocery Store in Hauser thought he saw a big logger walking down from the mill but he hadn't paid much attention because he was busy stocking shelves.

John "Nasty" Abernathy, alias Jake Sloan, had vanished.

There hadn't been a murder along this stretch of the Oregon Coast in years. There had been bar fights, axe handle fights and an occasional shoot-out, usually over women. "The Saturday Night Honor Society," as Henry called them. But there had never been a cold-blooded murder. Henry figured he might as well drop the rape charge. Spare the girl the humiliation of going to trial. Without Dodd, the prosecution would have a hard time getting a conviction. Yet murdering Dodd was hard for Henry to fathom: The premeditated murder of your only friend?

Henry rolled the crime over in his mind. For Abernathy, they might just crank up Old Tom, the electric chair, nicknamed after Thomas Edison, whose genius made electricity the miracle of the 20th Century. This guy deserves the chair, Henry concluded as he exhaled smoke from another Lucky Strike.

The Coos County Sheriff, Slim Haskins, and two state patrolmen reconnoitered with Henry in Hauser at one o'clock.

The quartet grilled Randy again. "Like I told Sheriff Stark," Randy insisted, "He was looking for a ride to Coos Bay."

"You must have talked about something," Slim pushed.

"I suppose we talked some," Randy scratched his head to show the officers he was trying. "Come to think of it, he mentioned that beach party. Said a girl was raped but I didn't know nothing about it and the subject was dropped."

"What else, Randy, anything?" Slim pushed harder. "You're lucky to be breathing. Help us out here."

"Well, come to think, when we passed Lakeside I let it slip that was where the rich folks lived, and . . ."

"And what, Randy?" A state trooper coaxed him, putting his arm around Randy's shoulder.

"He seemed interested, that's all."

"That's something," the good-guy state trooper assured Randy, patting him on the back.

Slim spread a map over the hood of his vehicle. "Three possibilities: One, he caught a ride to Coos Bay and beyond and is now halfway to California. Two, he caught a ride and he's laying low somewhere in North Bend or Coos Bay.

"Or..."

Slim made a sweeping gesture, "He slipped off into the woods around here. That's the one that worries me most."

"Let's get some roadblocks up," a state patrolman suggested.

"Better tell them 'armed and dangerous,'" Henry advised, "He might have a deer rifle."

The good-guy patrolman tried to add levity to the grim predicament "How about the Lost Tribe, Slim, think we could call them for a little help?"

It eased the tension.

"Hell, yes, let's send up a smoke signal," Slim joked. He turned serious. "We'll take all the help we can get. In the old days we'd bring in the dogs, but they cut the dogs out of my budget three years back."

He shook his head and reminisced, "I had a bloodhound that would have taken his scent off Randy's passenger seat. I swear to God that ole dog wouldn't have stopped until his nose was stuffed all the way up the bastard's ass."

The idea of a bloodhound's nose buried in Abernathy's ass provoked a riffle of laughter.

"Those were the days," Slim sighed.

* * *

Abernathy had started toward the mill office but it didn't feel right. Maybe Morgan was trying to detain him?

Have him wait in the office while he went down to the pond shack and called the police. No, that didn't make any sense, but what if? What if somebody had found Dodd and it was on the radio. The Pond Monkeys had radios. They'd say, "Hey Randy, hear about the murder in Reedsport? They're looking for a big guy."

Morgan would say, "Shit, I just gave a big guy a ride out of Reedsport."

He couldn't trust Morgan. How can you trust a coward? What if they found the body? What if it was on the radio?

The first place the cops would look for him was up and down 101. He could see the highway from where he was standing. Cars and trucks were shooting north and south. He could hear them – *whoosh, whoosh, whoosh*. Too bad he couldn't just whoosh himself inside one of the cars headed south, he thought.

Too bad he hadn't kept the Plymouth. No, he was right about the Plymouth. If the cops were looking for him, they were also looking for Dodd. The easiest way to find Dodd would be to put out an "all-points" on the Plymouth. He wished he had a map, a lay of the land.

Don't step back on that highway, the voice warned him.

Near the Hauser/101 junction there was an old logging road that ran northeast – into the woods – veering away from 101. Abernathy took it.

He hiked a mile and came upon a wooden bridge across a small, sluggish stream. The stream flowed north, which probably meant it didn't feed into the ocean. He guessed it fed Tenmiles Lake where the rich people lived. The logging road ended at a small mill that had been gutted by fire. Abernathy backtracked to the bridge and followed the stream. It was rough going through the dense forest of small spruce, black cottonwoods, red cedar, wild rhododendrons and ferns. When the brush became too thick he waded along the edge of the stream. He came across a tunnel through the underbrush made by black bears. He took his rifle out of the duffel bag, assembled it, cranked a live round into the chamber, clicked the safety off and proceeded. He wasn't concerned about snakes. There were no poisonous snakes on the Oregon coast.

Crawling through blackberry brambles was the worst. Many of the thorns were a half-inch long and all of them were needle sharp. He wished he hadn't dropped his seaman's hat at the beach; it would have protected his head and ears.

At four in the afternoon the fog began drifting in from the ocean. It was a thick fog and felt like light rain. It slid down from the treetops, rapidly covering the forest floor. By six it was too dark to continue. Should he make a fire? Why not. No one would see the smoke in the fog. The dry, dead limbs from fallen trees made perfect kindling. To assure his fire a fast start, he sought fallen branches laden with sap, found two, struck a match and just like that he had himself a crackling fire.

He thought about the canned goods back in the barn. Why had he passed up the chance to pack food? He forgave himself. How was he supposed know he'd be stuck in woods tonight? With any luck, he'd be through Coos Bay – if not in California.

Why did he have to end up with a coward taking piss-ant, peckerwood logs to a half-ass mill in Hauser instead of one of those powerful Mack trucks going into Coos Bay and a big mill and the freedom of a large crowd? What had he done to deserve a prick like Randy Morgan?

Take it easy, John, he told himself. Use your head. This could be a blessing in disguise. Maybe you'll come across one of those rich girls. He rubbed his crotch, thinking about a rich girl. He felt himself getting hard and began to talk to his penis. "Don't worry, Little John, we're going to find you a rich girl."

He remembered ripping the panties off the girl at the beach, he savored the scent of her terror, like buck rut, he thought, and he opened his fly and stared at his erection.

"Okay!" he said to it.

He began masturbating, stroking hard, furiously, to feel the pain. He willed himself to summon the image of the girl at the beach. He stroked harder and harder. He closed his eyes. The back of his eyelids became a movie screen. There she was, bleeding, screaming – harder, harder, bleed, scream – he felt an erotic rush and exploded his semen into the flames. He tucked Little John back into his trousers and fell asleep. He would not be visited by a bad dream tonight.

CHAPTER TWENTY-THREE

Greta glowed as she watched her son try on sport coats. The flighty girl with the hypocrite mother and pussy-whipped father were safely out of the picture. Jack had met another young woman, Kathy McDonnell. Her famous father might not like the idea of his daughter taking up with a saloonkeeper's son, but daughters have a way with fathers. An educated, worldly man like James McDonnell would be wise and wait for young love to run its course.

Fair enough, Greta thought. But if Jack was going to "go calling," one thing for sure, he wasn't going to look like he rode into Lakeside on a beer truck.

The balding, immaculately dressed, slightly effeminate salesman zeroed in on three coats: (1) Dark gray cashmere – herringbone pattern; (2) Classic two button camel hair – leather buttons; (3) Luxurious Irish wool – brown tweed. She could tell Jack didn't like the tweed. He was leaning toward the camel hair.

Jack's preference wasn't lost on the salesman. "You know, the college boys wear these with Levis and an open collar shirt for casual occasions. 'Cas' they call it.

"But on Saturday night, you slip into your blue button-down." He walked over to the shirt counter and produced a neatly folded, blue Oxford cloth dress shirt, "like this." He minced over to the tie case and selected a blue-red-yellow, diagonally striped tie. Painstakingly, he twisted a knot, placed the tie on the shirt, raised his eyebrows in appreciation and finished his pitch.

"And, excuse me, mam, I know we're talking about your son, but he'll have to fight the coeds away with a *Louisville Slugger*."

Greta smiled because she knew the salesman was performing for Jack, not for her – and because she knew the salesman wasn't far from the truth.

Jack wanted the coat but he'd seen the price tag: One penny short of one hundred and sixty dollars. The blazer they'd bought the year before at J.C. Penny had been thirty bucks. He said nothing.

"Do you like it?" Greta circled her son, checking out the coat, noting the 42-long was a perfect fit right off the rack.

"Yeah," Jack admitted. "Fits great, and it does look good with Levis."

"He needs shoes, too." Greta said. "And a belt to match. Cordovan penny loafers. No tassels. Then we'll look at belts."

They left with the shoes, belt, camel sportcoat, a pair of charcoal, worsted wool slacks, two of the blue Oxford cloth button-down shirts and two ties. Jack slipped into one of his new shirts before leaving the store. It was his mother's suggestion, "Why not wear your new coat to lunch?"

He sneaked another look at himself in the full-length mirror on the way out the door. Sharp, he thought. Wouldn't it be slick if he happened to run into Kathy today? Or Ellen. His mind flashed back to the booth in the drive-in. Tim and Ellen? He shouldn't be jealous, he told himself, but he was – just a little.

As Greta promised, they had lunch at the restaurant above the yacht club. It was déja vu for Greta – women of all ages checking out her "date." Women had looked at his father, John Portman, the same way. She ordered a glass of white wine with her chicken salad sandwich. "Chilled," she told the male waiter, remembering she'd seen the house wine sitting out on the bar.

"Of course," he said, approvingly, in the way good waiters have of flattering a customer through intonation. She tipped twenty percent instead of fifteen.

"Professional courtesy," she explained to Jack as she counted out the money and laid it on the table.

The only thing that spoiled the day was the roadblock on the way home. That's when they heard the news about an all-out manhunt for John Abernathy alias Jake Sloan. Considered "Armed and Dangerous." He was "Wanted for questioning regarding the murder of Terry Dodd."

* * *

Eleanor Reilly's Monday wasn't as satisfying as Greta's. Her daughter, Ellen, hadn't arrived home until three-thirty in the morning. When mother confronted daughter, Ellen snapped, "I'm not your little high school girl anymore."

Ellen had never rebelled before and it felt good. "What time I come home is my business," she added. Then couldn't stop. She proceeded to tell her mother that as a diploma-carrying member of the adult world, she would, henceforth, live her own life and come home whenever she damn well pleased.

Eleanor countered by calling Ellen an "ungrateful little slut." She immediately regretted the use of the word slut, but it slipped out in the heat of battle and there was no way to retract it.

"Who's calling who a slut?" Ellen fired back, "Everybody knows about you and Doc Stanwood."

Eleanor couldn't believe her ears. No one knew about her affair with Stan. They had always been discrete. She slapped Ellen across the face and hissed, "How dare you?"

Ellen glared at her, defiant. There was no shame or remorse on her face. Eleanor, the mother, saw only contempt. She realized she'd lost control of her daughter. Ellen obviously hadn't been with Pat because he'd called three times during the evening. She hadn't been with Jack Portman; she'd gotten that much out of Olive. She had been with Tim Budge.

Ellen turned away from the fray, and with a sexy swagger, marched defiantly up the stairs to her bedroom. Eleanor heard the bedroom door slam and tried to look on the bright side. The Budge family owned a respectable business on Lake Tahkenitch and they must have money because they'd bought their son a new car. Tim was a nice looking boy. He wasn't as good a catch as Pat Kelly, but if Ellen ended up with Tim, it wouldn't be a disaster. At least she hadn't gone back to Jack Portman. Unbelievably, her husband had defended Jack Portman. "Jack seems like a good kid to me," he'd said. "He's bright, knows how to talk to adults and his mother works hard. That saloon of hers is probably a gold mine."

What did he know? Men were stupid, Eleanor thought. Her husband was so obtuse he didn't even notice when she stroked Stan's thigh under the bridge table. She had a "man-joke" she shared with her closest female friends. Question:

"IF YOUR HUSBAND SPEAKS IN THE FOREST AND THERE'S NO ONE THERE, IS HE STILL WRONG?"

Her female friends all laughed and agreed, "Yes."

CHAPTER TWENTY-FOUR

John Abernathy awakened Tuesday morning just as the fog was beginning to lift. It was damp, but there were shreds of blue showing atop the green trees and gray sky. A light breeze pushed strands of fog across the treetops. Abernathy stretched. His muscles were stiff but he felt good. He was safe in these woods, at least for now, even if they found Dodd.

The voice assured him, *Keep your head and you'll find a way out of here.*

John communed with the voice. "Got money," he said. "Got I-D. All we have to do is get to California." He stood and began walking. He was hungry but he'd been hungry before. "Just don't think about it," he mini-lectured himself.

He was becoming acclimated. The soft *schussing* of the stream and the low *who-whoosh* of the wind were reassuring. The unrelenting conversations between hundreds of birds were comforting. He knew the time to worry was when the birds stopped talking. A hushed forest would mean he had company. He heard a sharp snap at one point, but saw nothing. Whatever it was, it hadn't frightened the birds. He ran his hand over the barrel of the rifle. It could be a deer or a bear.

He hoped it was a bear. He'd never killed a bear. He could hit a bull's eye at seventy-five yards – why not a bear's eye at twenty-five? But the woods were quiet again, except for the *schuss* of the stream, the *whoosh* of the wind and the chatter of the birds. The sharp snap must have been a deer, he determined. The deer had seen him and made a hasty retreat.

When the creek became wider and shallower, he left the bear trail and waded over the sandy bottom. Less than an hour later he arrived in a secluded cove on the southern edge of Tenmiles Lake. There was a natural meadow where the creek intersected the lake. As Abernathy stepped into the clearing he felt a profound sense of relief. Free of the brambles and thick brush, he sat down on a tree stump and sized up his situation. His clothes were ripped and torn, but he had one more change in his duffel bag. Clothing might be a problem later, but not today. Today, food was the first order of business.

A blacktail doe and her fawn walked into the pasture. Instinctively, John raised his rifle. Then thought better of it. The harsh crack of a gunshot would carry for miles across the lake and it wasn't hunting season. The deer responded to his sudden movement by bounding back into the trees. Soon, another doe appeared. She saw him, but seemed to have no fear of man. That told Abernathy there were houses nearby, at least within her range, which would constitute about five square miles. Applying this logic, he concluded the rich people who lived within her range were friendly to the local deer population.

The fancy folk would eat beef, pork, lamb and chicken as long as it came wrapped in clean, white butcher paper. But they didn't want to harm a hair on one of their precious Bambies. Most people were weak and cowardly. Even truck drivers were turning into cowards. Log truck drivers should be real men. They owned the roads – "I'm hauling logs, get out of my way."

Log truck drivers had real power. You see a log truck coming at you on a one-lane road and you better swerve into a pullover or start backing up fast. Maybe, John thought, he should get a job driving a log truck when he got to California?

Morgan was a disgrace to all the real log truck drivers. If he, John Abernathy, had gone to Korea, he would damn well have kept count. He would have notched his rifle, he assured himself, and they would have given him medals. When he came back to Florence he'd have worn his uniform with all the medals on his chest. When he walked into a tavern everybody would have stood in line to buy him a beer and shake his hand.

"That's the hand that killed fifty gooks," he would have said. *Fucking-A, man, he should have gone into the army where they appreciate a man who has the guts to kill the enemy and be proud of it.* He walked down to the lakeshore. Fish were rising, but he had no fishing line or hooks. As he explored the shallows near the mouth of the creek he saw a large population of crawfish. "Beggars can't be choosy," he said aloud, considering that a witty thing to say.

During the next half hour he stalked and captured twenty of the red-shelled crustaceans. He peeled the shells from the tails, made himself a small fire and roasted the plump chunks of white meat on a stick. "Not bad," he said, as if a uniformed waiter had asked. "Are the roasted crawfish tails to your satisfaction today, Mr. Abernathy?"

He heard the sound of an outboard motor in the distance. Hurriedly, he stomped out his fire and ran back into the woods. It was two minutes before the boat came into view. Abernathy was impressed with his keen sense of hearing. He sniffed the air, expecting his nose to tell him more about the intruder.

Full-blooded Umpqua Indian, Adams Armstrong, was the younger brother of Washington Armstrong. Unlike his brother, Adams never married. Before the Bureau of Indian Affairs handed him a check for thirty thousand dollars, he'd made his living handcrafting cedar shingles. There was a waiting list for Armstrong shingles. He could sell all he could make to the prosperous residents of Lakeside.

Adams lifestyle changed little after he came into government money. He did buy a used Chevy pick-up truck and replace his log cabin on Tenmiles Lake with a handsome A-frame structure with indoor plumbing. The Ambassador helped him build the house. Adams was impressed by The Ambassador's carpentry skills and considered asking how he'd come by them, but he didn't, assuming if The Ambassador wanted him to know, he'd tell him.

It took the two of them eight weeks to tear down Adam's cabin and put up the A-frame. Afterwards, Adams went back to crafting his shingles. This disappointed many of the locals, robbing them of an excuse to call him an "Uppity, lazy, no good Indian living on our tax dollars."

Adams enjoyed his late-model Chevy pick-up as much as the new house. It was more reliable than his previous vehicle, a decrepit pre-war Hudson, and carried ten times as many shingles. Once a week he would drive to The Dock Tavern and have one or two two beers. He had an arrangement with Greta Portman to never serve him more than two beers. He'd seen what alcohol had done to his father and vowed it would never happen to him.

Sometimes, Adams would drive up the Umpqua and visit The Ambassador. Adams knew The Ambassador was crazy, but judged it to be "a good kind of crazy."

The Ambassador insisted civilization was in ruins. He cited two world wars in less than half a century as proof. Adams didn't agree or disagree. He was ambivalent. To him, Europe and Asia were akin to distant stars in the heavens, faraway and irrelevant to his daily life. He saw no point in getting upset about any of it, although it was pleasant listening to The Ambassador. The Ambassador grilled beefsteak and treated him, Adams Armstrong, as an equal.

Adams often wished he'd been born before the white people had come to the Umpqua. But he hadn't been, so he wouldn't let himself dwell on the subject. He was proud to be an Indian; it just wasn't a very good time to be an Indian. He wished he had a woman but there weren't any Indian women left and white women didn't like Indian men. His brother had married the only Indian woman they knew, which was his brother's right because he was older. Adams wasn't jealous; he didn't like his brother's wife. She wanted to be like a white person and move into town, live in a house and go to church. She didn't understand. Even if she acted like a white person, she would always look like an Indian, and therefore, she would always be treated like an Indian.

Now she was insisting that her sons pretend to be white people. Adams feared this would eventually lead them to anger, and worse, self-hatred. They were nice boys, he thought, good fishermen, but he worried about their futures. It was not a good time to be an Indian. If there were such a thing as a Lost Tribe, they would be well advised to join it.

One thing was clear to Adams. Money would not make an Umpqua Indian white. Why couldn't the others see that? Adams tried to counsel his nephews but they wouldn't listen.

"If we had all the money in the world, they would simply change the money," Adams explained to the two young men.

"We once moved freely between the ocean and the low mountains, then the white men came and said, 'You can't do that any more because it is not your land.' But it was never our land; it was everyone's land. So, how did it become their land? They changed the rules to suit themselves. They will change the money in the same way."

Adams told his brother and nephews, "Indians will never be accepted by white people."

"I know," Washington Armstrong agreed with his brother. "But when I do what the woman wants, she leaves me alone, lets me fish and walk down to Carl's tavern where they let me play cards in the backroom. It's better than having her tell me to get a job and go to church with her."

The Ambassador once asked Adams if members of the Lost Tribe ever visited him. Adams pondered this and finally answered, "Yes." He answered yes for two reasons. First, because he knew it would please The Ambassador. Second, because in his dreams, he did see people of his race moving stealthily through the great trees and standing on high bluffs above the vast ocean. In some of these night visions, he would watch the migrating whales dance along the horizon. Then he would see the masts of tall ships and the blood of the whales mixed with the salty froth along the shoreline. Then he would wake up.

"Yes, I have seen the Lost Tribe, but only at night," Adams told The Ambassador.

The Ambassador shared his secret ambition with Adams, "I hope to be the first white man to be initiated into the Lost Tribe, but I know I'll have to earn my place."

"How will you earn a place?

"A time will come when I'm presented with the opportunity to do something exemplary."

Adams didn't know the word. "Exemplary?" He asked its meaning.

"Something outstanding. Something like," The Ambassador closed his eyes, "Something like saving the life of a worthy person, although, sadly, there isn't an abundance of them around. It's a difficult assignment, my friend, but not impossible."

CHAPTER TWENTY-FIVE

Jack sat on the edge of his bed and considered walking down to the marina. He dismissed the notion, yawned and let himself slip into a half-sleep. He visualized Kathy's face. Their last phone conversation played through his memory like a tape recording.

"I can't wait until Sunday to see you," she'd said.

They'd agreed he would come to her house "tomorrow night" – which was tonight. "Don't eat first," she had told him. "There may be a small dinner party, daddy enjoys having people over. If there isn't a dinner party, I'll have our cook make something special, just you and me."

Cook? They have a cook? Jack thought, impressed.

He heard his mother moving around and knew there would be a knock on his door. He waited, sure enough, *Knock, Knock.*

"Can I fix you breakfast, honey?"

"Thanks but don't bother. I'll have cereal. Can I use the car today?" He knew she didn't need the car. She'd work from eleven in the morning until midnight.

"I suppose," she said.

"And tonight?"

"What's tonight?"

"I'm going to see Kathy,"

Long pause.

"It's only Tuesday. Thought your date was Sunday?"

"We moved it up. How about the car?"

"I suppose, but don't be too late coming home tonight, there's a storm coming, heard it on the radio. . ."

Jack's day trip was a drive up to Tahkenitch to visit Tim. He found him applying a coat of green paint to a rental boat. The boat was upside down, resting on two sawhorses.

"Looks like fun." Jack said.

"Almost finished. Give me five minutes and we'll go over to the outlet and try for some bass."

The subject of Ellen didn't come up until they boarded an outboard-powered skiff to go fishing. Tim broached it first. "Suppose you're curious about what happened between your ex and me?"

"None of my business," Jack shrugged, dying to know – hoping to sound disinterested.

"Jesus, you really get me," Tim shot back.

Jack waited. Tim guided the boat out of the lake proper and into a wide channel leading to the outlet. The outlet was a small river in reverse. Instead of feeding the lake, it flowed from the lake through two miles of sand dunes and emptied into the Pacific. Tim rigged two casting rods with red and white plugs called Hot Shots. He handed Jack a rod.

"Ellen and I went to high school together for four years," Tim began, "and never said a word to each other, except for 'Hi.'"

Tim saw a telltale ripple in the water and instructed his friend, "Three o'clock, cast short of the lily pads."

Jack missed long and to the left (two o'clock). Tim shot his lure to the target with a skilled, wrist-action motion. He pointed the rod tip down and cranked the reel slowly, imparting a zigzag motion. The lure traveled less than three feet when there was a splash at the end of the line and the rod bent double. Tim set the hook, kept the rod tip up – the line taut – and coaxed the bass toward the side of the boat where Jack was ready with the net.

"Looks like the Lake Tahkenitch Resort will have 'Filet of Bass' on the luncheon menu tomorrow," Tim winked. He plopped the three-pounder into his Igloo cooler, shifted the out-board into low and moved the boat back into the current.

"So," Jack said, unwilling to wait any longer, "What happened after you got past 'Hi'?"

"A lot, but nothing," Tim began. "We left her old man's car in the lot behind the Teddy Bear and drove up here. I took her to the vacation house, turned on some music, found an open bottle of vodka and some Squirt, and I'm thinking, 'Timmy-me-lad, this is too good to be true.'"

Tim paused to light a cigarette. He exhaled slowly, purposefully, adding a touch of drama to his narrative.

"So I kissed her."

Jack quashed his resentment. He had no right to be jealous. "Then what?"

"She started crying. So, being gallant, I asked her, what's wrong? Her whole life story poured out, how her boyfriend is a twerp who only cares about clothes and cars, her mother is a hypocrite who doesn't care about anything but herself, her dad barely knows she's alive – how she thought she loved you, but you wouldn't fight for her.

"She said she didn't want to end up just another ex-cheerleader gossiping in the check-out lane at the IGA with a cart full of kids, hamburger meat and Cheerios."

"God," Jack said, "all that on your first date? We went together a year and she never told me anything. I don't even know her favorite color and I can't remember her birthday."

"Purple, a royal color," Tim paused, "April 26."

Jack laughed. "You're a piece of work, Tim Budge. I always knew there was a reason I liked you."

"Anyway," Tim continued. After that . . . with help from the vodka . . . she fell asleep. When she woke up, I drove her back to her car."

"That's it?" Jack was relieved.

Tim squinted at Jack. "You never made it with Ellen?"

"No," Jack answered. "Never."

"Ever make it with anybody?"

Jack shook his head *no*.

Tim flashed a bright smile. "Join the club, buddy."

Then he saw shadows in an opening in the lilies. Instinctively, he cast his lure and at the same time told his friend, "If you're still hot for her, I'll back off."

"I don't have any claim on Ellen," Jack answered.

The bass hit.

"Anyway," Jack said as he watched his friend reel in another three-pound bass, "I'm going with Kathy. I'm going to her house tonight. Did I tell you? They have a cook."

Tim raised his eyebrows, impressed, but he stayed on message. "So you don't have a problem with me dating Ellen?"

"Go for it, man."

CHAPTER TWENTY-SIX

On Tuesday, the first day of June 1954, according to the white man's calendar, Adams Armstrong took his small skiff onto the Tenmiles Lake. He adjusted the throttle on his five-horse out-board to 'SLOW' and lit the pipe The Ambassador had given him. He was in no hurry. He wanted to catch one trout for lunch and knew just the place; the cove where the stream emptied into the lake was good fishing in May and June.

As Adams approached the cove, he could see someone else had been there. The ground cover was depressed with indentations only men make and there was a hint of smoke from a smoldering fire. There was no boat, so whoever was there had arrived on foot. That made no sense. There was no road into this section of the lake.

Maybe someone had beached a boat earlier and gone ashore to catch crawfish for bait. No. There was no sign of a boat along the shoreline. Adams understood why people wanted to be alone in beautiful places. He knew another spot where the big trout lived. He turned his small craft, leaving the cove to the person who had built the small campfire.

* * *

The state and county police had distributed a flyer. It featured Abernathy's yearbook picture and physical description. Under the picture/caption it read:

WANTED
JOHN ABERNATHY
**Dangerous fugitive pictured here
may be in the Lakeside area.
Should you see anything suspicious,
please report it to the nearest authority. Do
not approach or attempt to apprehend.
Suspect is armed and considered dangerous.**

The flyer had been dropped on porches, slipped into mailboxes and tacked onto trees and telephone poles throughout the Lakeside community, including the eight mile long Hemlock Road, which ran along the lake's western shore. There were about twenty homes spaced along Hemlock Road, including the Kelly's, and at the very end of the road, Adam's A-frame.

The Kellys were an affluent family that lived in Coos Bay and kept a second home on Tenmiles Lake. The volunteers delivering flyers decided, "If nobody's home at the Kelly place, turn around. The Indian's place is irrelevant."

Needless to say, there was no flyer in Adam's mailbox.

After seeing the cove was occupied, Adams had motored to another of his secret fishing spots. He cut off his engine and baited a number 12 salmon-egg hook with a single, pale pink salmon egg. The water was calm. One split-shot took the egg to the bottom. Adams twitched the rod tip every ten seconds and waited. Within a minute he felt a gentle tug. He let out six inches of line. A few seconds passed. He felt the trout suck the egg into its mouth and he set the hook.

On his way home Adams saw a U.S. Coast Guard patrol boat. Strange. What was the coast guard doing on Tenmiles Lake? A boating accident? Was someone lost? Adams felt an urge to drive over to Wayne Grafton's store on 101 and find out what was going on. Maybe he'd buy a beer while he was there. Adams had presented Wayne Grafton with his self-imposed rule, "Never sell me more than two beers on any one day." Wayne had agreed but suggested Adams purchase a single, one-quart bottle instead of two stubbies or cans.

"Ounce for ounce, it's a better value," Wayne explained. "You get more beer for less money."

The more Adams thought about the beer, the better he liked the idea. Yes, maybe he'd purchase one quart of beer. Mathematically speaking, one quart bottle was actually one bottle less than his two-bottle limit. The trout would taste better washed down with the beer. He could also inquire about the coast guard. Wayne Grafton was among the five people who always treated him with respect. The Ambassador, Greta Portman, Sheriff Stark and James McDonnell were the other four.

The parking lot was full, so Adams parked on the road. The store was jam-packed. Wayne had an audience of two-dozen people, but when he saw Adams, he stopped in mid-sentence and sent a friendly wave in the direction of his regular customer. Unlike his brother, Glenn, Wayne Grafton lived by the successful merchant's code: *Customers first.*

"Help yourself to a quart, Adams – and anything else you need. I'll put it on your bill."

Adams selected a quart of Rainier beer. He liked the picture of the mountain on the label.

The flyers plastered around the store were meaningless to Adams because he'd never learned to read. With the quart cradled in his arm, he went outside just as a state patrol car pulled up.

"Excuse me, officer," Adams said meekly, having learned Indians had to be respectful when addressing uniformed representatives of the law.

"What do you want?" the patrolman snarled.

"I was wondering what the coast guard is doing on the lake."

"You were, were you, Chief? You were 'wondering?'"

"Yes."

"Look, why don't you take your beer and go back to your teepee, we got a real problem here and don't have time to talk about it with the natives, if you catch my drift."

Adams would never get used to being treated like a non-person, being brushed aside like a gnat. The Ambassador had attempted to explain it to him. "White people have a deep-down craving to feel superior. In the American South and big cities they have Negroes, but here on the Oregon coast there aren't any Negroes."

Adams had seen Negroes working on the railroad, and sometimes, fishing. He admired their appearance; the dark skin was attractive and practical.

"The fact is, Adams," The Ambassador droned, "you Indians are the only people of color around, so whites take out their latent prejudice on you."

"Latent?" Adams didn't understand.

"Means it's stored up inside them. Can't help it. We should feel sorry for them."

Adams didn't feel sorry for the state trooper. He felt like a gnat. He felt distrust and anger. He decided not to speak to anyone else. He wouldn't tell anyone that someone without a boat had built a campfire in the remote cove.

* * *

Sheriff Henry Stark paced his office. He was frustrated. Law enforcement had warned the communities of Lakeside and Hauser, called in the U.S. Coast Guard to patrol Tenmiles Lake, initiated road blocks all the way to Bandon (south of Coos Bay), and so far, nothing.

Well, that wasn't quite true. They'd had citizen complaints about "Gestapo type tactics" on U.S. 101 and had to abandon their roadblocks.

Henry did have more information about Abernathy. The bartender at the Teddy Bear and two customers identified him from the poster.

"Big guy, I wouldn't want to mess with him," the bartender remembered. "But easy going. Had ID in the name of Jake Sloan, drivers license and social. Said he was from Newport. Hard to believe he killed somebody."

The ID squared with what Randy Morgan said.

Henry checked on Jake Sloan through the Oregon Motor Vehicles Department and the Newport police. Sloan had left Newport two and a half years earlier with a plan to work his way down the coast and eventually get a job in California. His parents hadn't heard from him in over a year but weren't worried. They believed their son could take care of himself. "Probably left his wallet on the bar in a tavern," the father joked.

Henry didn't buy it. It was more likely Abernathy had taken it, which led him to suspect Terry Dodd wasn't Nasty's first homicide.

Two murders, Henry winced. Could he have made it to California? His gut told him John "Nasty" Abernathy was holed up in the Hauser-Lakeside area.

Henry checked the U.S. weather forecast for Wednesday and learned a storm was coming. A good, old-fashioned Oregon coastal storm with two or more inches of rain and gusts up to forty miles an hour. Nasty would have to look for shelter.

Henry paced his office. Assume Nasty made his way back to Lakeside because of the "rich girls" comment from the truck driver. Henry pulled out a map. "You're in Hauser," he said aloud, "You don't want to risk the highway, where do you go?"

Henry spotted a blue line on the map indicating a stream. Where there's water, there's a likelihood of a gypo mill with an unmapped logging road to service it. He remembered the logging road near the 101 Hauser junction.

He looked at the map again. Abernathy could have crossed 101. From there, being on the ocean side of the highway, he could have made his way to Horsefall Beach. From Horsefall Beach he could circle the bay to Glasgow. From Glasgow to North Bend – that would be easier than beating a trail into Tenmiles Lake. But Abernathy didn't know that. He wouldn't have a map.

Assume he acted on impulse: *Follow logging road, follow stream, find lake, rape and kill rich girl.*

Henry needed an airplane, preferably one with pontoons. He could fly straight to the spot where the stream emptied into the lake, follow the shoreline and identify Abernathy's targets of opportunity.

There wasn't time to go through the Coast Guard or law enforcement bureaucracy. Henry called the General Manager of U.S. Plywood.

The G.M. would have liked to help but the twin-engine Cessna with pontoons was being used to fly equipment into Loon Lake, and if it did get back early, there was a storm alert. They wouldn't be able to take it up again. The other plane was flying three middle-management types to Portland. The G.M. was sorry.

Should he call the judge? He dismissed the idea. Neither he nor the judge had jurisdiction in Coos County.

Henry cranked up his police-band radio and contacted his counterpart in Coos County, Slim Haskins.

Slim listened patiently to Henry's idea about an airplane. "Henry, we don't know for sure if the suspect is holed up there. If I had my dogs, we'd know which direction he headed. As it is, we don't. I've already got my ass in a sling for bringing in the Coast Guard. They're going all around the lake calling out for him to surrender. If he was in there, they probably ran him off. Let me handle it, it's my county. Smoke a couple of your cigarettes, drink a cup of coffee and be glad you're there and I'm here."

No dogs. No airplane. No Abernathy.

* * *

When James McDonnell heard Abernathy might be hiding along the shores of his beloved Tenmiles Lake, he called Ace Sheehy, Private Investigator. Sheehy's business card was designed to look like the ace of spades. "Stands out in a stack of cards," Ace boasted.

Sheehy started the rumor he'd served in Army Intelligence during WWII. McDonnell knew it wasn't true, he'd checked. He also knew Sheehy to be resourceful. Ace would know where to find reliable security guards.

By all accounts, the murderer was one-and-the-same as the Beach Night rapist. In McDonnell's mind, the rape was the more despicable of the two crimes. They gave murderers an appointment with Old Tom; they gave rapists a few years, if they could convict them. Convic-tions were difficult. The violated women were hesitant to step forward. They would have to face the accused again; and they would have to endure the ignorance of society's judgment. Did they "Ask for it? Was it their fault?" To these questions James answered, "No and no."

James felt anger surge inside him. Rapists could not be rehabilitated. They should all be shot like rabid coyotes.

CHAPTER TWENTY-SEVEN

Abernathy watched a coast guard boat cruise into his cove. A Coos County deputy sheriff was standing on the bridge. Through a bullhorn, the deputy bellowed, "John Abernathy, John Abernathy, if you're within the sound of my voice, come out with your hands above your head. You will not be harmed. I repeat, you will not be harmed."

Abernathy had the Coos County deputy in his sights. *Easy shot*, he thought, but not smart. The voice agreed. *Not smart*, it whispered as John lined up the shot. John had been watching the boat for twenty minutes. It was going all the way around the lake bull-horning the same bullshit plea.

The cops think I might be here, but don't know for sure, Abernathy reasoned. They tracked me to Hauser. They must have talked to that chickenshit truck driver. They must have found Dodd's body because they know my name. A phone call to Florence would link me to Dodd.

He chastised himself for not doing a thorough job of hiding Dodd's body. He should have weighted the body and sunk it in the tidal pool with the gym bag. No corpse, no murder.

Too late now, he thought. What was the saying? 'No use crying over spilt milk.'

He looked at the sky. A storm was coming. That precluded backtracking to Hauser, he'd never make it through the woods at night with the wind howling and rain swelling the creek. But the storm could work in his favor. Can't walk out of here in broad daylight. But at night?

In a storm?

He calculated – if he worked his way around the lake he'd find houses, he might even be able to steal a car. If he had to kill someone in the process, so be it. He settled down in his thicket to wait for nightfall.

Storm clouds gathered along the far edge of the ocean like an army preparing for battle. A regiment of gray, silver-lined clouds was first ashore. Low in the sky, the clouds moved quickly, riding gusts of wind as they sprinkled sparse but heavy raindrops on boats racing for shore. These outriders whisked over the houses and the highway declaring, "It's coming."

Darker, thicker clouds began a steady march toward land. They too rode the wind, a steady wind that bent small trees and chased the seagulls, snipe, mudhens and other birds off the water and out of the sky. These clouds brought an unrelenting downpour that would raise the level of small creeks by twelve inches in an hour.

With the sun curtained from view, nightfall arrived an hour early. In the sun's usual place on the horizon there appeared a fierce cavalry of black clouds. Their presence was trumpeted by cannons of thunder and flares of lighting. This third wave was accompanied by winds of forty miles an hour. Winds intercepted the falling rain, gathered it into sheets, and drove it on a horizontal plane against every boat, dune, dock, tree, car, house or person it could find.

When the light went out in the sky and the first raindrops began dimpling the lake, Abernathy disassembled his rifle and repacked it in his duffel bag. It was time. He was sure there would be houses along the western shoreline. Houses equaled roads. He made his way along the shoreline. All the boats were off the lake, so he had no fear of being spotted. With the wind coming from the southwest, the hills and tall trees that banked the lake provided a buffer. Still, he slipped and fell many times, but each time he picked himself up, cursed the rock, tree root or driftwood that dared to trip him, and kept moving. He slogged over a mile before he came across a pier with a boat dock at the end of it. The sky was pitch black, except for the occasional flash of lightning. There were no lights inside the house and it was fifty yards from the lakefront. Abernathy would never have found it were it not for the boat dock.

He crept to the back door and looked in the window. If anyone was home, there would be a light on. Even if the power were out, they'd have candles or a kerosene lamp. He tried the door. It was locked. He considered breaking the window, but thought better. Why leave signs of a break-in? He felt above the doorsill and in other obvious places for a key. No luck. He made his way around the house to the front door and continued searching for a key. His perseverance paid off when he lifted a small potted plant off of its decorative pedestal, revealing the house key. He opened the door. "Anybody home?" he yelled, thinking if someone was laying in wait with a shotgun, it would be better to act friendly. He would say he'd been fishing, his boat had capsized in the storm and he'd swum ashore.

No answer.

He ran his hand up and down the wall and found a light switch. The lights came on. He saw a table lamp. Quickly, he sloshed across the room and turned on the lamp. Then he sloshed back, switched off the overhead light and pulled the drapes.

"Not bad," he said aloud as he surveyed the house.

Abernathy had stumbled across the Kelly lake house. Patrick Joseph Kelly, Sr., father of Ellen Reilly's erstwhile boyfriend, Pat, loved this "Getaway Cabin."

Kelly Senior had a friend in the county courthouse. When "LAKESIDE, 3-ACRES W/CABIN" came on the docket for auction in 1950, he snapped it up before the gavel was raised. A childless widow had occupied it since 1936. Kelly purchased it for back taxes.

Ester Kelly accused her husband of acquiring the lake home to become a neighbor of James McDonnell. "So you'll be invited to one of those fancy McDonnell Sunday suppers.

Well, if you're invited, go by yourself. Mary McDonnell is too full of herself for me."

Kelly denied the accusation; pointing out the property was miles away from the McDonnell manor and his nearest neighbor was an Indian. "Hardly the high-rent district in Lakeside," Mr. Kelly rested his case.

The Kellys renovated the cabin by updating the kitchen and bath and adding a large shower-stall, master bedroom and garage. Mrs. Kelly gradually warmed to the idea of a second home. She paneled the walls with knotty pine and installed a mantle across the top of the stone fireplace. It was this mantle that drew Abernathy's attention.

Ester Kelly had arranged the equivalent of a family album across the fifteen-feet-long ledge. The selected family photos were all framed. Some of the frames were ornate, others quite plain. It was a photo history of the Kellys from their marriage in 1925, through the high school graduation of their son in 1953. In the middle of the gallery were pictures of a little girl, but she ceased being represented after the war years. She had been a casualty of the polio epidemic that swept through Oregon in the 1940s.

Abernathy was fascinated by the photo history of the Kelly family. His mother and father had never taken pictures of him. He had never seen a photograph recording his parent's wedding. There were no baby pictures of him. The only Abernathy "family photo" he knew of showed his father standing next to a six-point buck he had shot dead.

Abernathy picked up a picture of the daughter, Josephine. She was dressed for Easter Sunday. Still a little girl, "Josie" was on the verge of changing, physically, into a woman. She was chubby, but it was no longer little-girl chubby. There was a hint of breasts under the little-girl dress. One hip was thrust at a jaunty angle. She was smiling, confidently, hopefully, the way little girls smile when their parents assure them they are pretty and well on the way to being beautiful.

Confusing the image was Josie's Shirley Temple hairdo. Her golden ringlets had escaped from the Easter bonnet and tumbled across her face, hiding her right eye. Shirley Temple in a siren, Veronica Lake pose. Handwritten on the bottom of the photo was the simple legend, *"Josie, Easter, 1945."*

Looking at the chubby, pre-teen in the picture, Abernathy remembered another chubby pre-teen girl, Sarah, who had been nice to him in the seventh grade. Sarah sat directly in back of him because her last name was Appleton. Seating was alphabetical.

She had sent John an oversized Valentine. This had pleased him enormously because he always received fewer Valentines than anyone else in his class. He had adjusted to getting fewer Valentines. Who cared about all those itsy-bitsy Valentines anyway? But on this particular Valentine's Day, he received a great big Valentine: a giant red heart, surrounded by white lace. And it wasn't homemade. Sarah had parted with a good chunk of her allowance to buy it – at least twenty-five cents.

Young Abernathy carried the large Valentine in plain view for the rest of the day. Although he had received only three cards from his twenty-three classmates, in his opinion, quality trumped quantity.

A week later, when he looked at Sarah's notebook, he saw she had printed his name on the front cover. *Sarah A + John A.*

Other boys noticed and teased John during recess, "John has a girlfriend, John has a girl-friend."

Abernathy felt cornered. Real boys in the seventh grade didn't have girlfriends. Getting Valentines was one thing; actually having a girlfriend was another. He didn't want the other boys to think he was weak. He walked over to where the girls were standing, grabbed the notebook and tore it in half.

Then he wondered, why did I do that? I like having my name on her notebook.

Sarah started crying, and one of the boys taunted, "Hey Abernathy, farther from the bone, sweeter the meat."

The seventh grade boys laughed, although, honestly, they didn't know why they were laughing. It was just an insult they'd heard, a way to hurt someone's feelings if that someone was slightly overweight.

The mocking laughter sent John into a fury and he attacked. No one expected it. He was upon the other boys in a split second. He swung his right fist at the closest boy and connected. The blow crushed the boy's nose. John felt a rush of power.

He spun. Another boy, frozen in disbelief and fixated on his schoolmate's bleeding nose was standing next to victim number one. John aimed his left fist and connected with the boy's temple. The boy's knees buckled and he sagged to the ground.

The others ran, fleeing the path of the tornado. The boy with the bloodied nose staggered to his feet and John hit him again. The boy dropped to his knees and John followed-up with a kick to his rib cage. Then Abernathy put a chokehold on the boy.

It took two teachers and the principal to break it up.

The other kids said Abernathy started it.

It was the first time he was suspended from school for fighting.When his father learned of the suspension, he dispatched John to the riverbank to cut a willow switch. "I ain't beating you for fighting," he shouted, as he delivered fifty lashes, "I'm beating you for getting caught."

All this flashed through Abernathy's mind as he examined the photo gallery on the shelf-mantle above the fireplace.

Reality overrode his flashback. He was wet and cold. He clamped his jaw to overcome a mild case of shivers and began peeling off his wet clothing. He'd seen an electric washer and dryer in an alcove next to the kitchen. He tossed his clothes into the dryer, then fetched his last outfit from his duffle bag and tossed it into the dryer, too. Naked, he went into the Kelly's new master bedroom, pulled a blanket off of the bed and wrapped himself in it. It occurred to him that if the Kellys had a washer and dryer, they would certainly have lots of water. . . *hot* water. (His mother's houseboat didn't have a washer, or a dryer, or hot water.) He walked into the bathroom and found the new shower. He turned on the faucet and put his hand under the stream of water until it turned warm. Seconds later it was so hot he had to dial in some cold. He dropped the blanket and stepped inside. The water soothed him. He closed his eyes, reveling in the pleasure the hot water bestowed upon him. "This is the life," he said aloud.

As near-ecstasy spread through his body, he picked up a bar of Ivory soap. He washed under his arms, down his body until he reached his penis. He soaped his organ gently. "Little John" was small, limp and benign. He slathered it with soap and massaged it. Nothing happened. There was no more feeling than washing a foot or hand. This puzzled him. Why did he sometimes have such a fierce, undeniable urge to awaken it, and enlarge it, and drive it into a female body?

He would have never hurt Sarah, or the girl in the picture, he assured himself. He would only hurt girls who deserved it.

The hot water turned lukewarm. He had no idea how long he'd been in the shower. Maybe five minutes, maybe thirty minutes. He stepped out of the shower, found a towel and dried himself. He plucked a clean hand towel off a rack and wiped the steam from the mirror. He purposefully averted his eyes from Little John and huffed out his chest, asking himself, "Why don't women like you?"

"Fuck them," he answered. He liked the way he looked when he said that. He stepped back, turned sideways, but retained eye contact with the powerful, impressive fellow in the mirror. "Fuck them," he repeated in his best imitation of John Wayne. He wrapped the posh, terrycloth bath towel around his waist and left his bathroom-sanctuary in search of food.

CHAPTER TWENTY-EIGHT

Jack Portman nicked his chin with the razor. He placed a small piece of toilet paper over the cut and waited for it to clot. Slowly, he peeled away the paper. It worked. He splashed his face with Old Spice after-shave and checked himself over.

Should he wear the new sport coat? It was definitely going to rain like hell so he'd have to wear his knee-length yellow slicker over it. A fisherman's slicker over a college style sport coat would look goofy, he thought. He needed a real raincoat like the London Fog in the Coos Bay men's store. If he'd asked for it, his mother would have bought it. She had really been in a buying mode, he thought. He'd have to get one of those raincoats for college. In the meantime, he'd save his camel hair and new slacks for Sunday.

He elected to wear a crewneck sweater over his new blue, oxford cloth shirt. He'd only worn the shirt half a day so he considered it to be "still clean." He slapped a little after-shave under his arms just in case. What would Kathy's house be like? His mother said it was a "show-case" and pictures of it had appeared in magazines.

What were rich people like? The father, after the "mean son of a bitch" remark, had turned out to be a surprisingly nice guy. He remembered people saying, "It's as easy to fall in love with a rich girl as a poor one." Fall in love? Jack thought. You're getting ahead of yourself. What is love? He wondered – the longing and desire he'd felt for Ellen, or the sense of anticipation he was feeling for Kathy – who lived in a "showplace" with a hired cook?

Kathy told her father she'd invited Jack to their home. After he slowly nodded an Okay, she added, "I sort of promised him dinner."

James had assumed she would date the good-looking hero of Beach Night. He much preferred that the first date be in his home instead of a drive-in movie – or wherever else young people stole off to in this modern age.

"I'll have the Clarks over too," James said. "Liz is always happy to have an excuse not to cook and Nate loves to talk about his new project. Why don't you to tell Mrs. Ordway there will be six for dinner?"

Mary McDonnell overheard the father-daughter conversation. She'd been in a good mood. Off by herself, she'd been reading travel magazines, planning her still unannounced trip to Europe. Now, instantly, upon overhearing her husband and daughter conspire about dinner plans without consulting her ... Mary turned sullen, which in less than a-tick of the second-hand of a wristwatch, morphed into angry. She waited for her husband to go to his study and followed her daughter into the kitchen.

Kathy had attended many dinner parties and had observed that when it came to pleasing men, you couldn't go wrong with prime rib. She was suggesting this to Mrs. Ordway, the cook, when Mary burst on the scene.

"Prime rib?" Mary questioned, incredulous. "Prime rib?" She repeated an octave higher. "Pot roast would be more like it."

Fortunately for Kathy, her father wanted another cup of coffee and had circled back toward the kitchen. He'd watched his wife stalk his daughter and anticipated the confrontation.

Joining the melee in process he tried diplomacy, "Pot roast or prime rib? Both sound good to me."

Mary McDonnell wheeled toward her husband's voice, "Well, of course you'd take her side, wouldn't you? Fine. You two plan the dinner. From now on you can plan all the dinners. And why don't you invite those two thugs to join us?" She was referring to the two security guards James had hired through Ace Sheehy.

"I'll be in my room," she seethed, through her teeth. With measured dignity she exited the kitchen.

"I'm sorry, daddy."

"No need to be. She must of overhead us. My fault, I should have told her about it immediately." He put his arms around his daughter and patted her gently on the back.

Mrs. Ordway had stood in the kitchen with the anonymity of an appliance. She'd learned to ignore family spats. She just wanted to do her job. Mrs. McDonnell could be snooty and picayune. Mr. McDonnell's generosity more than compensated.

"So what's it going to be?" Mrs. Ordway asked, "Prime rib or pot roast?"

The cook's pragmatism was welcome comic relief. James laughed. "Make it prime rib."

He winked at his daughter. "What do you think, Kathy, should we invite our two security guards?

"Mrs. Ordway, you could extend the invitation."

He turned to the cook; "You could go outside and say, 'Mrs. McDonnell insists we set a place for you. Will prime rib be suitable, or do thugs prefer pot roast?'"

Kathy ignored her father's humor, "I can't talk to her anymore, daddy. I wish she would stay in her room."

"You know your mother, she'll come 'round. Half hour from now she'll act like this never happened."

* * *

The Ambassador relished the coming of the storm. When the sky darkened, he moved to his front porch and launched his oratory. "Do we have the courage to purge evil? Am I a messenger or messiah? An old fool or a prophet?"

The wind howled. The rain swept under the overhang on his porch and began to splash dark spots onto his buckskins. He took this as his cue to go to the kitchen. He had a row of canisters on the counter for flour, sugar, coffee and pot. He grew his own marijuana under the fir trees on the slope behind his house that overlooked the river. He opened a cupboard, surveyed his row of eight pipes and selected the Douglas Macarthur style corncob.

An LP record of Beethoven's Fifth was set to play on his Hi-Fi system. He clicked the start button, lit the pipe and slumped into his sofa. Long inhale. Slow exhale. The square corners of the room rounded. The room turned slowly, like a silent carousel in low gear. He asked the room, "Am I a messenger or messiah, am I either, neither or both? Why do turkeys crow and act like roosters? Why is life short and of the sort of thing that is a lie sometimes? If your life has been a lie, have you lived at all?"

The room answered, "Turkeys should be free to crow or gobble as they please. Life is short because in the grand scheme of things people need to die to make room for others. The jury is still out on your last question."

He smiled. The carousel stopped. Tomorrow, if there were a tomorrow, he just might get into his pick-up truck and visit one of the last of the pure people, Adams Armstrong. He would show Adams the crossbow he'd ordered from an ad in *Argosy Magazine*.

* * *

Abernathy opened the refrigerator and found a six-pack of *Miller's Highlife* beer, a dozen eggs and a pound of bacon. Bacon and eggs were his second favorite meal, beefsteak and potatoes being number one. He fried half of the bacon first. This was planned, as his method of cooking eggs required a pan full of grease. He reset the burner on the electric range, waited for the grease to stop bubbling and cracked open the eggs. With practiced dexterity, he dropped the eggs, one, two, three, four, five, six, into the bacon grease. Rather than turn the eggs, he spooned hot grease over the top of the yolks.

He felt at home in the Kelly lake house. He began imagining it was his home. He'd never lived in a house even close to this nice. He finished his feast, belched and opened another beer. Beer in hand, he returned to the photos on the fireplace mantle. What if I'd been born into this family? The boy, Pat, was small. A runt. The runt would have been his brother. Abernathy assumed other boys picked on the runt. He spoke quietly to the picture of Pat Kelly, "They wouldn't have dared pick on you if I were part of the family. I'd have beaten the shit out of any son of a bitch that looked sideways at you."

The girl would have been his sister. "I would have protected you too. It would have been nice growing up in a house like this." Undoubtedly, there was a grandmother's house where they went on Thanksgiving. There would have been a Christmas tree – a tall one with the star touching the ceiling. And underneath the tree there would have been real presents, like a Red Ryder BB Gun and a Schwinn bike. The mother and father would have been proud of him for his athletic skills. They would have come to the games and cheered him on. When he made a good play they would have jumped to their feet and shouted to everyone in the grandstand, "That's our boy!" They would have appreciated his protecting the brother and sister. He would have had nice clothes, and when he was sixteen, the father would have let him drive the car. Because he came from a nice family, and lived in house on the lake, other parents would have encouraged their children to be his friend. Every kid in his class would have sent him a Valentine. Girls would have liked him. Not just one girl, once, in the seventh grade, but all girls, all the time, in every grade. His sister and mother would have seen to that. They would have told him about girls and taught him how to talk to them. Some girls were probably as nice as his new sister and should be treated with respect. But how could he be expected to know which girls were nice if he didn't know how to talk to them?

The storm raged outside, but inside the lake house John Abernathy donned dry clothing and had a peaceful evening as a beloved member of the Kelly family.

CHAPTER TWENTY-NINE

The best thing about a storm, Henry Stark thought, is criminals don't like to get wet either. He called his deputy. "You're in charge tonight, Cal. I might have a drink or two, so don't call me unless there's news about Abernathy. If you do have to reach me, I'll be at Greta's place."

Henry changed into civilian clothes and set out for Winchester Bay. The rough sea had chased the fishing boats in early and The Dock was three-quarters full.

"What brought you out on a night like this?" Greta asked.

"I'd like to buy our sheriff a drink," charter boat captain, Harry Norton, called from a booth. "What are you drinking, Henry?"

"There you go," Greta smiled at him. "Famous lawman like you doesn't need money. Are you drinking tonight?"

"I wouldn't say no to a beer."

Greta served him a draft.

Another of Greta's regulars, the huge, bearded man every one called Swede, took the stool next to Henry's. "Hardly recognize you tonight," Swede said, referring to Henry's black dress slacks and colorful Hawaiian style shirt.

"They catch that guy yet?" somebody called from across the room.

Before Henry could answer, other patrons formed a circle around him.

"Not yet," Henry was loath to admit. "Not yet," he repeated, knowing it was an inadequate answer. The patrons didn't move. They were waiting for more. Henry shrugged. "Sorry. I don't have anything to tell you. This guy Abernathy, well, he's got animal smarts. He's hard to catch."

"He could be in California by now, laughing at us," one of the citizens ventured.

"More likely he's holed up somewhere on Tenmiles Lake," Harry Norton reported. "That's what the coast guard told me."

"Could be," Henry conceded. "He caught a ride to Hauser, so he could have doubled back to the lake, or, and this is just as likely, he could have walked over to Horsefall Beach or Glasgow."

"At least he ain't around here," a fisherman said.

"Doesn't seem so." Henry raised his empty beer glass toward Greta. "Hit me."

"We playing blackjack?"

"Checkers. I'm waiting for you to make a move."

A smile pried at the corner of her mouth, "Really? I keep thinking it's your move."

Somebody chose that moment to clunk a quarter in the jukebox. Hank Williams began to drone:

"I'd walk a mile for a smile from my mammy or pappy,
because I want them to know I love them so..."

* * *

Jack Portman did his best not to appear awed by the surroundings as Kathy escorted him into the McDonnell living room.

"You've met my father."

Jack stepped forward offering his hand. "Mr. McDonnell, nice to see you again, sir."

James took Jack's hand and sized up his daughter's beau. *Cleans up nicely, good hand-shake, not intimidated, not gawking around at the house and telling me, 'Gee whiz, what a neat place you have here, Mr. McDonnell.'*

Kathy continued, "These are our friends, Liz and Nate Clark."

Liz smiled and waved; Nate rose from his chair, walked over to the young man and offered his hand.

"Nice to meet you, Jack. Damn, you're tall. How tall are you?"

It was the same question his uncle and grandparents asked when they visited Winchester Bay during Thanksgiving.

"Six-two," Jack answered, wondering where Kathy's mother was.

After the altercation in the kitchen, Mary McDonnell had gone to her room where she bolstered her spirits with several ounces of vodka, fixed her hair, applied make-up and changed into a satin dinner dress. She waited in the wings, so to speak, choosing the moment after Nate's handshake to make her entrance.

"And last but not least!" Mary announced, with P.T. Barnum gusto. (Implying – "Let me direct your attention to the center ring.") "I'm Kathy's mother, so nice of you to come, Jack. It is Jack, isn't it? "Or is it John? Jack is your nickname?"

She didn't wait for an answer. "I've been so looking forward to meeting you. I understand you're a hero?"

She swished her satin dress, leaned forward on her tiptoes to brush a kiss across his cheek, a greeting she usually saved for more cosmopolitan cocktail parties.

Jack adjusted, instinctively, as he would in an athletic contest. He leaned down and accepted the lip-brush. "Very nice to meet you, Mrs. McDonnell."

He is handsome, Mary thought, *and he has poise. He's blushing, but it's minimal. Very male. Sure of himself. A lot of women will flop on their back for this one, but he's still a saloonkeeper's son from a pitiful little fishing village. Kathy can do better. Put him in his place.*

"I understand your mother is a bartender. I'd love a martini," she broke the brief silence. "Do you know how to make a martini, John, or should I say Jack?"

Jack absorbed the intended insult and remained composed. "Like you say, my mom is the bartender. She hasn't gotten around to teaching me how to make a martini."

James McDonnell was charmed by Jack's grace under fire and went to his aid. "I can give first hand testimony to the excellence of a Portman martini."

Kathy was mortified by her mother's behavior. What her mother thought clever was (in Kathy's estimation) blatant and obnoxious.

Yet . . . Jack had taken her mother's best shot.

Kathy knew everything would be fine once her father took control of the scene. James followed his endorsement with a full description. "Ah, yes, the legendary Greta Portman Martini.

"Rule number one, never bruise the gin . . ." James provided a narration as he mixed a martini for his wife. It looked and sounded so good, both Nate and Elizabeth Clark requested one too. Kathy maneuvered Jack to a large glass window with a view of the storm swept lake.

"Mother takes a bit of getting use to," she allowed, pressing her bosom against his arm. Were it not for the wind and rain, she would have taken him onto the deck and rewarded his performance with a kiss.

After serving the martinis, James led the small party to the baby grand piano. He sat down and began to play, and sing, although he didn't truly sing. He spoke the lyrics in a pleasant, rhythmic manner patterned after piano bar entertainers. James started with *"Nothing could be finer than to be in Carolina in the morning, nothing could be sweeter than to meet my honey greet her in the mooor-ning. If I had Aladdin's lamp for only one day, I'd make a wish and here's what I'd say, 'Nothing could be finer than to be in Carolina in the mooor-ning. . ."*

He executed a short, one-handed rift and segued into, *"Time after time, I tell myself that I'm, so lucky to be loving you..."*

James directed these lyrics at his wife. Mary stepped closer to him and placed a hand on his shoulder. For the moment at least, all was forgiven. The warmth of the music lured Kathy and Jack toward the piano. Jack began smiling without knowing he was smiling. *"So lucky to be, the one you run to see, in the evening when the day is done. I only know what I know, the passing years will show, you've kept our love so young, so new, and time after time, I tell myself that I'm, so lucky to be loved by you."*

James stood and ceremoniously bowed deeply from the waist.

"Play some more, James," Nate urged. "Play *Four-Leaf Clover!*"

"My friend, the secret of my success is that I know my limitations. Anything more than two songs exposes me for the musical-charlatan I am."

Meanwhile, outfitted in rain suits, two security guards patrolled the McDonnell property. Periodically, they passed one another and gave voice to the question, "What kind of fool would be outside on a night like this?"

* * *

At eight o'clock, Greta Portman announced, "The Dock will close at nine tonight . . .

"Except for you, Marine," she whispered to Henry Stark. "You can help me close up."

"Last call!" Greta declared at eight forty-five. The rain was slapping against the windows, the wind sounded like jet engines.

"Bottoms up!" Greta demanded at 8:58 p.m. "I want to see nothing but cash and empty glasses on the bar."

"Greta, my dear, gimme a six pack of *Schlitz* to go," a fisherman said as he placed his empty glass on the bar. He looked down the bar, "Hey, Sheriff, you ever worry that killer might circle back this-a-way and stow away in one of our boats?"

"Nope," Henry said. "That's not my worry."

"Why not?"

"Cause I know men like you can look after themselves."

"Damn right we can," the fisherman said as he placed three dollars on the bar. Greta pushed a six-pack of cold beer toward him.

"That's good," he said, nodding at the money, meaning, *keep the change.*

"Thank you, Charlie. You be careful driving home."

"And in the morning when you go to your boat," Henry warned.

"You're putting me on, right, Sheriff?"

"Yeah, I'm kidding. If I thought Abernathy was around here I'd be out looking for him."

"God damn," Swede pleaded. He was standing by the open door watching the rain swirl past in horizontal waves. "Can't you stay open another hour 'til this lets up?"

"We both know this storm won't blow over until midnight, Swede. If it were Saturday, I'd stay open. But you have to work tomorrow. Get going. You can use a shower anyway."

The regulars laughed. (Although none of them would dare say anything like that to Swede.) They donned their rain gear and followed the big man out the door.

Greta locked and bolted the door behind them, turned to Henry and asked, "You have anything to eat tonight."

"Come to think of it, no."

"Come upstairs and let's see what we can scare up. I'm famished."

She looked over at the dog, Sal. "You stay down here and keep an eye out, okay?"

Obediently, Sal laid down in his spot behind the bar.

"Famished," Henry thought. What a great word. What a great lady. And she was inviting him upstairs. She'd told him Jack had gone to Lakeside. Yet he was invited upstairs. She was going to fix him something to eat. He would have the pleasure of her company. It would be just the two of them. Upstairs. There would be no jukebox music or customers shouting for another round. Upstairs. There would be nothing to detract from the pure pleasure of her presence.

Greta suggested Henry take a chair at the kitchen table. She went straight to the fridge. "What are you hungry for?" she asked.

"Whatever you're having, I don't want to be any trouble."

"I've got a couple of T-bones in here and I've got some fresh flounder, caught this morning."

"You decide." He got up from the table. "Mind if I look at your art gallery?"

"Be my guest," Greta answered, pleased by his interest.

Walking along the row of local artist water colors and oils, Henry stopped in front of a fifty-dollar oil painting of a lone fisherman standing on the edge of a jetty. The fisherman was in the act of casting out to sea, oblivious to the dark clouds. It was titled, *One More Cast*.

"I like this one," he said.

Greta was curious. "Which one?"

"This one," he pointed. She walked over and stood beside him.

THE LAST BEACH NIGHT

"That's one of my favorites," she agreed, "Reminds me of Jack when he was in grade school. He was kind of a loner, never played much with the other kids. Loved to fish, though, so I used to let him go out on the jetty. When I'd go to get him, I'd yell, 'Jack, let's go!' And he'd always say, 'Just one more cast, mom.'"

"Fine young man," Henry praised her son. "He's impressed the hell out of me."

Greta wanted to kiss Henry. What had gotten into her? She really wanted to kiss him. Not yet, she warned herself.

"Here are the ground rules," she addressed Henry. Her voice was soft and promising. "I'm not feeling frisky tonight, if that's what you had in mind. But I do like you, and wouldn't mind getting to know you better."

"Sounds good to me. I'd like to get to know you better too. Let's spend some time together and see where it takes us."

She liked his response, although it wasn't what she expected. She expected him to put his arms around her, pull her close and whisper, "I want to get to know you better, too. *Right now.*"

What did she want from this man? What was the "Your move – Your move" exchange all about? One thing for sure, of all the men she'd met since her husband died, this one excited her the most.

"Right now," Greta said, maintaining her soft, promising tone, "You're going to sit down at my kitchen table and I'm going to broil some filet of fresh flounder and open a bottle of Sauvignon Blanc wine from the Sonoma Valley in California. "We'll ride this storm out together and you can help me worry about Jack getting his heart broken by that lawyer's pretty daughter in Lakeside."

"Jack will be fine. Just fine," Henry said, sitting down, while thinking, *I could have kissed her, but it's best to go slow. She has an artistic side, she's knows about wine, and she knows how to run a business. This is a woman of considerable class and great character and you need to let her know you're patient and responsible. Jack has been the center of her life, but she must know she needs a life beyond her son.*

Greta took a corkscrew out of a drawer and opened the wine. She selected two stemmed wine glasses from her cupboard and poured the translucent, almost golden liquid into the glasses. She clinked her glass against his. "To friendship," she toasted.

"And to your Jack," Henry responded, looking her in the eye. They clinked glasses again.

Henry took a sip. "This is good," he offered, "real good." He took another sip, as if to verify his original judgment. "What do you call this?"

"Sauvignon Blanc."

"Sauvignon Blanc," he repeated, committing the name to memory. "Had a lieutenant from Santa Rosa, bunch of us non-coms were shooting craps and drinking beer in the hold of the ship on the way to Iwo. He came down, brought two bottles of wine; it could have been this kind, Sauvignon Blanc. He said, 'Sergeants, I want to introduce you to the nectar of the gods, wine from the Russian River Valley in California.'

"Then he said, 'After the war, California is going to produce the best wine in the world.'"

"Did he make it?" Greta asked, referring to the lieutenant.

"Lieutenants didn't last long on the beach that day."

Greta saw Henry's eyes had teared up.

"I'm sorry," she said.

"Nothing you said," he assured her. "Memorial Day's coming up. I get real sad on Memorial Day. I can put it out of my mind most of the time, you know, the war, but... there are times you can't help but remember. Sorry to be such a fool, here we are, right in the middle of a real special evening and I get all teary-eyed on you."

"Sitting there, tears in your eyes, you've never stood taller in my estimation." She leaned over and kissed him.

First, it was peck on the forehead. But when he lifted his face, eyes glistening, her lips found his.

"Oh, God," she said, coming up for air, wanting him with a longing she hadn't felt since her husband's death. "What am I doing? Jack could come home any time."

Henry scooted his chair away from the table and pulled her down on his lap. "We can go away next Sunday, just the two of us" he told her. "We can get a nice room in Newport or Waldport, no one will know who we are..."

The compulsion to fulfill a hunger ignored for years was too great for Greta. She wanted him. She trusted him. She sure as hell was old enough.

She stood up. "Come with me," she urged him, perspiration forming above her lips and on her brow. She felt heat and longing deep between her thighs.

She led him into her bedroom. Henry was a fine man. He liked her art, appreciated her wine, respected her devotion to her son and had compassion for lost souls. It had been a long time. She was only human.

It was the first time Henry had seen a woman climax. In Hawaii and Southeast Asia they had pretended to climax, said they had climaxed, "Hey, Joe, you fuck good, I go bang, bang, bang, three-comes, you great lover, kiddo, want to see me again?"

This had been something else. No money, no game, no pretending.

Naked, but immodest, Greta walked into the kitchen and came back with the two glasses and the bottle of wine. Henry retrieved cigarettes out of his shirt pocket. He lit two.

She released the smoke slowly as she propped up her pillow and leaned against it. "So what do we do now?"

"How 'bout we close your place for a couple of days and drive down to Reno and get married?"

He was serious.

"That could be rushing things, Henry. Besides, it's not like our occupations go together. The sheriff and the saloonkeeper?"

"I don't care what people think," Henry said. "You're the finest woman I've ever known and I've been falling in love with you for years. Say yes, and you'll make me the happiest, proudest man on the face of the earth."

Greta was flattered and intrigued. She hadn't thought about marriage, but Henry was a good man. Best man she knew. She could love him. He loved her. It was going to get lonely when Jack went to college. They were comfortable together. They were sexually compatible.

"That's sweet, honey," she said, consciously replacing Henry with honey, "But you have to give a girl time to think things through. And don't you have a bad guy to catch?"

CHAPTER THIRTY

Ellen stood on her porch waiting for Tim. When she saw his headlights, she buttoned her raincoat and ran down to the curb. She'd be damned if she'd subject Tim to the ordeal of meeting her mother.

Rainy nights were good movie nights. People living in Reedsport liked to joke, "What do you want to do tonight? Go to a movie or go to the movie?"

The feature, which started on Sunday and would run through midweek, was *A Star Is Born*, with Judy Garland and James Mason. Tim and Ellen entered the theater and Tim bought a large box of popcorn and two Cokes. There was a moment of hesitation as they walked through the velvet curtains into the theater proper. Should they sit in the right hand aisle with the high school kids? Or sit in the middle row with the adults? They didn't consider the left aisle; it was seventh and eighth grade territory. Nor did they consider the balcony. Things could get rowdy up there. The balcony was the domain of single men who worked in the woods and sawmills. You could smoke in the balcony, and as long as you didn't flaunt it, you could drink beer. There were females in the balcony too, unmarried women in their twenties who had tried being "nice girls" long enough and were looking for a little fun.

Tim steered Ellen down the right aisle and chose two seats in the back of the middle section. The lights dipped – *Movietone News* began. "Can you believe this?" Ellen whispered.

Tim didn't know what she meant. Believe what? Should he ask her what she meant? Or pretend to understand and shake his head knowingly? He elected to do the latter and offered her popcorn. After they finished the popcorn and Cokes, Tim took her hand. During the more intense scenes, she squeezed his hand, looked at him and smiled.

Should he put his arm around her? Try to do some mild necking? No, that was high school stuff. Besides, he found the movie interesting, the tragedy of a fallen matinee idol contrasted against the rising success of his adoring wife and protégé. Tim averted his eyes to watch Ellen as the movie reached its predicable, tragic ending. The broken but dignified figure of James Mason's Norman Mane walking toward the ocean depths, making the ultimate sacrifice: setting his lovely, wonderful, sensitive and multi-talented wife free to achieve her destiny as America's greatest star.

Ellen didn't cry. "That was really unfair of him," she said, jaw set.

Her reaction took Tim by surprise. "How was it unfair?"

"All he had to do was stop drinking. Or he could have gone off to Europe. To flat out kill himself was unfair to her – because even if she knew it wasn't her fault, something deep inside her will always think it was her fault."

"I see what you mean," Tim said.

"What did you think?"

"I think they should give Judy Garland the Academy Award."

The lights came on and they stood up, slipped into their raincoats and worked their way through the crowd. They nodded hellos, but didn't stop to talk to people they knew. Outside, the rain was coming down hard. Tim said he'd run and get the car.

"Let's run for it together," Ellen said and dashed ahead of him. April 26, Tim thought. Taurus. Inside the car they wriggled out of their raincoats and tossed them into the back seat. The rain continued pounding down outside but it was cozy inside. Tim started the engine, turned on the windshield wipers and the defogger. The windshield wipers went slap, slap, slap. Tim tried the radio but there was too much static. They didn't speak for three minutes, both thinking about what to do next.

"It's only nine," Tim broke the silence, "we can go to the Drive-In Café."

"Or somewhere else," Ellen said. "We could go back to the cabin on Tahkenitch Lake."

"I can't go back there. My dad checked the cabin. He might be on to me."

"I know a place."

"Where?"

She turned and leaned toward him, "Kiss me, and if it's a really good kiss, I'll tell you."

Tim maneuvered around the steering wheel and kissed her. The cramped quarters of the Henry J made serious necking a challenge but they were committed. A tight-lipped exploratory kiss turned into a long, open-mouthed passionate kiss. She pulled away from the embrace while placing his hand against her breast – letting him know she wasn't rebuking his advances. "I know a place in Lakeside," she said in a husky voice. "The people who own it never go there during the week. They'd never go on a rainy night. I know where they hide the key."

CHAPTER THIRTY-ONE

James McDonnell stood at the head of the table wielding a long, slim, Swiss-made carving knife. The matching fork was in his left hand. He plunged the tines of the fork into the prime rib and raised the knife into a ready position. "Liz, if memory serves, well done?"

He sliced off the browned end of the prime rib and ceremoniously placed it on the top of the six dinner plates stacked in front of him.

"Lovely," Liz said.

It was a simple menu: salad with bleu cheese dressing, asparagus (extra-slim spears) and baked Idaho potatoes.

"Mary likes her prime rib medium," James narrated as he carved, "Nate is medium-rare. Mr. Portman, you're the unknown quantity."

"To tell the truth, Mr. McDonnell, I'll take prime rib any way you slice it."

"Well said, but you may be more selective. Do you prefer pink, pinker or pinkest?"

"Pinkest," Jack said, tacking on a "Thank you."

James nodded approval. "Man after my own heart."

"Damn it, Jim," Nate intervened light-heartedly, "get on with it. Carve the damn meat and sit down so I can make a toast."

"I see," James winked, "as the local bard you're looking for an excuse to be clever."

Nate raised his glass, "Not clever. Just sincere. To our new graduates. To the realization of dreams, whatever they are, wherever they may take them."

Five people raised their glasses. Nate made a point of reaching across the table to clink glasses with Jack and Kathy.

Mary McDonnell did not acknowledge the toast.

"So, Jack," Nate said between bites, "What are you going to do this summer?"

"I have a couple of choices: I can work on the green chain at E. K. Woods in Reedsport; or, on one of the..." (He almost said 'pukers', but caught himself)... "Charter boats out of Winchester Bay?"

"You haven't decided?" Liz asked, keeping things going.

"Hours are better at the mill, but I can make more money on a boat."

"Isn't it dangerous?" Liz asked.

"Not with a good skipper. It does get boring, and you don't have many days off."

"How much can you make over a summer?" Liz asked.

"With a little help from the weather, close to $3,000," Jack answered.

"That's a lot of money," Liz said, impressed. "Why aren't there more wealthy fishermen?"

"Short season," Jack explained. "It's all over by October."

James changed the subject. Jack had been under scrutiny long enough. "Nate, how's your epic going?"

Nate swallowed a gentlemanly sized chunk of prime rib and pondered the question. "Interesting," he began. "Interesting," he repeated, "It's interesting how you get into this material and can't find your way out of it.

"I found an intriguing new character, man named John Colter. He was with Lewis and Clark. The Corps of Discovery was on the way back in 1806 when they encountered a group of trappers coming up the Missouri. With Lewis' permission, Colter signed on as guide and headed back into the wilderness. Colter was the first of the real mountain men. I'm thinking of putting the TV series aside and writing a historical novel based on Colter's life."

Nate bounced the conversation back to Jack.

"They teach you anything about America's mountain men in school, Jack?

"A little," Jack answered. (In the 1950s the Oregon Public School system taught more Oregon history than U.S. history.) "The mountain man I liked best was Joe Meek."

"Controversial figure," Nate remarked.

Nate explained to the entire table, "Joe Meek was the first U.S. Marshall in the Oregon Territory. He tracked down and hanged Chief Tomahas in retaliation for the Whitman massacre."

James joined in, "He also went to Washington D.C. as the Oregon Territory Representative. He was a colorful character. The press loved him."

"All that happened after he was a mountain man," Jack said confidently. "I like the story about Joe Meek and Mountain Lamb."

"Mountain Lamb?" Kathy encouraged him.

"She was a Shoshone Princess, daughter of a chief. In 1831, after Rendezvous, she rescued Joe and William Sublette."

Not to be completely one-upped on his own subject, Nate interjected, pleasantly, "Sublette was a Captain in the American Fur Company. Rendezvous was the annual convention for mountain men – but go on Jack, Mountain Lamb is news to me."

"It's kind of a long, sad story," Jack said.

"That's perfectly all right," Liz spoke up. "We're accustomed to long, sad stories."

Fortified by the glass of wine, Jack began. "Joe and Sublette ran into a Shoshone war party that chased them into the Shoshone's main camp."

He looked around the table; everyone was listening, including the mother. "With nowhere to go, Meek and Sublette rode up to the Medicine Lodge and scrambled inside, figuring it was sacred ground and the Indians wouldn't come in after them without a powwow. Anyway, while the Indians argued about what to do, Mountain Lamb took two ponies and slipped around to the back of the Lodge. She sliced it open and Joe and Sublette were able to escape."

Jack paused for effect, then continued. "Mountain Lamb was beautiful, and neither Joe nor Sublette could get her off his mind."

Jack had heard this story from his uncle, who in addition to running his popular road-house in Wemme, read and collected obscure history books about the American West. His uncle assured Jack this story was true.

"Anyway," Jack transitioned, "Sublette had a big advantage, being a Captain and all, so the next spring he went back to the Shoshones with a string of ponies and bought Mountain Lamb from her father, the chief."

Jack felt Liz Clark's eyes on him; she was staring at him as if she were spellbound. He met her gaze and began telling the story just to her. "But Mountain Lamb was really in love with Joe, and Joe felt the same about her. A couple of years passed and Sublette decided to quit the mountains and run his business from St. Louis. Since he had a wife in St. Louis, he gave Mountain Lamb to Joe."

He felt Kathy's gaze. He turned to her, and spoke only to her. "But it wasn't like it sounds, it wasn't a white man-squaw-sort-of-thing with Joe and Mountain Lamb. They had a big wedding. The whole tribe came and Joe gave Mountain Lamb a beautiful white horse as a wed-ding gift."

Jack made himself look at the other guests, going from left to right, person to person, just as he'd learned in Speech class. "They were married four years, and they were happy."

Jack paused. He didn't like the ending.

"What happened to them?" Nate asked. "I know he didn't bring her to Oregon."

Jack looked at Nate. "They were on their way to Rendezvous in '38 and crossed paths with a group of Bannock braves. The braves wanted to trade for Mountain Lamb's big white horse and Joe said 'No way.' The Indians didn't like the answer and one of them whipped out his bow and sent an arrow in Joe's direction. Mountain Lamb saw the brave with the bow and arrow but Joe didn't, so she jumped in front of him and took the arrow. Right after that, Joe set the white horse free to run with the wild mustangs and left the mountains forever. That's when he came to the Oregon Territory."

"That's one helluva good yarn," Nate said, "but I don't believe a word of it."

Liz spoke up, "Make a good movie! Joel McCrea as Meek and that actress who played opposite Jimmy Stewart in Broken Arrow, what's her name?"

"Debra Padgett," Kathy answered.

James joined in. "Victor Jory would be perfect as Sublette."

"Oh, yes, that would make a fine movie," Mary McDonnell entered the conversation, her voice chilled with sarcasm. "The classic tale of a noble savage, bought and sold like a slave for a string of horses, and finally sacrificing her life for a man whose greatest claim to fame was hanging a few defenseless Indians."

The lively buoyancy that had filled the room moments before . . .evaporated.

James McDonnell had been amused by Jack's story and the group's ability to instantly hollywoodize it. He was feeling genuinely pleased with the evening. Now this! Why did his wife have to be so viciously contrary?

He affected a cheerful demeanor and said, calmly, "Why don't you tell us how you really feel, Mary? Don't

THE LAST BEACH NIGHT

sugar-coat it, don't hold back, we're all terribly interested in your insights."

Mary glared across the table. He had done it to her again. It had taken her two minutes to compose her put-down. It was bad enough listening to Nate babble about meaningless dead men, but, definitely, she shouldn't have to put up with more of the same from a lowlife from Winchester Bay. Now her husband had taken him off the hook – and put her on it. She had no response. She could get up from the table and go to her room, but if she did that, in front of the Clarks, James would be the winner. There was also the matter of the trip to Europe she wanted to take. She smiled. "Touché, darling. Let's have our coffee in the living room."

Jack felt Kathy's hand on his knee; he turned toward her and saw a reassuring smile: An everything-will-be-okay smile.

"You go ahead," James responded to his wife. I want another glass of wine, and I want to hear how Jack got to be such a history buff.

"I second that motion," Nate said.

Liz was caught in the middle. She'd been enjoying the dinner conversation. She resented Mary's vitriolic attitude. However, it would be humiliating for Mary if she didn't join her.

"I'll have coffee, too," she said, pretending to like the idea.

"So then, Jack," Nate said. "You didn't hear that story in a history class at Reedsport High School. You mentioned an uncle."

"Yes sir," Jack said. "My uncle is a history nut. I spent the summer between my sophomore and junior year with him and my grandparents. My mom wanted me to get to know the rest of the family.

"So, you believe it's a true story?" Nate asked.

"True or not, my uncle loved telling it," Jack answered with a smile.

"This uncle of yours," Nate asked, "He ever say anything about the Lost Tribe?"

"Says it's a myth, the *Babe and the Blue Ox* of the Oregon coast. But if you want to know about the Lost Tribe, you should talk to the Ambassador."

"The Ambassador?" Nate questioned.

James enlightened him, "He's a character around here. I like to think he's a lost, gentle soul who saw some awful things and retreated into his imagination."

"He told my mother his ambition is to parlay with the Lost Tribe," Jack added.

"Does she believe in a Lost Tribe?" James asked, genuinely curious.

"No." Jack answered. "But she says The Ambassador does, and that makes it true."

James liked the answer; after all, truth was no more than subjective conviction. If enough people hold the same conviction, it becomes a fact – until someone disproves it, which can take a split second or a thousand years.

James nodded toward Jack, indicating he agreed with his mother. He finished his wine and shifted his attention to his daughter, "We're going into the other room to make peace. You two should go down to the rec room and wait for the storm to die down – play pool, play mu-sic..." He laughed. "But don't play around." He winked at Jack.

Downstairs in the expansive recreational room, Kathy became exuberant; taking on an air of gaiety. She turned on the Hi-Fi.

"You were wonderful," she proclaimed, spinning around the room as if she were dancing. "I can tell daddy really likes you." She spun again. Her dance step ending with her body pressed against his.

"Your mother doesn't much care for me," Jack said, slipping his arms around her, loosely, as if they were dancing.

"She doesn't like anyone who isn't in the social register," Kathy said, lightheartedly. "But mother doesn't matter. Only father matters and he likes you."

Kathy changed the subject but not her mood. "Am I shameless?" she asked, as if it were a line from a movie, "The way I throw myself at you?"

She wrapped her arms around him and pressed her pelvis against his thigh and then she spun away, playfully, and asked, "Would you rather have me play hard to get? I could be distant, aloof, unattainable."

She had her hands on her hips, a mock sultry look.

"I like you the way you are," Jack assured her. "Even though I don't quite know who that is... yet."

"Maybe you never will, maybe I'll just keep changing, maybe I'll be so many different girls you'll never want to date another."

He stepped toward her. She met him half way. "Oh, Jack," she whispered. "Do you feel the way I feel?"

He answered with a kiss, a pleasurable kiss, warm, and soft, sensuous but restrained. He held back for fear of where he might go. Sometime, in some other place, they would go there. It was inevitable. But not tonight. Not while in the sphere of James McDonnell's omnipresence.

She leaned away from the kiss, took a deep breath and looked into his eyes. "Jack Portman, I think I'm falling in love with you."

They couldn't resist. They kissed again, open-mouthed, tongues exploring. They slow-danced to the couch, the record player pounding the erotic beat of *Bolero*. His hands roamed over her body until they finally found their way under her dress. He slipped one hand under her panties, cupping one buttock; he massaged and squeezed it gently, which made Kathy sigh from never-before-experienced bliss.

He whispered in her ear, "If you want me to stop, just so say."

"I don't want you stop, but daddy is upstairs." Contrary to her words, she wriggled under him, "I want you to press against me. I want to feel you." She arched her back and thrust herself against him. They found each other's rhythm and began the motion of sex without the sex. Here I go again, Jack thought. Almost, but not quite – what if I just pulled off her panties and unzipped my fly and kept going? The thought of yielding to carnal instinct and forcing himself inside her scared him. He pulled away. Kathy clung to him, surprised that he would want to stop doing anything so pleasurable. She had never gone this far before. No boy's hand had ever touched her fanny or bare breasts before.

"We have to stop," he whispered. "I want you so bad I can't stand it."

"I want you too, it's just . . ." She didn't finish her thought. She didn't have to. "I love you," she confessed.

He sat up on the couch. She wriggled out of the love-making position and sat beside him. "It's times like this I wished I smoked," he joked. "It always looks so cool in the movies."

"Are you making fun of me?" Kathy wondered aloud.

"No way. I just had to say something stupid to get my mind off what I want to do to you."

"What do you want to do to me?" She teased, knowing full well.

"I think you know."

"How do you feel about me?" She'd used the "L" word. It was his turn.

Good question, he thought. He wanted to have sex with Kathy; that much was for certain.

"I think I love you too."

He knew it was what she wanted to hear. He watched her relax. She'd been biting her lower lip – slowly, she unclenched her jaw muscles and smiled, displaying her perfect teeth.

"You have a great smile," he said. He leaned over and kissed her gently on her beautiful smile.

James McDonnell watched, approvingly, from a window as Kathy walked Jack to his car. Although under the cover of an umbrella, the presence of the guards restrained them from a goodnight kiss.

The boy has the good sense to know when to go home. McDonnell thought. Jack had scored four out of four on the McDonnell rating scale: INTELLIGENCE, POISE, COM-MONSENSE, VERBAL SKILL.

He loved his daughter more than anything/anyone in the world. If she fell in love with the wrong young man, what would he do? How could he save her without losing her? Parental obstacles didn't detour young lovers – they inspired them. "Us-against-the-world" motivated many elopements. Kathy was eighteen. If she wanted to marry the wrong man all she had to do was get in her car and drive to Nevada.

James experienced a leap of logic. If he was proactive, he could choose and mould his daughter's mate, thereby assuring her happiness and his own legacy. He saw it as clearly as one might see a solitary goldfish swimming in a solitary glass bowl.

A few phone calls early in the day had disclosed Jack Portman to be an excellent student, fifth in his class, despite his participation in athletics and other activities. He scored in the 98th percentile in the Iowa student evaluation tests. His I.Q. was in the 120s. He was intelligent, athletic, tall and physically attractive. He was ambitious to better himself; he retained information and could articulate it. McDonnell admired the way Jack recounted the Joe Meek story, complete with names and dates. Jack Portman had the qualities necessary to be a successful lawyer.

Lately, James McDonnell had been in touch with his own mortality. How much time did he have left on this earth? What would be his legacy? He had a daughter but it was a rough road to success for a woman, regardless of qualifications or connections. But with the right man married to his daughter, a dynasty could be launched. There was time to influence several grandchildren. Jack Portman would be relatively easy to guide and influence. There would be no competing interest from the family of the groom. No strong father-figure on the other side with his own ideas for his son. Jack was pure – a clean canvas upon which to paint. Greta Portman would embrace a relationship with a successful family, and in fact, "Son of a Widowed Saloonkeeper" would play well should Jack go into politics. And why not? Governor? Better yet, U.S. Senator? Senator would be an attainable goal. That would be a legacy a man of influence and subtle power could view with pride. There would be a son, of course. His name would be James McDonnell Portman, make that U.S. Supreme Court Justice, James McDonnell Portman.

James poured a snifter of brandy. It was, at the very least, a theory worth further exploration. "Yes, yes," he uttered aloud, congratulating himself on the genius of his "Assure Kathy's Happiness" strategy. He walked onto the deck and looked out onto his lake. The storm clouds had parted enough to reveal the moon hanging high in the sky, reflecting a rippled glow along the surface of the dark water. He stared at the moon's reflection as if it were an omen.

An omen of what? He cross-examined himself. Are you sacrificing your daughter to your own ambitions? He answered the question with an emphatic "No." She was falling in love for the first time. First love was the one love no one ever forgot. She would never be completely happy with anyone else. The greatest gift he could give his daughter, he concluded, was the man she loved.

"James?" He heard his wife's voice. It was her soft, inviting voice, not the shrill, sarcastic voice he'd dealt with earlier in the evening. She was wearing a sheer silk nightgown. "Why don't you come to bed?" she asked.

"Go to bed, or come to bed?"

"Come to bed. With me."

"God, you're beautiful," he told her, amazed how easy he was to manipulate. Her nipples were pressing through the thin fabric of her nightgown.

"I'm sorry I was such a bitch tonight, darling. I don't know what got into me."

"I hate scenes in front of guests," he replied. He said it carefully, not wanting to spoil the mood.

"There wasn't a scene," she answered, "because of you. You always know the right thing to say or do. I'm so very fortunate to have you to protect me – 'so lucky to be loved by you,'" she cooed, reciting the words of the song he'd dedicated to her earlier in the evening.

It had been three weeks since she'd invited him to bed. She placed her hand on his crotch.

"Are you coming to bed, or do you want to fuck me right here?" she teased him, rubbing her hand against his growing erection. "We could show your guards how the rich folks do it."

He could never account for how aroused he became when she talked like that. He swept her up into his arms and carried her to her bed.

CHAPTER THIRTY-TWO

Tim Budge squinted through his rain-splattered windshield. "I think I saw a light on inside." He switched off the headlights, but left the engine running. The light from inside had been faint, fleeting, but it was a light. He had a strong urge to shift into reverse and drive away.

"There's no car here. I'm sure no one's home," Ellen said. She'd show Jack Portman and Pat Kelly. She would do "it" with Tim in Pat's house. Then she and Tim would get engaged. When they were engaged, it would drive her mother, Jack and Pat crazy!

Tim had a queasy feeling in the pit of his stomach. This was Lakeside. The people who lived here were rich. If caught in the house, a Coos County deputy would toss him in jail for breaking and entering. How would a felony conviction on his college application look? But did he dare back down? Would there ever be another opportunity like this? What about Ellen? Does she really like me? Or is she using me to get back at Jack? It would be great to make it with a girl like Ellen. Ellen was the kind of girl a guy would be lucky to marry.

"Come on, Timmy," Ellen urged. "The light you think you saw was probably just a reflection of your car lights passing a window. "If someone was here, there'd be a car."

"Maybe not," Tim said, thinking fast. "The garage door is closed."

"There's no room for a car in there. That's for the boat and the water skis."

"The Kellys could have dropped someone off, loaned the house to a friend," Tim improvised. Tim's reticence irritated Ellen. He was ruining her plan. What she envisioned as her final victory was slipping away.

"You stay here and I'll go check," she volunteered.

She had wriggled back into her raincoat and was reaching for the door handle.

"What will you say if someone's there?"

"The only people who could be there are the Kellys. I know them. I'll say we got stuck in the storm and ask to use the phone, I mean, it's not a big deal, and they know me. But I'm sure no one is home."

"Wait, I'll go," Tim said, too late. She was out the car door and darting through the rain to the front porch.

Abernathy had fallen asleep, awakened, dressed in his warm, machine-dried clothing and then fallen back to sleep. The sound of tires crunching over the gravel drive awakened him. He'd seen car lights rake across the room, and then go off. Was it a police car checking the place out? He cursed himself for not turning off the light and quickly flicked it off. Instinctively, he retrieved his rifle from his duffel bag and crawled to the front window.

He peeked outside. It was a small car, one of those sissy Kaiser cars, definitely not a police car.

Could it be members of the family? His new family? If so, he wished them no harm. But if they were family, why did they sit outside? Were they burglars? Were they local hoodlums taking advantage of the storm to rob the Lakeside houses? By God, if they were, they had picked the wrong house to rob. The Kelly house would not be robbed on John Abernathy's watch.

He saw a female open the passenger door and run toward him. Was she a relative?

Ellen knocked on the door. John held his breath. She knocked again. "Hello!" She shouted. "Hello! Anybody home?"

When there was no response, she turned away from the front door and faced toward Tim, hands on her hips, "I told you nobody was home!"

This confused John. Why would you visit the Kellys if you thought they weren't home?

The girl didn't return to the car. She reached for the key under the potted plant. It wasn't there. She turned the doorknob. The door opened.

"Come on, Tim," she shouted, "They forgot to lock the door."

Tim was sure he saw a shadow move across the front window. He shouted back, "No, Ellen, come back! Let's get out of here!"

Abernathy made his decision. There was a car in the driveway. He needed a way out of here; he needed to reach California and his new life in the Redwood forests near Samoa. He stepped out of the doorway and swept Ellen into a viselike grip with his left arm. With his right arm, he leveled his rifle at the driver's side of the Henry J.

"You!" He shouted in Tim's direction, "Get out of the car or I'll break her neck!"

Tim considered his options. He could duck, throw the car into reverse and probably get away. But he couldn't leave Ellen. The brute on the porch had a stranglehold on her. It could be John Abernathy, the murderer. The rapist.

Alternatives exploded in Tim's head like fireworks in the night sky. Get away? Get Help? Save yourself? Leave and Ellen will be raped and murdered.

Tim opened the car door and raised his hands. "I'm getting out of the car, don't hurt her." It seemed surreal, this wasn't really happening. The guy with the gun would let go of Ellen, laugh, and say, "I really had you kids going, didn't I? Well, that'll teach you not to sneak around other people's houses. Now get the hell out of here before I call the cops."

But it was real. *Damn*, Tim said to himself. *He's a big son of a bitch. Stay cool. Stay calm. You can't out fight him; you've got to out think him. Don't let him know you know who he is.*

"Sorry to bother you, sir, I know it's late," Tim called to Abernathy, flashing an innocent grin. "You must be a friend of the Kellys too. You must know Ellen, she's Pat's cousin from Reedsport. We were driving by, saw the light, thought Pat might be here."

Keep talking, Tim told himself.

"But if Pat isn't here, heck, we'll just be on our way." Tim looked at his watch, "It is late, later than I thought, sorry to bother you..."

"Shut the fuck up, asshole," Abernathy blasted. He'd never liked fast-talking, slender, good-looking blond men. Probably a faggot, he thought, although he wasn't quite sure what a faggot was, other than it was worse than a queer, and a queer was a man who screwed other men.

But Tim had managed to plant a seed, *cousin*. Was this girl a cousin? If he, Abernathy, was an honorary Kelly, and this girl was a cousin, then he shouldn't harm her.

He hadn't had a good look at her. Her hair was wet. The rain and the brief petting spree after the movie had removed her make-up. The raincoat hid her feminine curves.

"Are you really a cousin?" Abernathy asked Ellen.

She nodded yes and he relaxed his grip. He still held her, but loosely, so as not to hurt her.

"Who are you?" Abernathy demanded, looking at Tim as he swung his rifle in line with Tim's chest.

"Just a friend," Tim said.

"He gave me a ride, that's all," Ellen said, gathering her wits. "We're sorry we bothered you. I should have called first. Why don't you let go of me and we'll be on our way, please?"

"If you're a cousin, you'll help me." Abernathy said, a plan taking shape. He dropped the menacing tone. "What's your name?" he asked Tim.

"Tim."

Tim, Abernathy thought, that's a faggot name if there ever was one, but this Tim could be useful. He didn't want to do anything to him now, not in front of his newfound cousin. He wouldn't leave a live enemy, but there was plenty of time to deal with Tim.

"Tim, huh. Good to meet you, Tim. I'm Jake Sloan, how 'bout you helping me out. You and my cousin here, you could really help me out."

"Sure, whatever, Jake, be happy to help."

"See, I've got a job waiting for me in California, but my car broke down. So, of course, the Kellys, they said make yourself at home 'til you get your car fixed, but it's the damned transmission, and I'll have to wait three days and if I wait three days I just might lose the job. Understand?"

"Sure do," Tim said. "Look, you're welcome to borrow my car."

"No, wouldn't want to do that. Better if you drove."

He released Ellen. "If you're my cousin, you'll help me," he told her. "Help me and nobody gets hurt. You understand?"

"Yes," she said, beginning to shake.

Abernathy saw this. "Don't be scared. Help me, and nobody gets hurt," he repeated. "Now go inside and get my duffel bag, a blanket and my shoes. And get the four beers outta the 'frigerator."

He swung the rifle back in Tim's direction. Ellen did as she was told.

"Please, God," Ellen pleaded with devout sincerity as she packed the bag, "I'm sorry I have these evil desires, but if you let us live, I promise I'll be good and never do anything like this again for the rest of my life."

Abernathy's first idea was to get into the back seat with his cousin and have Tim drive. That didn't work. The back seat was too small for his large body and the girl, so he squeezed into the back seat by himself. There was no legroom but by shifting into a sideways position he was able to make himself comfortable. He could also scrunch down out of sight if necessary. Once settled, Abernathy pushed the rifle barrel through the crease of the fold-down seats, positioning the point of the barrel firmly against Tim's rectum. "Try anything funny and I'll send you to hell in a shower of shit."

Tim started the engine and checked his gauges. "I don't have enough gas to get to California," he reported. He was sweating like he was sitting in a sauna, but he sounded calm and matter of fact.

"You got enough gas to get through Coos Bay?"

"Yeah, but barely," Tim answered.

"Then we'll fill up there. Got it?"

Tim turned off Hemlock Road onto Lakeside Boulevard.

"Drive normal," Abernathy warned. "Don't do nuthing to attract a cop."

* * *

Jack Portman stopped at the end of the McDonnell driveway, shifted into neutral and leaned back in his seat. He needed to gather his thoughts. What an evening. The elegant home, the sophisticated dinner-patter – and wouldn't it be cool to play a piano like Mr. McDonnell or write books like Mr. Clark? And if he was patient, he could and would get to make love with Kathy. All he had to do was get her alone.

He wondered, in exchange for her virginity, what would Kathy expect? He should go to a drug store and buy a condom. How do you stop in middle of passion . . . and get one on . . . What if he botched it? What were Tim and Ellen doing right now? Don't think about it! He liked Kathy, maybe even loved her, but what would it be like with Ellen? And how about all the girls he was going to meet in college?

He saw a car coming on Lakeside Boulevard. It passed through his headlights. Unmistakably, it was Tim's Henry J. Who else would have the word *Intelligencia* painted on the door?

Tim saw the two-tone green Chevy coupe at the edge of the McDonnell driveway as he passed by.

How many of those could there be?

It could be Jack; Jack's new girl lives in Lakeside. *Please, God, let it be Jack*, he prayed. How could he signal him?

Jack recognized Ellen in the passenger seat. What were Tim and Ellen doing driving around Lakeside on a stormy Tuesday night? He shifted into gear, eased onto Lakeside parkway and followed. Should he honk? Should he pull up beside them when they reached the 101 inter-sections and say hello?

Or, should he ignore them? What business did he have butting into their business? Still, it was weird. Tim was sitting up straight in the driver's seat. He usually slouched. Ellen was sitting on the far right, looking straight ahead. Normally, the girl leaned over, close to the driver. Maybe they'd had a fight? There was something odd about Tim's car. Jack figured it out. It was riding too low, way too low. It had a heavy load in the backseat or trunk.

Tim pulled up to the stop sign at 101 and flicked his blinkers indicating a right turn, north. When the traffic cleared, he turned left instead. South, toward Coos Bay.

"What are you doing?" Jack said aloud. "Why aren't you going home?"

Tim was thinking, *Please, Jack, you're our only hope. Follow us. Don't let us be alone with this crazy bastard. He's going to kill me the instant he doesn't need me and God only knows what he'll do to Ellen.*

An instinct, maybe telepathy, told Jack to follow his friend. Jack waited for a southbound car to pass and pulled onto 101.

"California, here we come!" Abernathy whooped. "Where's that beer, cousin?"

"It's in your duffel bag,"

The bag was on the floor in the back seat. Abernathy reached down and found the zipper; he wagged his hand through the blanket and clothing and found a cold bottle. "You get an opener?" he asked Ellen.

"I forgot," she admitted, worried the response would displease him.

"Well, hell, real men don't need openers." He stuck the top of the bottle between his back teeth and crunched the cap off. He spit the cap into the front seat of the Henry J and repeated, "California, here we come!"

The car immediately behind the Henry J became impatient with Tim's strict adherence to the 50 mph speed limit. When the driver saw a straightaway with no oncoming headlights he gunned his Olds '88 past the compact. This allowed Jack to move up and get a better look inside Tim's car. The moon was up. The rain had all but stopped. Jack saw the hulking figure in the backseat.

As Abernathy drank beer, Tim felt the pressure of the steel barrel against his anus relax. Abernathy had let go of the rifle.

Tim had seen Jack's car pull out behind the Olds. Jack was now directly behind him. His thought: If I slam on the brakes, everything would go forward. The gun will go forward and I can grab the barrel and pull it toward the front seat. Ellen and I can jump out of the car and run to Jack and this nightmare will be over.

But what if he couldn't grab the rifle? What if it stuck between the fold-down upper seat and the driver's seat?

What if it wasn't Jack? The car following would swerve around them and keep going, shake a fist and yell, 'Crazy kids!'

Abernathy will be furious – shoot me, grab Ellen and drive off.

No, Tim decided, better to bide his time.

They came to the Hauser turn off; Abernathy shot his middle finger in the air and shouted, "Fuck you, Randy."

A roadside mileage sign posted North Bend 5, Coos Bay 7. Abernathy saw the sign. "Once we get through Coos Bay, how far to California?"

"Over three hours. If we fill-up in Coos Bay we can easily make it to California. There's a Shell station between North Bend and Coos Bay that's open 24/7, I'm thinking we should stop there."

"I'll tell you where to stop. I'll pick the station." Tim felt the pressure of the gun barrel push hard against his buttock.

"You're the boss." Tim glanced in the rearview mirror. The headlights were there. Was it Jack?

"God damn fucking right, I'm the boss," Abernathy boomed. "So how would you like to sing for me?"

"What do you want me to sing?" Tim was eager to please his captor.

Ellen eased down in her seat, trying to make herself invisible. She could see the soft glow of lights emanating from North Bend and Coos Bay. She remembered there were stoplights on the stretch of highway after the bridge. When Tim stopped, she thought, she could open the door and make a run for it. If she got away, she could get help. She could run up to another car, there would surely be lots of cars on the road, even if it were late. But what would happen to Tim? She'd gotten him into this. He'd tried to talk her out of going up to the lake house. It was her fault. How could she just run away?

"You know that driving song, *Ninety-Nine Bottles of Beer on the Wall*?" Abernathy said. "We could sing that. We used to sing that on the bus on the way home from football games."

Abernathy fished another beer from his duffel bag, bit off the cap and began to sing, "*Ninety-nine bottles of beer on the wall, ninety-nine bottles of beer, if one of those bottles should happen to fall, ninety-eight bottles of beer...*"

"I bet you were a great football player," Tim ventured.

Abernathy took a long swallow of beer, "I was pretty fucking good, I was a fucking good boxer too, but I couldn't afford no manager. That whole racket is crooked. I could have boxed or played football in college if I wanted. Couple of years ago Reedsport had that hot-shit fullback, Bookman, or whatever the fuck his name was. I was as good as him but I didn't want to go to no fucking college – how 'bout you, Timmy, you a college boy?"

"Not me. Just a working stiff, got a job gassing boats and guiding tourists at that little resort on Lake Tahkenitch."

Hearing this, Abernathy hated Tim a little less. "How's the pay?" he asked, genuinely interested. That gave Abernathy an idea. "Throw me your wallet and I'll see for myself."

Tim followed orders.

It was too dark for Abernathy to read denominations, but there were five bills in Tim's wallet: a five, three ones and the portrait of Benjamin Franklin. Abernathy stuffed all five into his pocket and tossed the wallet back into the front seat. "Thanks, shit head, it's all for a good cause."

They reached the Coos Bay Bridge. As they drove uphill toward the center of the span the little engine lugged down. Jack slowed too. He'd seen enough *film noir* detective dramas to understand the strategy of following a car.

Assume the worst and act accordingly, Jack had concluded. Tim and Ellen are hostages. There was only one person on the Oregon Coast who would take hostages. If he, Jack, didn't intervene – Abernathy would kill Tim, rape Ellen, and then kill her. Jack's mind spun back to a pivotal moment in his life: the locker room confrontation with Eldridge Olsen. It worked then – it could work now.

Don't think about it. Attack.

The issue was how and when? If he failed, what would happen? The question was mute. He had to take the chance; otherwise, Tim and Ellen were going to die. The Henry J reached the apex of the bridge span and regained speed on the downgrade. Jack closed the gap. He had an idea. To execute it, he would have to stay directly behind his friend's compact.

Inside the Henry J, Abernathy took notice of the increased traffic. He reached into the front seat and rapped Tim on the top of the head with his knuckles. "Remember, fuck-head, we don't stop in Coos Bay until I tell you."

Abernathy continued to sit tall and look around. He was trying to stay alert, although the feminine being in the front seat increasingly diverted his attention. Every mile they'd driven from Lakeside had taken him farther away from his fantasy-family. He wondered what this girl would look like without her raincoat. He'd find out, he promised himself. He'd look for a lonely road leading back to a campground or beach and he'd tell Tim to pull over so he could take a pee. He'd crush the faggot's skull with one swift swing of the rifle stock and haul the girl out of the car, rip off her raincoat and whatever else she was wearing and slam his manhood so deep inside her she'd bleed from her mouth. She was a cousin all right but not a kissing cousin. She was a fucking cousin.

The light at the end of the bridge was green and Tim cruised through the intersection. He caught a green light at the next intersection too. The third light was red and he eased to a stop.

Abernathy approved, "That's a good boy, Timmy, you keep driving smart and you and my little cousin here are going to be just fine." He reached over the seat and patted Ellen on the head.

Attack. You can do this. Jack hit the gas and rammed his front bumper into the rear end of Tim's car, pushing the Henry J into the intersection – causing an immediate commotion.

Brakes squealed as vehicles swerved to avoid the Henry J. Horns honked and fists waved.

"What the fuck," Abernathy yelled, turning to look out the back window.

"Run for it," Tim shouted. He opened his door and dashed toward the Shell station on the corner.

Jack saw Tim escape and moved swiftly toward the Henry J's passenger door with one thought, save Ellen.

Abernathy saw Jack coming and reached for his rifle, but the force of the collision had pushed it forward. It was jammed tight. His next reaction was to reach for Ellen. He ended up with a fistful of raincoat. Jack opened Ellen's door. His eyes met Abernathy's. He sized up Ellen's predicament – she was trying to lurch free of Abernathy's grasp. *Attack.* Jack grabbed her raincoat on each side of the lapel, ripped hard, and the buttons popped. He leaned inside the car, took aim with his right fist and smashed Abernathy in the face. The blow landed on Abernathy's right eye and cheekbone. It startled Abernathy, distracting him, momentarily. In that split second, Jack grabbed Ellen by the front of her sweater and yanked her out of her raincoat and the car. Abernathy shoved the front seat down and followed them. For the two-to-three seconds it took Abernathy to disengage from the backseat, he was vulnerable. Jack coiled, and sprang toward him, swinging his forearm across Abernathy's jaw. The blow sent Abernathy sprawling to the pavement. He rolled once, regained his balance and sprang to his feet.

Teeth bared, he charged. Jack stepped sideways, avoiding full-force contact, but Abernathy was rattlesnake quick. He feinted right, lunged left and grabbed Jack in a bear hug. Jack writhed and kicked his legs trying to break away, but the air was being crushed from his lungs. He saw a blur, heard a thunk and the monster's arms relaxed. Abernathy stepped back and looked around, confused.

Ellen had wrestled the rifle free from the car seat. She didn't know how to shoot it, but she knew how to swing it. She'd grabbed it by the barrel and whacked Abernathy on the back of the skull.

Jack heard sirens. He saw Ellen. He staggered to her side, took the gun and pointed it at Abernathy.

The sirens were closer. Seconds away.

Abernathy didn't counterattack. "Hey," he said to the gathering crowd, "This is just a misunderstanding." He backed away. "A family quarrel, that's all." He backed out of the circle of befuddled bystanders, turned, and sprinted into darkness.

Jack raised the rifle to his shoulder, took aim and pulled the trigger. Click. He worked the bolt action, aimed and fired again. Click. No bullets.

"Drop it! Drop the rifle or I'll shoot."

A policeman was pointing a revolver at him.

"You stupid shit," Ellen screamed at the policeman. She was jumping up and down, pointing into the night. "That's Abernathy, the killer."

"Drop it," the cop commanded. Jack obeyed.

As the rifle clattered onto the pavement, Jack's adrenaline rush subsided. His chest ached and his right hand was throbbing. "Call Sheriff Stark in Reedsport," Jack said as the cop forced him to spread-eagle on the street.

"Shut up, shit head. Point a gun in Coos Bay and you go to jail."

Hearing this, Ellen resumed her rant. "You stupid fool, he's a hero. You're letting the killer get away."

"Cuff her too!" The cop yelled.

It took an hour to sort things out with the Coos Bay City Police and Coos County Sheriff office. Fortunately, the night attendant at the Shell station had called his boss, Art Wagner, and described the wild melee in the intersection. Wagner said he'd be right over.

When Wagner saw Jack in handcuffs he confronted the officers. "This is a mistake. I know this boy; his name is Jack Portman and he's a good kid."

Tim finally stepped forward. He was ashamed because he ran and even more ashamed for not joining the fight. He didn't know how he'd ever face Ellen or make it up to Jack. He had to start somewhere. "That's my car," he pointed at the Henry J. "Ellen and I were kidnapped in Lakeside and forced to drive here. He wanted to go to California. Jack saved us."

The story was so preposterous it had to be true. A county deputy had seen the wanted poster. He retrieved it from his car and showed it to witnesses. They agreed, "That's the huge guy who ran away."

The Coos Bay Times dispatched a reporter, Len Fletcher, to the scene. He had a B&W Polaroid camera and arrived in time to snap Jack and Ellen in cuffs. He shot a dozen "instant" pictures and interviewed witnesses. This headline writes itself, he chuckled:

HEROS IN CUFFS, ALLEGED KILLER ESCAPES

Yeah, he'd lucked into a good one: statewide for sure, maybe national. The girl, Ellen Reilly, was a rich vein to mine. She described the terror she'd felt while being held hostage at gunpoint in the car. "With every mile we traveled, I felt I was getting closer and closer to a ghastly death."

Tim Budge was less forthcoming. He was too mired in shame-induced self-pity to give a good interview. He did provide background detail. "We decided to go for a ride after the movie. Ellen remembered she'd left a sweater at the Kellys. We drove up, the light was on, so, she went to the door, and this huge guy comes out waving a rifle."

"You're all from Reedsport. What were you doing in Lakeside?" Fletcher asked Jack when he finally had a chance to question him.

"Visiting friends. Look, Mr. Fletcher, I just happened to be in the right place at the right time. Tim Budge deserves the credit. He recognized my mother's car and was smart enough to figure a way to signal something was wrong. He was the one with the gun pointing at him."

"Right," Fletcher said, jotting down Jack's words, grinning. The hero was both brave and humble.

"But," Fletcher shifted to the meat of the story, "you were the one who pulled Ellen Reilly out of the car. You were the one who physically confronted him."

"Tim had to think Ellen got out of the car the same time he did," Jack answered.

County Sheriff Slim Haskins had been called to the scene. He interrupted the interview.

"Sorry about all this, son."

"It's okay. I was aiming a gun. If I was a cop, I'd have arrested me too."

Fletcher jotted it down.

"I talked to Henry Stark," Slim said. "Told him there's no citations. The girl's daddy is driving down to get her. Henry asked if either of you boys need anything."

"Gas," Jack joked.

Slim laughed and patted Jack on the shoulder. Henry and Art Wagner are right, he thought, this is a terrific kid. "Too bad the rifle wasn't loaded," Slim opined as he walked away.

"Yeah," Jack nodded, wondering, what if I'd killed Abernathy? He decided that would have been okay – after what he'd done to Betty Wagner.

* * *

Abernathy doubled back in the direction of the bridge, found a through street and ran toward the waterfront with its myriad of loading docks and warehouses. After ten minutes he realized he wasn't being pursued. He slowed to a fast walk and began analyzing his newest quandary.

His dream of going to California would have to be abandoned; the faggot and bitch would tell the cops he was headed for California. He'd been so close. Where did Portman come from anyway? He remembered Jack Portman from football. Good tackler. He'd watched him play basketball too. He was no faggot. Packed a good punch for a slim guy. He had guts. Was the gun loaded? He thought he'd loaded it. Portman could have shot him and didn't. He owed him one. He had him whipped though, if the bitch hadn't blindsided him. He felt the lump on the back of his head, it was tender but he'd been hurt worse. Best thing to do was ignore it. The little gal was feisty, though. A fighter, maybe she wasn't a bitch. He'd bet she'd kick, bite and scratch, not just lay there, crying and whimpering.

John cut through an alley between warehouses. A side door was slightly ajar. He slipped inside. The warehouse was like a concrete football field with a roof. It was filled with rows of plywood on pallets awaiting export. He pulled the door shut behind him. Good place to hole up and think things through. He'd lost his duffel bag and rifle, but he still had money.

He'd find a way.

CHAPTER THIRTY-THREE

"God, that was unbelievable," James McDonnell said to his beautiful wife after his breathing returned to normal.

She sat up in the bed and slipped her nightgown back over her head and shoulders. "When you're nice to me, I can be nice to you," she purred. "I've been thinking," she continued. "We haven't gone anywhere in a long time."

"New York," he reminded her, "last September; San Francisco in March."

"But they're both in America and we go there all the time," she said, sweetly. "I was thinking of somewhere different."

"Somewhere different?" he sighed. "Life here is a perpetual vacation for me. I don't covet 'different.' We have our friends, interesting guests, the Clarks, our dinner parties."

"I know, James, but they're really your friends, your dinner parties. I don't want you to think I don't enjoy them, but it would be lovely to get away for a while, I mean really *away*."

"What do you have in mind?"

"Europe," she whispered. She slipped her hand beneath the sheet and began stroking his abdomen. "Wouldn't that be fun? Romantic? I have some brochures and magazine articles. It would be an adventure."

"When were you thinking about taking this trip?"

"Why put it off?" she cooed. "We have our passports so all we need do is make the bookings. The travel writers warn against going in August so we should leave soon."

The last thing James McDonnell wanted to do was join a horde of camera-toting American tourists traipsing through Europe in the summer.

"It would be hard for me to get away right now, Mary, I try not to bother you with a lot of detail, but I have a few irons in the fire."

Mary anticipated this. "It would be awful to go without you but if you're busy, you're busy."

She continued to lightly stroke his tummy. "What if Kathy and I went? Shouldn't a girl have the experience of seeing Europe before going to college? Wouldn't that give her a new perspective on the world? There's that great museum in Paris, those famous ruins in Rome."

The Louvre and the Coliseum, James thought, she could at least know the names. 'A new perspective on the world?' That had to be a direct quote from one of her magazine articles. Still, all things considered, it was fortuitous. It would separate Kathy and Jack while he further evaluated the young man and made sure he was worthy of being "chosen."

"Mary, my dear, if you want to go to Europe, you should go to Europe. Invite your sister as well." He expected her to ask about taking her sister, so he figured, might as well bring it up himself and get credit. There would be more sex between now and Mary's departure.

"Kathy needs a companion, too," James continued. "I'd like to do something for the Wagner girl. I believe a change of scenery might be excellent therapy."

He got out of her bed. "We'll talk about it in the morning. I'll call Ruby at the travel agency and have her get started on itineraries."

"Thank you, darling." She patted the place in the bed he'd vacated. "Sure you don't want to spend the night?"

"You forget how I snore." He leaned over and kissed his wife good night.

* * *

Abernathy hunkered between the pallets of plywood and began thinking about his next move. They'd be looking for him, but they'd probably wait until daylight. That meant he'd have to be on the move before daylight. He was near the docks, which meant there were freighters and rail cars. He could try to stow away in one of the freighters or he could slip into a boxcar on an outgoing train. But he was near the water.

Steal a boat, the voice told him.

"Yeah," he agreed with the voice. That would be the least expected. They'd sure as hell check boxcars and they'd get the word out to all of the longshoreman and merchant seaman to be on the lookout. A small boat with a one or two man crew would be the easiest to over-power. There were hundreds of small craft in Coos Bay, Abernathy calculated. Once in the bay, he could slip out into the Pacific and follow the coastline north to Winchester

Bay. He could make that trip in a skiff equipped with an outboard. Early in the morning he might find a boat like that unattended, maybe even gassed up and ready to go.

Everybody thought he was headed for California. They'd never look for him in Winchester Bay. That's what big male cougars do, Abernathy remembered, they double-back. Hunters stomp through the woods – looking straight ahead – not knowing the cougar has circled around behind them. The hunted becomes the hunter. Better yet, the hunter/warrior quietly slips away to freedom.

A watchman stopped by the warehouse at two in the morning. He'd heard about the murderer on the loose and had been instructed to report anything suspicious. He didn't look very hard. At a buck and a quarter per hour, he reasoned, they didn't pay him enough to tangle with a murderer.

At four in the morning, according to Terry Dodd's wristwatch, Abernathy slipped out of the warehouse. The rain had come back but was now a light drizzle. The moon was behind the clouds. The watchmen were sitting inside their tiny offices. Abernathy made his way to the docks. He passed Pier 6 where a Norwegian freighter was docked. A Japanese freighter was tied up at Pier 5. John kept moving until he saw what he was looking for: a row of smaller boats tied up at a smaller, unnumbered pier.

There was a tin shack at the entrance. He watched the shack for five minutes and detected no movement. The boats bobbed gently, temptingly, against the string of old tires nailed in place to protect the hulls. He sized-up the boats: two rowboats, two inboard cruisers and an open boat built along the classic lines of a whaler's longboat. The rowboats didn't interest him. He'd never been on an inboard cruiser, let alone operated one. *That's the one,* Abernathy thought, eyeing the longboat. Sixteen feet long with a deep hull and a high bow; it was designed to cut through the choppy waters in the bay – and when necessary, make short runs into Pacific. It was a working boat, used primarily to run supplies and equipment out to the tugs. The only question was, did the outboard have a security chain to guard against theft?

He stopped at the tin shack on his way to the boat. The door was unlocked and the shack unmanned. Abernathy's eyes were accustomed to the dim light and he spotted a yellow, water-resistant poncho and a five-gallon gas can. He slipped the poncho over his head and picked up the gas can. Nearly full, he noted, sloshing the contents. He took a second look around. There was a rusty screwdriver, pair of pliers, pack of Marlboro cigarettes and a book of matches on the table. He pocketed the items, closed the door and made his way to the longboat.

The boat was unsecured, gassed and ready to go. "What a dumb ass," he said aloud, referring to the boat's owner. He felt an immediate bond with the craft and spoke to it in a friendly, reassuring tone, as if he were a horse wrangler calming a high-strung mare. "If I owned a boat like you, I'd use double chains and double padlocks and I'd keep the keys on a chain around my neck. Well, hell, it looks like I own you now."

A task force of law officers hit the docks at six. They canvassed warehouse-to-warehouse, pier-to-pier, boxcar-to-boxcar and vessel-to-vessel. They rousted the winos from their hideaway shelters and questioned every seaman and longshoreman. Their search stymied dockside operations for the entire morning but they didn't find their fugitive. He'd followed the buoys to and through the Coos River channel and was headed north toward Winchester Bay. The boat he'd stolen wasn't reported missing for hours because the boatman assumed his boss had commandeered it for a special run. After all, that's why he had standing orders to leave it gassed and ready for action.

CHAPTER THIRTY-FOUR

Harold Gilbert was in his office by eight, early for him. But it was Wednesday and they were putting the paper to bed. The graduation special was extra work but worth it, considering the six hundred bucks it added to revenue. He wished he could afford an assistant. Editing copy blurbs for ninety graduates was tedious, eye-straining work.

The front page remained a question mark. They'd saved space for the big murder story, hoping the killer would be captured in time to run it as a half-page feature. But that hadn't happened. Harold had suggested they run a story critical of the state police action during Beach Night, but Karl had been adamant. "We don't need to infuriate the authorities and risk losing our county and state printing contracts."

Harold typed:

BODY FOUND, POLICE SEEK
FLORENCE MAN.

He stared at the words. Not bad but not great. He leaned away from the typewriter and sipped from his coffee cup. He felt the warm fluid slide down his throat. He closed his eyes and waited. Sure enough, a sense of contentment spread through his body as if it were vapor escaping from a just-opened jar. With the contentment came confidence. He looked at his faithful Underwood, and said, "Clock's ticking, what's our angle?"

The phone rang. Harold reached for it, grateful for the delay. "*Umpqua Valley Journal*, Harold Gilbert, Editor, speaking."

"Hello, Mr. Gilbert, you're just the man I want to talk to. This is Larry Smith with the *Oregon Journal*."

The Journal was the afternoon newspaper in Portland. Smith was a statewide reporter and he had taken the story of the hostage rescue off of the wire from Coos Bay. It had all the ingredients of real news. Best of all, he could scoop his paper's cross-city rival, *The Oregonian*, which had delivered its morning edition without one line about the daring young man who had saved his classmates from the clutches of a madman.

The suspect had a colorful nickname, "Nasty." That could juice up the headline. **NASTY BUSINESS IN COOS BAY** had already popped into Larry's head.

"How can I help you?" Harold said, warily, wondering what news had transpired locally that he didn't know about. Harold didn't have the advantage of a wire service and had yet to receive his comp copy of the *Coos Bay Times*.

Larry Smith began. "Have you heard about the rescue last night with three of your Reedsport High kids?"

"Haven't got all the details," Harold stalled.

Reporter Smith could tell the editor of the little paper knew nothing. But Smith wasn't in competition with a boondocks weekly. He needed some details about the kids involved; something to flesh out his feature story. For that, he could afford to humor the small town editor.

"Well," Smith began, "I got this off the wire. I'll tell you what I know; maybe you can help me out with some background on three of your high school grads. Fair enough?"

"Works for me," Harold said, thinking, thank God, with Smith's information, he might have a timely front-page story after all. Harold took copious notes as the reporter walked him through the wire report.

"Now," Larry Smith said, having completed his part of the bargain, "What can you tell me about Jack Portman?"

Thanks to the graduation special, Harold had his 1954 *Chieftain Yearbook* handy.

"His mom is a widow, runs a tavern over in Winchester Bay," Harold answered off the top of his head. He thumbed to the page in the yearbook with Jack's picture and continued. "Jack was a three-year letterman in football, basketball and baseball. Captain of the football team last season; he was on the honor roll, voted most likely to succeed by his senior classmates – and let's see," he continued referencing the yearbook, "he was in the junior class play. He likes sports and reading. Plans to go to the University of Oregon."

At the reporter's bidding, Harold read the credits for Tim Budge and Ellen Reilly.

"So, Hal," Larry Smith quizzed, "what do think? What the hell were those three doing in Lakeside?"

"Hard to tell. It's only a few miles south on 101 to Lakeside, be like you driving from Portland to Beaverton."

Harold wanted the reporter to know he knew his way around Portland.

"You say the Portman kid's mother runs a tavern?"

"Correct. It's a popular place. I stop by there myself from time to time."

In truth, he'd stopped going to The Dock regularly because Greta's customers didn't treat him with the deference he felt his position as editor of the newspaper deserved. His favorite watering hole was the Y-Café. He kept an eagle eye on bartenders and there was no doubt in Harold's mind that Tony, the bartender at the Y, held the bottle over the glass at least a half-ounce longer than Greta.

"You have the mother's phone number?" Larry Smith asked.

Harold pulled out his directory, looked up the number of The Dock and dutifully gave it to the reporter. He made a mental note – if Smith asked, "Where's a good place to get a drink?" He would recommend the Y.

"What do you know about this Abernathy character?"

"One of those bad apples. Our sheriff was on to him from the start, we printed the wanted poster right here in our back shop."

"Oh yeah," the reporter said, encouraging Harold to continue.

"I saw the big ape eating breakfast at the Y-Café here in town..."

Harold elected to elaborate. "The Y is a good place for dinner, too, serves the best steaks in town and they pour a fair-sized drink if you know what I mean."

The reporter had no interest in Harold's 1954 Guide to Dining & Entertainment in Reedsport, Oregon, but he listened patiently.

"That's good to know, Hal."

Smith gently steered Harold back to the subject at hand. "You actually saw the suspect, Nasty Abernathy? How was he acting? What was his demeanor?"

"He was cool as a cucumber, but that was before I saw the poster. When I got back to my office, the posters were sitting on the counter and I told the sheriff, 'If you're serious about interrogating the man on your poster, I suggest you get yourself over to the Y and hope he stuck around for a second cup of coffee.'"

Harold was pleased he had used the journalistic word 'interrogating.' So pleased, he rewarded himself with another sip.

"But he got away?" the reporter asked.

"Slick as whale shit sliding to the bottom of the ocean." Harold liked that metaphor. He'd heard a traveling salesman say it and had filed it away for use on just such an occasion as this. "Hitched a ride on a log truck," Harold continued. "Sheriff tracked him to a sawmill in Hauser but by then he'd dropped out of sight. They had roadblocks – even had the Coast Guard looking around Tenmiles Lake – but he laid low, holed up somewhere near Lakeside until he hijacked those two kids."

Smith was shuffling through his notes; he realized he was missing the dates. "This wanted poster, Hal, when did the sheriff print the wanted poster?"

"Monday morning."

"They didn't find the body until Monday. How was it your sheriff got a poster out so fast?"

"The poster was for rape, alleged rape, I should say."

"What rape?"

"At the Senior Beach Night, Saturday night, there was an attack on a girl. The Portman kid was the one who rescued her. That's why the sheriff was looking for Abernathy in the first place. I covered the story myself on Saturday night."

"And what's this sheriff's name?"

"Henry Stark, he's the county sheriff in Reedsport. We're too small to have our own police force."

Rape, murder, kidnapping, a daring rescue and a heroic young man – to cap it off, the villain was still at large.

"How long does it take to drive down there from Portland?" Smith asked.

CHAPTER THIRTY-FIVE

"Sorry to wake you up, Mr. McDonnell, but you told me to call if I heard something . . ." It was Ace Sheehy.

"What have you got?"

"This is so good, the *Coos Bay Times* stopped the presses and held the front page for it," Ace began.

He relayed the full story and waited for instructions.

"Let's give the police a little help, Ace. Hire whomever you need to hire, spend whatever you need to spend. See if you can track the son of a bitch, Abernathy, down."

Ace asked the $64 question, "What do we do if we find him? He doesn't appear the type who's going to put his hands in the air and march off to jail like a good little boy."

McDonnell knew what Ace was asking. He settled upon an inexact, but easily interpreted phrase. "Defend yourself. I'll take care of any messy details."

"Yes, sir. If we find him, we can do that."

McDonnell hung up and went back to sleep. It was going to be a busy day and he needed his rest.

A few hours later he awoke, showered, dressed in casual clothing and went outside for the newspaper. From there he went to the kitchen. Kathy, still in her pajamas, was eating a bowl of Rice Krispies.

"Would you like to know what Jack did after he left here last night?"

She looked up, startled.

"No, he didn't have an accident, did he?"

"Not in the traditional sense." He recognized the fear in her eyes. It was not the time to be droll. "He saved two of his friends from Abernathy."

"What?" She put her hand over her mouth, expressing fear, pride and delight – all at once.

He laid the newspaper in front of her. The banner headline screamed:

YOUTH FOILS KIDNAP: RESCUES CLASSMATES!

The subhead was:

COPS CUFF HERO WHILE MURDER
SUSPECT ESCAPES.

"My goodness," Kathy nearly swooned. "How can he be so brave? So wonderful? He could have been killed. She did a double take. "Why did they handcuff Jack?"

"Read the story. He had Abernathy's rifle when the police arrived. Tried to shoot the sick bastard but the gun wasn't loaded or it jammed."

James watched as tears formed in his daughter's eyes. "He is an impressive young man. I want you to know, I thoroughly approve of him."

Her excitement was instantaneous. It stopped her tears in their tracks. *Her father approved!*

"Later, this afternoon," James said, "we'll hop into that spiffy little sports car I gave you and drive to Winchester Bay. Let's not tell your mother where we're going."

The idea thrilled Kathy and she sprang from her chair to hug her father.

"There is something I want you to do for me," James said.

Kathy leaned back, arms still wrapped around him. "You know I can't say no to you."

"Your mother wants to take you on a little trip."

"A little trip?" Kathy released him and turned away.

"Europe. It could be great fun."

"With you and mother?"

"With your mother, your Aunt Jane and perhaps a companion your own age."

"Jack?" She asked mischievously, facing him again.

"A girl friend," he laughed. "I was thinking about Betty Wagner." He became serious. "I've talked to women who've been through the same ordeal. Based on what they say, it could do Betty a world of good. She'll always carry emotional scars, but – new, positive experiences are the best medicine."

His suggesting Betty Wagner didn't surprise Kathy. She knew her father was compassionate and philanthropic. She knew he'd paid the doctor bills when Mrs. Ordway's daughter had a baby. She knew he had purchased a lakeside tract for the local Indian and informed everyone it was a U.S. Government Land Grant. Beyond a shadow of a doubt, he was the best father in the world and more than made up for her mother. If he wanted her to go to Europe, she would go.

"How long will I have to be away?"

"Not long. A month. And don't worry, absence makes the heart grow fonder."

"The second verse of that song, Daddy," Kathy quipped, "is 'For somebody else.'"

"If you do this for me, I'll look after Jack. I promise."

"How will you do that?"

"I have an idea. I'll get Nate to hire him as a researcher for the summer. Of course I'll pay, but Jack needn't know that. I'll make him a regular for Sunday suppers. I'll make friends with his mother. I'll be a mentor. Trust me, I'll keep him so busy he won't have time to meet another girl."

She liked that. She twirled, grabbed the newspaper, threw him a kiss and bounded off toward her room.

CHAPTER THIRTY-SIX

A ringing sound awakened Henry Stark from deep slumber. He fought for consciousness. He couldn't tell if it was the alarm clock, phone or doorbell. Tuesday had been a long, eventful day-into-night odyssey. First there was Greta. Second, the phone call from Coos Bay.

He'd held Greta's hand until her son walked safely through the door at two-thirty in the morning. Once he tucked himself between his own sheets, it took another half hour for sleep to overtake his thoughts about Greta, her brave son and the two kids who, by his reckoning, had escaped death by the narrowest of margins.

If only he'd gotten the wanted posters printed Sunday evening . . .

Ring, Ring, Ring, Ring.

"Yeah," he yawned into the mouthpiece.

"Henry, I'm sorry to wake you..."

Hearing Greta's voice invigorated him. "No problem, you did me a favor, got me up, I can't afford to sleep, got too much to do today."

"Well," Greta said, laughing softly at her lover's eagerness to please her, "Maybe you can do me a favor?"

"Anything, name it."

"A reporter from the *Journal* up in Portland called. He wants to do a feature story on Jack. Said he'd be here this afternoon. 'Portrait of a young hero,' he called it. I don't know, it doesn't feel right to me."

"What does Jack think?" Henry asked.

"He doesn't know. He's asleep."

Henry had an inspiration, "Tell Jack you asked me – better yet, say I called." Henry chose his words carefully. "Say I called and requested he not discuss any aspect of this case until the suspect has been apprehended."

"So, you have a funny feeling about this too?"

"I don't think it's a good idea to splash Jack's face all over the papers until we have that crazy, Abernathy, locked up. He got away. God know's where he's going."

Henry paused, rolled to the side of his bed and started to put yesterday's socks back on. He changed his mind and tossed them toward his dirty clothes hamper. "You know," he whispered into the phone, "I meant everything I said, including the part about Reno."

"I know," Greta said softly. "We'll talk later. I don't trust these phones."

"Yeah, I know, If that reporter calls me, I'll tell him Jack is off limits. I'll get over there as soon as I can. You and me will stonewall him together. How's that sound?"

"Sounds good, honey." She hung up.

Henry was wide-awake now. Greta was right; the operator often listened in and Greta had called him honey. So what? He was proud of Greta and he was going to marry her. He went into the shower. Love, he thought. Imagine that! Me, in love. You're acting like a teenager, he chided himself. Too bad you can't be as cool as young Jack.

Jack would have been the one to rush the machine gun bunker, he thought, and reconsidered. Maybe not. He wasn't reckless. Jack had a sixth sense. He seized exactly the right moment to make his move. He'd make a great marine. An officer. And his mother was something, and he, Henry Stark, had slept with her. She was different afterwards, less...what was the word? Less brassy. Less sassy? Less what? Neither brassy nor sassy were right. She'd come out of her shell, that's what it was. The protective layer had fallen away. He remembered how she undressed, the way she had stepped out of her panties and tossed her bra to the side. The tough, wisecracking saloonkeeper disappeared. In her place, a soft, beautiful, loving and generous woman materialized. He closed his eyes and imagined her lips touching his, her legs touching his, her breasts touching his. He was going to marry her. If she said no, he'd just keep asking her. He'd wear her down. . .

Operating the switchboard was a boring occupation, unless you were, as Elsie Brown described herself, "A people person, interested in everybody and everything."

To say Elsie knew everything going on in town might be an overstatement, but it's safe to say she knew most everything people talked about over the phone.

As Henry's home number rang and rang, she'd told Greta, "No one is answering."

But Greta insisted she continue ringing.

How was Greta so sure the sheriff was home?

Elsie had been forced to listen.

Then she started ringing her circle of friends.

"So guess who calls the sheriff 'Honey?' Guess who the sheriff wants to run off to Reno with?" Elsie asked Lucy Baldridge.

Elsie was confident – whatever tidbit she passed along to Lucy – would go straight to Rosie Grafton, who was carrying a torch for Sheriff Stark. Ever since Rosie's record business had taken off, Elsie judged, she'd been way too big for her britches.

CHAPTER THIRTY-SEVEN

Ace Sheehy pondered his conversation with McDonnell. How could he, Ace, beat the cops to this Abernathy? If he could take care of this, McDonnell would take care of him.

Ace had an ace in the hole. Tom Houghton had been with Pinkerton. He was a widower and now retired. He'd moved to Coos Bay from Los Angeles to be near his daughter and two grandchildren. Tom liked to make extra money so he could buy things for the grandkids. Tom liked the action too.

Tom Houghton was on the docks by ten in the morning. He looked around and asked the logical question, "How would I get out of this place?" He began poking around. Tom was a medium sized man with an easy way about him. In his mid-fifties, he had dark bushy hair, streaked with gray, and a matching mustache. He wore khaki pants and a dark blue seaman's sweater. He fit in on the docks. By noon he'd located a tug-runner with a missing boat.

"You report it to the police?"

"Didn't find out she was stolen 'til hours after she was gone, then couldn't get through to the cops on the phone. I'll have to go down to the station and wait in line.

Fuck us taxpayers, right? I'm just a water-monkey with a missing boat. One of those yachts disappear and it's a different story, right?"

"You have insurance, don't you?"

"Sure, but my boat is missing, not wrecked. That's the shit-end of the cow. Missing! I have to wait thirty days before I collect a dime. So I'm screwed. I got a contract with Pacific Tug. What am I supposed to do, sub-contract to a competitor?"

"Tell you what," Houghton said, "I'll try to find that boat for you. Give me a description and your phone number."

The tug-runner became wary. "What's it going to cost me?" It crossed his mind this could be a scam. One guy steals it, the other guy finds it.

"Nothing." Houghton put his hand on the man's shoulder. "I'm already being paid, but don't forget to report it stolen. Get the clock started on your insurance claim in case I come up empty."

Earlier in the morning, Abernathy had steered the boat out into the bay. Two hundred yards from shore he nearly ran into the black hull of an anchored freighter. He could hear the bells from the buoys but couldn't see the blinking red lights. He tucked his boat against the freighter, shut down his motor and waited for sunrise.

The sun finally came up. Stubbornly, it squeezed light into the darkness. But even when there was light, the fog hung heavy over the water, blocking visibility. John didn't panic. If his boat were reported missing, they couldn't look for it in the fog. If he couldn't see, they couldn't see. There was a chill in the air and he was grateful for his newly acquired poncho. He lit a cigarette and waited. Coffee would taste good right now, he thought. Black coffee, steaming hot. He held the cigarette smoke in his mouth, trying to simulate the taste of coffee.

He concentrated on listening. At first he heard only fog-horns and the slap-slap of the water against the freighter. Next, he heard the seagulls begin to squawk, and in the distance he picked up the ding-ding of marker bells. Finally, he heard the entire waterfront come to life. He recognized the squeaking noise a crane makes as it hoists cargo onto a docked ship. He heard bullhorns and sirens, more seagulls, and the slap-slap of the water against the freighter's hull. It made him feel safe, like when he was a kid – after a beating – when he crawled under his bed.

Slowly, the fog inched off of the water, leaving a sight-line about two feet above the surface. He could see to navigate even if larger boats and tugs couldn't. He started the outboard and made his way toward the sound of the bells. He found the channel and saw three salmon boats heading to the fishing grounds. They were traveling at 12 knots per hour, making up for lost time. Abernathy opened his throttle and steered into the wake of the trailing fishing boat.

He followed the fishing boats over the Coos River bar and into the wide Pacific. The sun was at his back, which was due east. Turn right, he told himself, north. There were thick patches of fog, but not enough to obscure the shoreline. About thirty miles due north was the mouth of the Umpqua and Winchester Bay. No one would look for him there. If he were going to be caught, it would have been last night, but he'd slipped away easy as you please. He would keep going north. Seattle was a big city. It would be easy to disappear in Seattle. Better yet, he could go to Canada. He could get a logging job and start over. His logging boss had told him, "You're quick as a cat and strong as an ox. Learn to get along with the other men and you'll have a future in this business."

Yeah, damn fucking right, he had a future.

In Canada. New country. New identity. Start over. Maybe find a woman, a woman like the feisty one in the car last night who pretended to be his cousin. If she hadn't known who he was, she might have liked him. She was spunky, all right, he remembered, he liked that. And un-der the raincoat, when he finally got a peek, she had great tits. He wished he'd made her take off the raincoat in the car so he could have looked at her tits, maybe grabbed them. If he had a woman like that, he may not need the other women. They could all go to hell. One woman, the right woman, and he could settle down. Work his way up in a logging operation and get a house like the one on the lake. Canada had logs. Canada had lakes. Canada was a much, much better idea than California. He'd find a pretty Canadian woman and be real nice to her.

He imagined himself sitting in a Canadian café, sipping coffee. A pretty waitress, who looked exactly like Ellen Reilly, came up to him and said, "You sure look strong."

Shyly, he peeked up from his coffee and smiled back at her. "I can be strong and I can be gentle," he imagined himself saying.

Then what? What would she say next? She wouldn't come on to him like a whore. "Hey big man, let's get your rocks off." He'd paid for a whore once. Three of them came to the logging camp with their own trailer. When it was John's turn, the woman just laid there. He went soft and she laughed at him. When she laughed, he slapped her – once, twice, five times, which made him hard and he ejaculated on her naked belly. She complained to the boss-whore, who told her to shut up. "What ever cranks his engine, we didn't come here on an Easter egg hunt."

The girl in the café was the exact opposite of a whore. With her, he would be gentle. But how would they get together? There'd probably be a loudmouth in the café, and the loudmouth would make a pass at her.

In his fantasy, the loudmouth looked like the Black boxer who'd beaten him in Eugene. Except the boxer was now a blonde like Tim Budge. "Hey, baby, how 'bout I pick you up after work and you and me have some fun?" The pretty girl looked helpless, like a possum caught in the middle of the road, frozen by the headlights. "I... I already have plans," she stammered, not wanting anything to do with the guy who looked like a Black boxer with blonde hair.

"Oh yeah, with who?" Loudmouth said, getting mean.

John Abernathy rose to his feet, to his full height. "With me," he said. He was wearing his new Pendleton shirt, which had never been bloodied, so he hadn't thrown it away. He didn't go over and beat the hell out of the loudmouth. Instead, he stared him down, until the loudmouth began backing toward the door, a cowardly dog with his tail between his legs.

"Hey!" Abernathy commanded. "Believe you forgot something."

"I'm sorry," the loudmouth whimpered to the lovely waitress. "I'm sorry," he whined to Abernathy, thinking Big John meant he'd forgotten to apologize.

"No, loudmouth, you forgot the tip!" Abernathy delivered his punch line with gusto and good humor, demonstrating to everyone in the café he was an all around good fellow.

The Canadians in the café roared with laughter. Best of all, John and his true love had met without her coming on like a whore – and without him having to grovel or beg for a date. Somebody played a song on the jukebox, *That Old Black Magic*, and when Perry Como sang the lyric, "The mate that fate had me created for . . ." the beautiful waitress came over to John and placed her dainty hand on his.

Canada is a good plan, the voice inside John's head assured him.

"A great plan!" Abernathy said aloud. He was so engrossed in his fantasy, he hadn't noticed the increased boat traffic.

"That's got to be Winchester Bay," he said, continuing to speak out loud, sharing his observation with the voice and his noble steed, the long boat.

Winchester Bay. What if he kept going north? How long would his gas last? He didn't know. He might have enough to get to the next port, Florence, but everyone knew him there. He might get to Yachats, but that was a small harbor where people not only noted the comings and goings of every boat, they knew every seagull by its first name. Many of the townspeople knew him. He needed to get to Waldport or Newport. Newport would be best. No one knew him in Newport.

Winchester Bay should be safe – if he was careful. It was a small town but it had a big harbor. He could avoid the main port and marina; find a place to tie down, go ashore and buy gas at a service station. "Let's see," he told the boat, "ten gallons should be enough to get us from Winchester Bay to Newport. More than enough!"

As he thought about buying gas, he remembered the money he'd taken out of the faggot's wallet. He pulled the crumpled bills out of his pocket and couldn't believe his good fortune. A ONE HUNDRED DOLLAR BILL! This is the omen I've been looking for, he thought. Everything made sense now. Was it an accident he hadn't discovered the $100 until he started thinking seriously about Canada? No. It was part of a master plan. When he got to Newport he would gas up again. Next stop, Astoria. It would be easy. He'd pinball his way up the coastline. He'd lay low, behave himself and ignore the women. He had a better woman waiting for him in Canada. He had a sturdy boat, plenty seaworthy. The boat would make it. He would make it. His true love was waiting. This was going to work, he assured himself. First thing he'd do was take care of the gas. He'd be on his way north by afternoon.

CHAPTER THIRTY-EIGHT

Ace Sheehy's key selling point for his detective agency was his exclusive *ACE System*, his acronym for "Advanced Communications Exchange." Two hundred in cash had bought him a dozen walkie-talkies and a half-dozen two-way radio set-ups at a U.S. Army surplus auction. The walkie-talkies were of little use, but the two-way radios worked brilliantly. He provided his field men, he called them *Operatives*, a unit and antenna for their cars. This allowed him to receive on-the-spot reports in *HQ*, his office. Ace was partial to military jargon. For himself, he chose the code name "Dealer." Not very military, but it did go nicely with his moniker, Ace. Operative Tom Houghton was assigned the pseudonym "Sailor."

After talking to the boatman, Tom walked back to his car and reported in, "Dealer, Dealer, this is Sailor, do you read me." He felt self-conscious about the jargon, preferring plain words and old-fashioned telephones. But Ace said telephones weren't secure, claiming his firm dealt with "sensitive and delicate matters."

There was a squeak-squawk sound, and Tom heard Ace answer, "Roger, Sailor, I hear you loud and clear. Report."

The radios had a peculiar effect on Sheehy, Tom thought. Ace would never say, "Report" if they were face-to-face in an office or café. He'd say, "Whatcha got for me, Tom?" Tom shrugged this off.

"Found a fellow down here missing a boat. Boats don't go missing around here so chances are it's your bad-boy. Over."

Ace dropped the jargon. "My client doesn't think he'll go south. Why don't you drive up to Winchester Bay and sniff around. Over."

"Makes sense," Tom said. "Over."

"One more thing, Tom. Nobody is going to be picky about how they receive this sack of shit. They'll take him dead or alive. Catch my meaning? Over."

"Look," Tom said, reading Ace perfectly, "if he's in Winchester Bay, I'll find him, I'll tell you where he is, but that's as far as I go. Over."

"Roger, Sailor, find him and report. Over and out."

Squeak-squawk.

CHAPTER THIRTY-NINE

Greta spent the morning on the telephone. There were calls from Jack's friends asking if he was all right. Two of his high school teachers called, more out of curiosity than concern. The Chevrolet dealer phoned and offered to repair her front bumper and grill for free and provide a loner while the car was in the shop. The superintendent of the Plywood Plant in Gardiner offered Jack a summer job. The most unexpected call came from Eleanor Reilly.

"Greta, I know we've had differences, but I think it's time for us to move past that."

"What differences are you talking about?"

"You know, I... well, I discouraged Ellen...because I didn't want them, Ellen and Jack, to become too serious... while they were still in high school."

"You won't get an argument with me over that," Greta responded in a placid tone.

"I don't want you to think it was because I didn't like Jack. He's a fine young man."

"Yes he is."

"And now, he actually saved my daughter from ... from... heaven knows what, and I just want him to know he will always be welcome in our home."

"That's very gracious of you," Greta said, not hiding her sarcasm.

"Yes, well, anytime Jack wants to see Ellen, I just want you...and Jack...to know he is welcome. We are just so grateful."

She's trying to keep from crying, Greta detected with a sliver of compassion. The instant she hangs up, she'll burst into tears.

"Eleanor, it was nice of you to call," Greta changed her tone, "I'll tell Jack what you told me. But," she paused, she couldn't resist, "I'm sure you know Jack is dating someone else, Kathy McDonnell from Lakeside. You may have heard of her father, the lawyer, James McDonnell?"

Greta didn't wait for acknowledgement. She'd made her point. "It's a good thing, too – for Ellen's sake," Greta went on. "You realize, if Jack hadn't been a dinner guest at the McDonnell Lakeside Manor last night, he would never have seen Tim's car..."

There was a loud knock on the outside door. "I'm sorry, Eleanor, someone's at the door, I have to go, but thanks for calling."

"Miz Greta, you in there? You okay?" It was Champ, her bartender. She was supposed to have opened the front door of the saloon for him at 10:00 a.m.

Clutching the front of her bathrobe, she answered her upstairs door.

"I tried to call," he apologized.

"I know, the phone's been busy."

It was ringing again.

She ignored it.

She gave Champ the key to the tavern and went to her son's room.

"Rise and shine, superman. I know you're awake. No mortal could sleep through that phone ringing."

He was on his back, topless, his right arm slung over his eyes to shield the daylight. "Been awake for hours, lying here, thinking."

"You can think later, sweetie. You need to get moving. We've got a busy day."

CHAPTER FORTY

Abernathy steered his boat into Winchester Bay and sized up the lay of the land, or, as was the case, the lay of the water. The majority of boat traffic was along the north shore. Bigger boats could follow the main Umpqua River channel up river – inland. He didn't want to go up river. He slowed his boat to trolling speed and began exploring the south shore where the bay sloshed into a marsh covered with tulle grass. His keel hit bottom and he pushed himself free with his oar. Surveying the wetlands, he couldn't help but think, under different circumstances, he could take a flat-bottomed row boat in there and dig himself a gunny sack full of mud clams.

Then he'd smoke a cigarette, drink a beer and wait for the tide to float him back into the bay proper. The idea of mud clams, chopped up, mixed with onions, rolled in flour and then fried into fritters made him hungry. His girl in Canada worked in a restaurant and would know how to cook them. As he continued along the nearly deserted shoreline, inevitably, Winchester Bay's abandoned cannery came into view. It was a low-slung, sheet metal building with more rust than shine. What interested him most was the dilapidated dock. He cruised under the dock and saw steps leading up the steep bank. Perfect hiding place, he thought. The risky part came next. He was going to have to find gas. He sloshed the five-gallon can he'd swiped from the guardhouse. Quarter full. No reason to lug it to a gas station. The solution would be one ten gallon can, or two fives, just as he'd figured earlier. Ten more gallons would be enough to make Waldport.

"Well, hell," he said out loud, "Ten gallons of gas between me and being free. 'No hill for a stepper.'" He liked that saying. His logging boss used it whenever the task ahead was difficult but doable.

John made his way up the steps to the abandoned cannery. The pilings were sound although the planks on the unloading platform were rotted. He peered inside the metal shell of a building. One sniff told him the cannery had become a bat rookery. He didn't like bats; there was something eerie, even scary about them, although he'd never admit to anyone he was afraid of bats. He walked around the perimeter of the building. A gravel road ran right up to a long-ago abandoned office and loading dock.

There was a small house trailer sitting in the parking lot. The trailer had once been silver, but salt air had corroded it to a brownish, rusty color. A boy about twelve years old was playing in front of it. The boy was wearing a dirty white tee shirt, jeans and black high-top tennis shoes. Intent on his game, the boy didn't hear Abernathy's approach. The game was simulated baseball. He would select a piece of gravel; pick out a target and go into a baseball wind-up. "Stee-rike!" He yelled after each toss,

"Hey, kid!"

The boy nearly jumped out of his shoes.

"That was a ball, a foot outside," Abernathy said, flashing a friendly smile.

He didn't want the boy to bolt and run. How could he gain his confidence? Jack Portman had been a football, basketball and basketball star from this area, he remembered.

"Do you know my buddy, Jack Portman?"

The boy considered the question. He and his friends idolized Jack Portman. Not only that, Jack had stopped to talk to them when they were fishing off the marina dock. Jack had even let him pet his dog, a police dog, which Jack had pointed out, was really a German Shepard.

"Yeah, I know Jack," the boy answered.

"He's not only my buddy, he's maybe my best buddy," Abernathy declared. "He's the one who told me about this cannery."

The boy relaxed.

"So, you and me, we got a mutual friend," Abernathy said, widening his disarming grin, "and friends help each other out."

"I suppose," the boy said.

"You help me and I'll help you. Pay you real good. Enough to buy yourself a real baseball."

"Doing what?" the boy asked, interested.

"Running a few errands, that's all."

"What kind of errands?"

"Well, I got my boat down below," Abernathy began, "and I've got engine trouble. Nothing I can't fix, but I need gas and a can of engine oil, you know, the kind you mix for outboards."

The boy nodded. He knew about outboards.

"Top of everything else, I'm hungry. Hate to just walk off and leave my boat to go into town. Figured maybe you could get the gas and groceries while I fix my boat."

"How much?" the boy asked.

It was no time to dicker. "How 'bout ten bucks?"

"Ten bucks!" the boy repeated. He cocked his head. Ten bucks was a whole summer of Hershey bars and Royal Crown sodas. "You teasing me?"

"Just trying to be fair. See, you're going to have to scare up a ten gallon can, or maybe two fives, then lug it back here full of petrol."

"I can do that."

"Then you'll need to make a quick trip to the grocery store."

"I don't mind, not for ten bucks. You really going to pay me ten bucks?"

"Hell yes, no sweat. But there's one other thing," Abernathy said as he pulled out his wallet. "I don't want nobody to know I'm here, or ever was here."

"Not even Jack?"

"Not even Jack. I don't want him to get in trouble over me."

"You on the lam or something?" It was an expression the boy learned in an Edward G. Robinson movie.

Lies came easily to Abernathy, "Well, you see, what's your name?"

"Edward."

"You see, Eddie, I bought this car in Coos Bay and the damn thing wouldn't run for shit, so I refused to pay. I gave 'em the keys and told 'em where it was, but damned if they didn't send a bill collector after me. You'd think I was a murderer or something the way they've hounded me. So I'm skipping out, got a good job and real pretty gal waiting for me up in Canada, unless that bill collector finds me first."

Abernathy could see the boy believed him. The next step would be to make Edward like him. "Where's your ma and pa?"

"Ma is working, cracking and picking crabs. Don't have a pa."

"Yeah, that gives us something in common. I didn't have a pa, either." John read trust on the boy's face, a kind of kinship. He, John Abernathy, was changing, he decided. He was being kind and understanding to this boy, and – as he'd just confided to his new little pal – he had a girl waiting for him in Canada.

"Here's twenty bucks," Abernathy said, pulling the twenty that had been in Dodd's shoe from his wallet. "That's more than enough for the gas, oil and the can. Get the gas first, and then we'll make out a grocery list."

"Okay," the boy said, wide-eyed. The twenty-dollar bill was the most money he'd ever held in has hand. He stuffed it into his front pocket and trotted out of the cannery parking lot and down the gravel road.

CHAPTER FORTY-ONE

Tom Houghton took his time going to Winchester Bay. He figured it was like hunting dove with a 22-caliber rifle. The birds were impossible to hit in flight. You had to wait for them to land. Perched on a tree limb, a dove was any easy shot.

He drove to a roadside diner on the outskirts of North Bend. There was a hand-written sign in the window promoting "Breakfast Anytime." It was almost noon, but breakfast food appealed to Tom. He ordered two eggs over easy, a stack of buttermilk pancakes and a side of link sausages. There was a *Coos Bay Times* on the counter. He picked it up and read about the heroics of Jack Portman. When the waitress refilled his coffee, he tapped the article and said, "Helluva kid, huh? The way he risked his neck to save his friends."

"Yeah, but that creep is still out there," the waitress responded as she slid two plates of food in front of him. Her face registered genuine concern. "Two cops were in this morning. They said Nasty Abernathy was on his way to California, but 'til they catch him, I'm keeping a shot-gun under the counter and my door bolted at night."

"They'll catch him," Tom assured her as he began shoveling food into his mouth. He was tempted to tell her that he, personally, ex-Pinkerton man, was hot on the trail – but he never spoke with his mouth full.

Plates and mouth empty, Tom looked up. "Where's the restroom?" He felt pressure building in his lower abdomen. Tom loved link sausages but they gave him gas.

"I'd recommend the Chevron next door."

He paid his bill and mince-stepped to the filling station. He was thankful no one was in the men's room because he barely made it. Sitting on the toilet, he amused himself by reading the graffiti. There's the classic, he thought and grinned. It seemed like it was written inside the stall of every men's room on the nation's highways.

Here I sit brokenhearted, came to shit and only farted

That's not my problem, Tom thought. He scanned the other messages, several replete with crude, lewd drawings. There are a lot of sick people running around, Tom told himself, but damn few as sick as this Abernathy character. Alleged rapist, alleged murderer. Alleged, my ass, he thought. They had him dead to rights. All "alleged" meant was they hadn't proved it in a court of law. He thought about his grandchildren and how the world could be a mean place, especially if you were a woman and found yourself in the wrong place at the wrong time. This made him decide to spend more time with his grandchildren. He began to daydream about the small inboard cabin cruiser he'd looked at in the Bandon boatyard, thirty-five hundred, brand new and fully equipped. Be a great boat for kids. He wouldn't take them out in the ocean, but lakes and bays were safe. He finished his business in the stall, cleaned himself carefully, washed his hands and headed for his car.

Tom was convinced the world would be a better place for the waitress and his grandkids if vermin like Abernathy were removed once and for all. He'd been too quick to climb on his high horse when Ace said "dead or alive."

He cranked up Ace's two-way.

Skipping the military jargon, Tom got right to the point. "So, Ace, let's say I find this scumbag, and let's say it looks like he might get away again, or, let's say he comes after me? Over."

"Self-defense," Ace assured him. "You'll be home free. The best lawyer on the west coast will be looking after your interests. You've got my word on that. Over."

"Ol' Jim McDonnell? He your client? Over."

"Not saying he is, not saying he isn't. But if there's any problem, he'll be the one looking after you. Over."

Tom was nodding his head. "What's in it for me? Over."

Ace answered, "What's fair? Over."

"Thirty-five hundred cash, clean and sweet under the table. Over."

Ace said "Whew," into the speaker, as if the number was a lot more than he thought it should be. After an appropriate pause, he relented. "That's a deal, Sailor. Contact me if you get the deed done, or if you have any other news. Over and out."

* * *

That afternoon Greta's saloon drew people as if it was a magnet and the citizens of the lower Umpqua were metal shavings. Sheriff Henry Stark took over a booth and became the unofficial Sergeant-at-Arms. Greta sat next to him and let Champ keep up with drink orders as best he could.

Around four-thirty, the reporter from the *Oregon Journal*, Larry Smith, finally gained an audience with Greta. His editor had assured a front-page story but Larry knew it would be below the fold. If he could have called in by two o'clock with an update, he might have been bumped up to the second lead and gotten a byline. But the local-yokels had stonewalled him. Still, until the law caught up with Abernathy, it was a breaking story and there'd be another paper tomorrow. Keep digging, he told himself. He was face to face with the local sheriff and the mother of Jack Portman.

"Look, Mrs. Portman," Smith pleaded, "I'd just like to talk to your son for a few minutes to verify the facts."

"What facts might those be?" A tall, lincolnesque looking man said, sliding into the booth. The man extended his hand to the reporter, "James McDonnell, I'm the Portman's attorney. . ."

"Greta, Henry, how are you?" James McDonnell continued. He fixed his eyes on Larry Smith. "Again, what facts have eluded you?"

"Ahhh, the facts about the rescue..."

"I read today's *Coos Bay Times*, I believe the facts were correct as reported. Wouldn't you say so, Sheriff Stark?"

"I'd say so," Henry said. Although he hadn't read the paper, he'd heard the whole story from Jack.

James extended his hands above the table, widening them to help make his point. "Well, there you have it, the full story, verified." He paused and added, "Anything else?"

Smith recognized James McDonnell. The Coos Bay lawyer was big time. Rich and powerful, they called him the Clarence Darrow of the Oregon Coast. What the hell was he doing here? Family lawyer, my eye, Smith thought. What the hell is going on here? It smacked of a cover-up, but what was there to cover up?

Smith appealed to Greta. "I've come all the way from Portland to interview your son. I tried to talk to the Reilly girl, but I can understand why she's upset. I tried to interview the Budge kid too, and again, I can understand why he's not talking. But Jack? He's a true hero. He deserves his place in the limelight."

Greta didn't yield.

Smith played his last card. He squared his shoulders and became righteous. "The public has a right to know."

"Precisely," McDonnell countered. "The public does have a right to know and the *Coos Bay Times* reported it. Accurately, according to the sheriff, and Sheriff Stark's word is held in high regard around here. Face it, my man, you've been scooped."

"Well, then...may I ask you, sheriff, how is the investigation going?"

"Henry," McDonnell said, "Do you have any news for this honorable member of the fourth estate?"

"Only that the search for Abernathy is concentrated on Coos Bay and points south. The fugitive fled my jurisdiction on Sunday. It's not my case anymore."

Smith was, justifiably, frustrated. He'd driven four hours through intermittent rain, put up with the rummy that ran the local newspaper – and he couldn't get a statement from the hero. He tried again. "You don't think there's a possibility he might return to the scene of the crime?"

Henry reached for his Luckies. "That's always a possibility," he said slowly, tapping his cigarette as he spoke, "and we've taken precautions."

An opening! Smith thought. "What precautions?" he shot back, leaning forward.

"Not at liberty to say." Henry placed the cigarette in his mouth. "If I tell you, everybody including the suspect will know, so what would be the point of taking precautions?"

Greta felt sorry for the reporter. "Look, Mr. Smith, hell, I'm going to call you by your first name. Look, Larry, you're fighting a losing battle. But this is a friendly little town so why don't I buy you a drink and you can hang around as long as you please – but you're not talking to my son until..."

McDonnell tag-teamed Greta, "Until the suspect is apprehended." He freed a Crook cigar from his shirt pocket and peeled off the cellophane wrapper.

"That's it," Henry added. "That's all she wrote. Sorry, end of interview." He raked his thumb over the little wheel on his Zippo and a flame sprang to life. "Lights first time, every time," he said. He lit one of his Lucky Strikes and offered the flame to James.

"Thank you. I have one of those, too," James said, guiding his cigar into the fire, "Finest lighter I ever owned."

CHAPTER FORTY-TWO

Kathy had driven to Winchester Bay with her father. They parted at the entrance to The Dock as she went around the building to the outside stairs. Both the screen door and French doors were ajar. She let herself inside.

"Jack."

An hour earlier, Ellen Reilly walked up the same wooden stairway. The doors were ajar then, too. Ellen heard music and entered the apartment without knocking. As if the god of irony was keeping vigil, the lyric, *"If ever a pair of eyes promised paradise, Jezebel, it was you,"* by Frankie Laine was playing on the phonograph.

"I love that song," she said, moving her feet and swaying her hips to the beat.

Jack was startled. "Ellen." He rose to his feet.

"Door was open. I heard the music."

"Well, sure, come on in."

"I'm in," she said, looking around. "I've never been up here before. It's nice."

Jezebel ran its course and a new record dropped into place: *"Jum-bo-li and a crawfish pie and a me-o-my-o, we gonna have big fun on the bayou..."*

Ellen squared her shoulders. "You saved my life last night."

"And vice versa," Jack said. "You were really something. He had me until you cracked him in the head."

She slipped closer and abandoned her script. They put their arms around each other and swayed with the music.

She spoke in a murmur, "I just wanted to see you, thank you."

He brushed an innocent kiss across the top of her head and inhaled her scent. She smelled of her favorite perfume, *Evening in Paris*. He remembered seeing the blue bottle on her dresser. They continued to sway to the music, holding each other gently. She closed her eyes. "I almost died last night. It made me think, you know, about how silly I've been."

He started to protest, "You're not . . ."

She placed her hand over his mouth. "Shush," she whispered, "just listen. It made me think – ask myself, 'what do I really want to do with my life?' It made me think about all the things I've never let myself think about."

She stopped swaying, leaned away from him and looked into his eyes. "You know how you want to go to college?"

It was rhetorical so he didn't answer.

"I'm not going to stay in Reedsport either. I talked to my dad about it this morning. He's going to pay to send me to secretarial school in Roseburg. He said he'd send me to college but I don't want to wait four years to get out into the world. When I get my credentials, I'm going move to Portland and get a job. I'm going to have my own apartment. You can come visit if you want to and we can be friends. After what we've been through, we should always be friends."

"We'll always be friends," he assured her and kissed her forehead.

The record finished. The apartment was soundless except for their breathing.

Click.

The next record dropped onto the turntable. It was the Ink Spots' rendition of *Paper Doll*, one of Greta's records. *"I'm going to buy myself a paper doll to call my own, a doll that other fellows cannot steal..."*

Jack thought about the nights he'd tossed and squirmed in his bed dreaming about Ellen. All the mornings he'd awakened with soiled sheets from love dreams. They had helped each other grow up, he thought, without either of them knowing it. They should always be friends.

"If you ever need me, just call," Jack whispered in her ear.

"Or . . . just pray, like I did last night?"

They held on to each other for a minute or two – then released each other, exchanged smiles and light kisses as tears welled in Ellen's eyes. More tears than when she'd handed him his Letterman ring after the baseball game a million years ago. She went to the door, pausing to blow a kiss as she passed through.

Jack said, "Tim's a great guy."

She replied, "I know, but he's no Jack Portman."

* * *

"Jack?"

Ellen had been gone less than ten minutes.

"Hey, come in," he called, surprised and happy to hear Kathy's voice.

He and Ellen were now "friends", whatever that meant. Close? Even if faraway?

Emotionally bonded by a shared trauma? It was impossible for him to decipher his feelings toward her. It wasn't marriage type love, yet it was a forever love.

He greeted Kathy with a question: "You hear about last night?"

"Yes, of course. Everybody's heard about it." Impulsively, she rushed to him. "That's why I came over." She clutched him. He smelled faintly of lilacs and a cheap perfume. She lurched back.

"You smell like perfume."

"Really, Kathy," he said. "Ellen came over to thank me, the girl from last night. We hugged each other. She'd been through a lot."

He put his hands on Kathy's shoulders and looked her in the eye. "Abernathy might have killed her last night and God knows what else."

He turned away from her, walked into the kitchen and opened the fridge. "I'm going to have a beer. You want one?"

Kathy had followed him and saw it was Olympia beer – their beer – and wished she'd never mentioned lilacs and cheap perfume.

"I'd love one," she said, thinking this bottle didn't have to have four dots; she already had a four-dot label in her panty drawer.

CHAPTER FORTY-THREE

Tom Houghton parked in the community lot near the fishing docks. A light mist had settled over the harbor. Planning for various contingencies, he'd brought a rain-proof jacket along with binoculars and his 30-30, lever-action Winchester rifle. The rifle was in the trunk. "Dead or alive," he said, staring at the rifle.

The rifle was too obvious; the army issue 45 Caliber Browning Automatic sidearm he carried under the front seat was a better option. He strapped on his shoulder holster, slid the hand-gun into its holster and patted it. He slipped on the rain jacket to disguise his intentions, picked up the binoculars and walked down to the marina.

He followed procedure. First, check out the obvious. He walked up and down the docks until satisfied his prey had not stowed the missing longboat in the main marina. Next, he rented a skiff with an outboard and slowly toured the north end of the harbor. He checked at the floating Gas 'N Bait store. The owner said he would have remembered a long boat. The north harbor tour took about an hour and a half. When he returned the skiff, he showed the attendant his Pinkerton ID. "I'm looking for a stolen boat. If you wanted to hide a sixteen-footer, what would you do?"

The man shrugged indifferently.

Houghton handed him a five-dollar bill.

"I'd go up river, there's a thousand places to hide a boat between here and Reedsport."

Houghton dismissed this. He didn't think Abernathy would go up river. If he was here, he was somewhere on the bay.

"Where else?"

"Well, the south side of the bay is shallow, no place to really put in over there, except, maybe by the old cannery, but that docks gone to rot. Still, I suppose, in a pinch, you might be able to stick a boat in there."

"This cannery, where exactly is it?"

"You drive here from Coos Bay?"

"Yeah."

"Remember passing a Flying A station?"

"Sure do. On the bay side of 101."

"There's a gravel road just past the Flying A. Turn right, it'll wind around a hill and take you back to the bay, right to the cannery."

* * *

The boy, Edward, returned to the cannery lugging two five-gallon gas cans. John helped Edward carry the cans down the steps to the boat.

"Where's the oil?" John asked.

"Already mixed," the boy said proudly. "Eight to one, that's what Mr. Sylvester told me."

"What'd you tell him?" John asked. "Did you remember it's a secret I'm here?"

"Told him some tourist-type fishermen ran out of gas and I was helping them out. He said if I brought the cans back he'd refund the ten-dollar deposit. Gas and oil was just over five bucks."

"That's all you told him."

"He was busy, didn't ask me anything."

"He believe you?"

"Sure. People run out of gas all the time, that's why he has all the cans."

John relaxed. "You did good, Eddie. Hell, you did great! Now you need to go for groceries." He began listing them: "Bread. Squeeze it first and get the softest loaf of white they have. Cheese. Two pounds of baloney, a jar of mustard, crackers, sardines, get a couple of cans of sardines, the kind with the key on top...and peanut butter...you going to be able to remember all this?"

"Yeah, sure, I go to the store for my ma and her boyfriend all the time."

"They let you buy cigarettes?"

"If I say they're for my ma, they do, she smokes the long kind in the red pack, Pall Malls."

"Well, we don't want to make the storekeeper suspicious, get a pack of your ma's cigarettes, too.

"What else?"

"Couple of Almond Joy bars. For you." John reached over and rubbed the top of the boy's head. John didn't know the boy's last name, but he felt close to him. Go figure, John thought. Oddly enough, he had a good feeling about Portman too. Portman hadn't shot him because Portman respected him: the warrior's creed.

If he were in the army, he'd want a guy like Portman in the foxhole with him, another warrior, not a sniveling coward. Portman was willing to fight for his woman . . . hell, Jack was probably after the faggot for messing around with her, and he, John Abernathy, just happened to be in the car. The more John thought about it, the more the explanation made sense. The faggot had sure as shit run like hell when he saw Portman headed for his sissy-ass little car.

Before the kid and Portman, the last person he'd taken a liking to was Terry Dodd.

But even the kid, Eddie, had a lot more spunk than Dodd. Come to think of it, he hadn't liked Dodd all that much; he'd liked his car. When he sold his boat in Canada, he'd buy a pick-up.

"Sure you'll remember everything at the store?" Big John asked Edward.

"Bread, baloney, cheese, mustard, crackers, sardines-with-key, peanut butter, Pall Malls and Almond Joys," Eddie recited.

John rubbed the boy's head again. "Good. Tillamook cheese if they have it." He reached into his billfold and pulled out another twenty. He pressed it into the boy's hand, "Whatever is left over is yours. Now get going, I'm half starved."

Abernathy gassed up, stowed his fuel and waited a half-hour for Edward to return. Then he began to fidget. How long could it take to go to the store in Winchester Bay?

What if somebody who knew the kid saw him packing an armload of groceries and started asking questions? Any number of things could go wrong. The cops, dumb as they were, could be looking for him north as well as south. He had his gas, why push his luck? Maybe he should move on, cruise along the shoreline until dark. After dark he'd be safe; he could drop anchor, catch some sleep and wait for the sun to peep over the hills. He'd get in line with the fishing boats just as he'd done in Coos Bay and follow them over the bar into the Pacific. Simple. Easy. Canada.

And Debbie, his fiancé in Canada, now had a name, the same first name as his favorite movie actress, Debbie Reynolds.

He told himself he worried too much. Relax. No one was looking for him here. He could trust the kid. Probably a long walk to the store. Eddie would be back soon. Eddie would go as fast as he could, take every short cut, he was a great kid. Couldn't be easy living in a trailer, John thought, only thing worse than a houseboat was a trailer. No place to hide in a trailer when the kid's mother serviced her boy friend. Kids would tease him about being trailer trash and he wasn't a big kid, couldn't beat the shit out them, but maybe he was a ballplayer. If he was a good ballplayer they wouldn't tease him. It looked like he had a pretty good arm, John thought, remembering Eddie's motion when he was throwing rocks. Yeah, the kid will be back soon, John assured himself, and the first thing he'd do is make a baloney sandwich, slathered with mustard. He felt saliva rise in his mouth as he thought about the sandwich.

What about the gas station? Did Mr. Sylvester, or whatever the grease monkey's name was, believe the boy? Or would he call the sheriff and say there was something strange going on at the cannery? But why wouldn't the guy in the gas station believe the boy? Why would he think twice about it? He'd been paid, what did he care?

Still, just to be on the safe side, it might be smart to wait someplace where he could keep an eye on the parking lot.

* * *

Homer "Sly" Sylvester's mind was on the valve job he was performing on a '48 Chrysler, so, in point of fact, he hadn't thought twice about the kid buying gas. Wishfully, he hoped the fishermen would keep the gas cans. They'd only cost him a buck each.

Tom Houghton drove up to the gas pump. "Fill it up with the Ethyl."

"Yes, sir. Want your oil checked?"

"Nope, just had it changed, thanks for asking though. Say, you have any strangers show up here today? Big guy, probably on foot, looking to buy gasoline?"

Sly shook his head *no*.

Tom pulled out his wallet and flashed his expired Pinkerton ID.

"I'm a private investigator. Friend of mine's boat was stolen in Coos Bay. I'm trying to help him find it. My friend is a workingman like you and me, needs his boat to make a living. I thought the sneaking bastard of a thief might bring the boat up here and stow it 'til folks stop looking, then sell it."

Sly was impressed with the official looking Pinkerton card. He finished pumping the gas and hung up the nozzle.

"I'd remember if a big guy had come by," he offered, "A kid was in here a while ago. Normally, he don't have two cents to rub together but he bought two cans and ten gallons of gas and paid with a twenty. Had me mix for an outboard. Said some tourists ran out of gas. They do that, you know, come down here, rent a boat, don't have a clue about boats or fishing, so I didn't think much about it, except, generally folks only buy one can of gas."

"And why would they send a kid?" Tom raised his eyebrows.

"Dunno," Sly answered. "Why don't you ask him? Lives just up that road." He pointed. "Him and his old lady bunk in the trailer parked in front of the old cannery."

"I'll do just that, and I thank you," Tom said.

CHAPTER FORTY-FOUR

A few miles away, holding hands, Jack and Kathy walked down the wooden sidewalk toward the pier and Marina. Without realizing it, Kathy was taking deep gulps of sea air, unconsciously trying to purge the scent of the other woman from her memory. If Ellen and Jack had a weird bond, Kathy thought, she and Jack had a stronger bond, a l-o-v-e bond. But why was he waiting? She'd said it. She'd committed. Why didn't he?

"Is there something you want to tell me," she probed.

He sensed she was asking him to say he loved her. She's very pretty and has a great body, he thought, remembering how lithe and supple her bare fanny had felt in his hand. He was, after all, now a grown-up. She was rich and was hot for him. Her father's bark had been a lot worse than his bite. He wanted her. The key was saying he loved her. Not "I think I'm falling in love with you . . ." but flat out, " I love you."

He stopped, showed her a wry smile and said the three little words.

Girlishly, she slapped him on the shoulder. "Now was that so hard?" She put her arms around him. "Kiss me. Right here in the open in front of the world."

He had no choice but to oblige. Kathy hoped Ellen Reilly was watching.

* * *

The Ambassador awakened about noon on Wednesday. He'd fallen asleep in his buck-skins. He went into his bathroom to urinate. Afterwards, he took a critical look at himself in the mirror and the image startled him. He looked absurd in buckskins. Indians didn't have facial hair. He looked like an old mountain man. Such irony, he thought, a wolf in sheep's clothing, and even if he shaved the beard, he was still, irrevocably, Caucasian. The revelation incited his thinking process. Within the next few days – or so – he would visit his friend, Adams Armstrong, and show him his crossbow. He'd sent for the mail-order crossbow on an impulse. It had been advertised in *Argosy Magazine*. Its arrival teased his imagination. He employed the old "what if" game. "What if all weapons post-dating the crossbow were banned by the United Nations?"

There would be no guns. No tanks. No bombs.

It seemed an elegant solution to mankind's escalating weapons race. However, development of his thesis was stalled by lack of information. When was the crossbow invented? Fourteenth century? Could there be a loophole? When had the Chinese invented firecrackers? Would that legalize gunpowder? Hadn't the Huns used crossbows against the Romans in 200 A.D.? That certainly predated the advent of explosive powder. Leave it to the Germans, he sighed. But he needed to know for sure. He would write his brother in Boston. His brother, a Harvard professor, would send him the definitive books on crossbows and Chinese fireworks.

Maybe he couldn't save the world, yet there was no harm trying.

His path to the next level of enlightenment decided, he made coffee, filled one of his pipes and began examining his crossbow.

As he fiddled with his new toy, he launched into a lecture, one of his favorites. He'd delivered it many times before – verbatim.

"Freedom is a narrow ridge to walk. To define it is next to impossible but remarkably easy, because freedom is the essential contradiction. If you're totally free you answer to nobody. Yet, my friends, if you're truly free you answer to everybody. That's the narrow ridge. Because it's not about your freedom, it's about everybody's freedom."

The Ambassador took a deep breath. "You wonder why they call you crazy? You should get one of those tape recorders and play yourself back. You'd say, 'Listen to him! He's one crazy old white man.'"

The Ambassador burst into laughter and walked out the door, still carrying his crossbow. He walked over to his favorite vantage point of the Umpqua, the platform he'd built just above the concrete steps that led down to his dilapidated wooden dock. The great green river was a nearly a half-mile wide at this point. There were several boats trolling for salmon fifty yards from shore. He wondered if he could shoot a salmon with his crossbow.

CHAPTER FORTY-FIVE

Glenn Grafton returned to his store from lunch at the Horseshoe Café and found his daughter, Rosie, in tears. This troubled him because Rosie was the only person on earth he cared about. In contrast to her mother, Rosie was a fine cook and a tidy housekeeper. His late wife, Melanie, had been a bad housekeeper and had asked him to buy far too many material things. Why would you spend good money on something as frivolous as window coverings? Melanie had also stopped giving him sex. Sex should be a husband's right. For a woman, sex should be like taxes; you pay whether you like it or not.

Although he hadn't told his daughter, Glenn Grafton was more relieved than saddened when his wife died of stomach cancer. Her time had come; it was as simple as that. It wasn't his fault. Nothing he could do about it. Walking around with a black armband and acting grief-stricken would serve no purpose – it certainly wouldn't get the special order for the Barney's kitchen counters finished any sooner. Besides, as the preacher said, "She was in a better place."

His brother, Wayne, who in Glenn's estimation had always been a lazy, loud-mouthed sneak and liar, had closed his grocery store in Lakeside in order to maintain a vigil next to Melanie's deathbed. This hadn't fooled Glenn. He knew Wayne did it to show up his older brother and make points with the townspeople. Glenn suspected Wayne of wanting to sleep with Melanie when she was healthy. The Bible said it was a sin to *covet thy neighbor's wife*, therefore, by comparison, *coveting your brother's wife* had to be a real whopper of a sin.

He wondered if Wayne coveted Rosie, too. He didn't see overt signs this was the case, but he was watchful. Twisted as he was, Glenn didn't covet Rosie, either, at least not any more. She was his creation. She was the one and only decent human being on the planet. Now, returning from lunch, here was his Rosie sitting in front of the cash register, sobbing, and saying she didn't know how she'd be able to face any one in Reedsport ever again.

He finally got her to tell him what happened. With her heart crushed and her self-esteem in tatters, Rosie's rendition of her relationship with Sheriff Stark mixed fantasies with facts. According to Rosie, Sheriff Henry Stark had lured her to his bed with promises of marriage.

Now, according to an irrefutable source, the sheriff was carrying on with Greta Portman, *whom everybody knew was a loose woman*.

"God only knows what goes on in that apartment above the saloon," Rosie's informant had said. One thing Rosie knew for certain, thanks a close friend of the telephone operator, was the sheriff had proposed to Greta when he should have been busy trying to catch the murderer, John "Nasty" Abernathy. But Rosie didn't blame Greta. It was the womanizing sheriff who had betrayed and humiliated her.

Grafton listened to the story and pondered Rosie's plight for a full fifteen minutes. His daughter had been "betrayed and humiliated" by a man who was supposed to represent the law. It was the proverbial *Last Straw*.

Calmly, Glenn told his daughter, who was feeling better for having gotten everything off her sizable chest, "Don't you worry, Rosie, I'll look after you. I'll take care of that sheriff too."

Glenn Grafton owned a Marlin 22-long rifle with a peep sight. He used it to plunk crows brazen enough to invade Rosie's vegetable garden. He hadn't decided if he would merely wound Henry Stark or kill him. One way or the other, he'd teach him a lesson. No man could play fast and loose with his daughter and get away with it. He figured locating the sheriff would be easy enough; he'd stake out Greta Portman's tavern in Winchester Bay. Hang out in the community parking lot. Sooner or later, Henry Stark would show up there. He'd shoot him, jump in his car and escape while everyone was running to see what happened. No one would suspect *him*.

* * *

"Care for one of your martinis, Mr. McDonnell?" Greta asked after reporter, Smith, had skulked away from the booth.

"Please, call me James."

"James it is," she smiled. "Then, James, may I offer you a martini? On the house."

"Little early in the day, but what the hell. I might end up having two and making Kathy drive me home. She went up your backstairs to see Jack, I'm assuming he's home."

"He is, and I'm sure he'll be glad for the company."

She turned to Henry. "How about you, sheriff? Can I get you anything?"

He said, "You can both call me Henry." The three of them exchanged smiles.

"I'm on duty," Henry answered the question, "but if I weren't, I'd sure take a glass of your Sauvignon Blanc."

Twinkle-in-the-eye may be an over-used description, but there was definitely one in Henry's eyes, which Greta noticed – and returned, that is, twinkled, back.

"When you come off duty I'll scare up a glass. Might even join you." She excused herself and went to the bar.

James didn't miss the exchange. "You didn't strike me as a wine connoisseur."

"Well, you know what they say about a book and its cover."

"She's a fine woman," James said, adding, "Her Jack is a fine young man too, which leads me to the obvious question. What are you doing to protect him?"

The deftness with which James had switched subjects caught Henry off guard. *Protect him?* Henry thought for a second. "You mean from Abernathy?" Another pause. "You think he might come back here?"

"Can't dismiss the possibility," James leaned forward, inviting Henry to join him in a confidential discussion. "He told those two kids he was going to California. Wouldn't surprise me if he did the opposite. My source tells me he might have stolen a boat. This is the first harbor north of Coos Bay."

"Is your source the Coos County Sheriff?"

"No. The police, present company excluded, have gotten nowhere. For God's sake, Henry, they put Jack in handcuffs last night while the killer got away. I hired a private detective."

Henry nodded. "Him doubling back crossed my mind. That's why I didn't want Jack talking to reporters."

"That was your idea?" James sounded impressed.

"Yeah. You don't have to be Einstein to figure Abernathy might want revenge."

"I agree."

"Mind you, I believe Jack is perfectly safe. I doubt if Nasty reads a newspaper with his morning coffee. Probably doesn't know where Jack is. Still, it's better if Jack keeps a low profile until this is over and done with."

Greta returned with a gin martini, straight up, olives glistening through the clear glass.

James took a sip, closed his eyes and smacked his lips. "Arrest this woman, sheriff, this martini is too good to be legal."

Greta accepted the compliment and went back to work. The afternoon charters were coming off the water, unloading their catch and making a beeline to her saloon.

And the two men, now on first name basis, clearly had more to talk about.

"Let's say Abernathy did come back to Winchester Bay" James resumed. "Let's say my detective located him and called me. Off the record, how would you deal with it?"

His cigar had gone out. James plucked Henry's lighter off the table, flipped the lid, thumbed the wheel and watched as a new flame sprang to life. "Every time," he said, nodding his head in appreciation.

James blew a series of smoke rings toward the bar and waited for an answer.

CHAPTER FORTY-SIX

Tom Houghton turned onto the gravel road and followed it to the cannery. He pulled in front of the trailer and waited. Usually, if you park in front of a trailer, who ever lives inside will peek outside. No one peeked. Tom got out of the car and rapped on the door. Nobody home.

He felt a rush of adrenaline. Could Abernathy be hiding under the dock in back of the abandoned cannery? If so, had he killed the kid who fetched the gas? From what he'd read in the paper, Abernathy was capable of killing his own mother. What chance would a kid have.

Part of him hoped it wasn't Abernathy who sent the kid for gas. The other part hoped it was. There was a lot of money at stake. It was time to find out. He opened his trunk and removed the 30-30 Winchester. Quietly, he pulled the lever, moving a round into the chamber. "Ready or not," he said under his breath. He left the trunk lid open. The slam of a car trunk was a sound that carried. The soft crunch of tires on gravel, the rap on a door, those sounds were absorbed by the wind and the waves, but a trunk lid coming down, metal striking metal, that would send a warning signal.

Tom crept around the side of the cannery, dropped on his belly and inched forward to peer down the embankment. There it was, the stolen boat. Just as the owner described it. But there was no one in it.

Abernathy watched Tom Houghton from the moment the car turned into the abandoned cannery's parking lot. He wasn't a cop, Abernathy decided. Eddie had said he had no pa. Maybe the guy was one of his ma's boyfriends, an old lecher stopping by for a poke from Eddie's old lady. But what the hell was he doing with the rifle? Maybe he was one of those salmon-lovers who liked to shoot seals from the bank – but Abernathy hadn't seen any seals in this part of the bay. Maybe, maybe, maybe...John thought. Best to watch.

Tom walked around the side of the cannery. He's going to see my boat, John realized. What will he do when he sees my boat?

Tom returned to the parking lot just as Eddie arrived with the groceries. Both Tom and Eddie stopped in their tracks. Tom spoke first, "Hi, kid, don't get the wrong idea. I'm not here to hurt you."

"Then what are you doing with that gun?"

Good kid, John thought. It was obvious the boy didn't know the man. Eddie had not betrayed him.

"I'm a police officer," Tom said.

"You don't look like a cop. Your car don't look like a no cop car."

"I'm a private policeman, I can show you identification, son. If I show you my ID, will you answer some questions?"

The boy nodded, a reluctant yes. He had already decided not to tell the man anything. If the old guy was looking for his new friend because he hadn't paid for the lousy car, well, it was just too bad.

Abernathy watched Tom walk slowly toward the boy. Option one was to work his way behind him, get as close as he could and rush him – bust him across the head, grab the rifle and the groceries and make a run for it, either in the old guy's car or by boat. But, old or not, the man looked like he could handle the rifle. It was a big parking lot. Running on gravel was noisy. The man could wheel and shoot in the blink of an eye. John didn't want to die; it wouldn't be fair to Debbie.

Option two: slip back to the boat and gun it into the bay, get lost among the other boats and somehow get back into the Pacific, or...go up river. He had gas, he could last another day without food. Debbie was waiting in Canada. He backtracked to the boat. The engine started on the second pull. By the time Tom heard the outboard and ran to the decrepit pier, Abernathy was fifty yards from shore. Tom didn't have a clear shot. In frustration, he pointed the barrel into the air and reeled off three shots before racing back to his car. Huffing and puffing, he contacted Ace via the *Advanced Communications Exchange*.

Ace knew exactly where his client was. He placed a phone call to The Dock Tavern. So close, Tom thought. Thirty-five hundred bucks, gone like a dove clearing the treetops. But he should still be in line for a bonus. He'd done something the cops couldn't do. He had located the elusive Mr. Abernathy.

* * *

Greta paged James to the phone. He listened, said "Good job" and placed the phone on the receiver. He walked back to the booth.

"He's here. My man spotted him leaving a shut-down cannery over in the south side of the bay. He has a '16-foot outboard of the open, longboat design'," James said, repeating Ace's description.

"We're in business," Henry said, snuffing out a Lucky. "Since he knows he's been spotted, he'll likely head out to sea. Wait while I call the Coast Guard."

Henry hurried to the phone. The bar was noisy; people were talking loudly so they could be heard over the jukebox. He wasn't worried about being overheard. As he waited for the Coast Guard dispatcher, he scanned the faces of the fishermen lined up along the bar. Harry Norton was there.

The dispatcher picked up on the third ring. Henry identified himself, described the fugitive and his boat and asked them to block the route over the bar into the Pacific.

He tapped Harry Norton on the shoulder. "Need to talk to you outside, Harry."

"Am I under arrest?" the skipper joked. He was in a good mood, they'd boated two Chinook, one over 25 pounds.

"You will be if you don't set your beer down and get your ass outside."

The skipper obeyed.

Henry could feel Greta's eyes on him. With a head gesture, he directed her to the end of the bar. James joined them. "Abernathy is boxed in out in the bay. We're going after him. I don't want the others to know. If we get a lot of boats out there trying to help, it'll turn into a circus."

Outside, Henry advised the confused skipper. "I'm conscripting your boat, Harry. You are going to help us catch us a bad guy."

"Why me?" the skipper started to complain.

"I've offered a five-thousand dollar reward," James told him. "We get him! Half of it is yours."

The skipper smiled. "I volunteer." With that, Harry bolted toward his boat to fire up the engine.

From their conversation earlier, Henry understood what James McDonnell didn't want. He didn't want Abernathy in jail. He wanted him dead, right here and now. That had left Henry's own ethics twisting in the wind. But James was persuasive. "What have you really got on this sick son of a bitch, Henry?"

"I can put him in Reedsport the night of the rape. The Ambassador saw him driving up Main Street. The Preston kid at the Texaco told my deputy that Abernathy asked for directions to Lighthouse Beach. The Ambassador and kid put him in the proximity."

James shook his head. "That adds up to zero. Further, it's only relevant to the rape and Betty Wagner can't identify him. There goes your rape charge. As for the murder," James argued, "maybe you can connect him to the car, but so what? His buddy gave him a ride? Even if you have fingerprints, it's circumstantial. And whom did he kill? A prominent citizen? No. A hapless, out-of-work mill worker nobody gives a damn about.

"I talked to the coroner," James continued. "Cause of death was a broken neck. They'd say Dodd fell from the loft in the barn. I could make mincemeat out of the prosecution's case. Hell, even a half-ass, local attorney should get reasonable doubt. But we wouldn't be that lucky. This has been front-page news, so you know some fire-in-his-belly attorney from Portland will take the case to make a reputation."

"What about the kidnapping?" Henry asked.

"What kidnapping? That'll end up being four kids on a joyride. Nasty forgot to load his rifle. The police on the scene assumed Jack was the lawbreaker. They'll say Tim Budge and his what's-her-name girlfriend made up the story to cover the accident – to protect Jack, whom, the cops who cuffed him will testify, was drinking. Or they could say all three *teenage* boys were fighting over the girl. Jack used to date her, you know. Worst case, they'll call me to testify and under oath, I'll have to admit Jack was drinking wine in my home. Jack is a wonderful young man and I don't want to put his future in jeopardy. No, Henry, we need to end it here and now, because this Abernathy will rape again and kill again and when he does, the guilt will be ours to share."

Jaws set, the co-conspirators strode side-by-side toward the marina.

"James, can I ask you one question?"

"Certainly."

"Do you know Judge Stoval in Roseburg? What I mean is, do you know him well enough to get him out of my hair?"

"Even better, I will make the judge your staunchest ally." James felt a smidgen of guilt for having sicced the judge on Henry in the first place.

Henry took a deep breath. He was comfortable with his decision. He took two more regular-length strides and shifted into double-time. The long-legged James McDonnell followed closely behind, inhaling sea air into his lungs, feeling himself gain strength with every stride.

Skipper Norton was waiting for them – his idling engine gently stirring the bay water.

Impulsively, Henry made a theatrical, sweeping gesture. "Climb aboard, Admiral. Or should I say, Deputy James McDonnell? Let's get this thing done."

CHAPTER FORTY-SEVEN

Jack and Kathy were sitting on the end of a pier, legs dangling, a school of baitfish churning the water below them.

Jack had told her about following Tim's Henry J into Coos Bay. He'd told her about the *accident*, Tim's flight, the fight, the gun and the handcuffs. He left out the part about squeezing the trigger. Hearing the story, Kathy understood why Ellen felt compelled to visit him. Still, she sensed that Ellen was after *her* Jack. She had competition. Too bad for Ellen, Kathy thought. He loves me, but, to be safe, she would need to seal their love. Surely, after that, Jack would be faithful.

"Do you want to go back?" Jack asked.

She squeezed his hand. "Can we just sit here for a few minutes? I have something to tell you."

"Sure. Tell me."

"I have to go away for a while. My mother wants to go to Europe. Not for long, a month, I think. Are you going to be good while I'm away? Will you wait for me?"

"You know I will." It was what his mother called, "A little white lie." The kind intended to hurt no one. Besides, he just might wait. Probably would. How did he know? Everything was happening so fast. All he'd been able to do was *react*; there had been no time to think beyond *react*. Jack also felt a jolt of jealousy. He imagined a handsome European with a sexy, romantic-sounding accent approaching Kathy in a sidewalk café. One thing would lead to another.

"The question is, will *you* be good?" Jack countered.

"You never have to worry about me, darling." She meant it. This was her man. She was thinking they should go to college together. She wanted to tell him about the summer job her father was inventing for him. *No.* It would be best if he heard about it from Nate Clarke.

"Remember our second beer?" She snuggled close. "Four dots. I kept the label. I knew we were meant for each other the first time we kissed."

"I remember," Jack assured her.

"Before I go to Europe," she wanted to sound nonchalant, "we're going to do something about our four dots."

It was what Jack wanted to hear and he squeezed her hand.

"But you have to make me a promise, Jacky?"

She'd called him darling and Jacky. What should he call her? *Lamb* – as in Mountain Lamb? Lambs were weak and submissive. She was about to be submissive, but she wasn't weak. She was demanding. So be it. The word *Baby* came to mind. Bogart used it. Good enough for Bogart, good enough for him.

"Sure, Baby." He agreed to make the promise.

"Promise you'll never drink Olympia beer with another girl?"

"That's it?" Jack said "That's easy. I'm thinking about switching to martinis."

Three gunshots sounded in the distance.

"What was that?" Kathy wasn't alarmed, simply curious.

"Probably somebody shooting seals or sea lions."

"Why would they do that?"

"They eat the salmon. No salmon, no fishermen."

"That's sad," Kathy said. "The seals can't help it. They were here first."

"I suppose," Jack acknowledged, "but the fishermen don't see it that way."

Jack's eyes were drawn to the action on the bay, specifically, to an approaching boat. It was moving fast, dangerously fast considering its distance from the marina. He saw the large man in the stern. Could it be Abernathy? It looked like Abernathy. He felt peculiarly cavalier. It was definitely Abernathy and he didn't care. He knew he should leap to his feet – race back to the tavern and alert the sheriff and Coast Guard. He should be a modern day Paul Revere, "Abernathy is coming, Abernathy is coming . . ."

But he just sat, dangling his feet. The boat veered away from the marina and toward the center of the bay. Jack averted his eyes. Abernathy wasn't his problem. He felt an abnormal kinship to the brute from Florence – a macabre brotherhood.

Rescuing poor Betty and challenging Abernathy were the best things that ever happened to him. It had turned him into the town hero and elevated his love life from non-existent to very, very promising. His mind flashed to the good-looking waitress at the drive-in. If Kathy was going to Europe, well, he was tired of being the town monk. The confrontation with Abernathy forced him to examine his own dark side. He could attack without remorse and pull a trigger without thinking of the consequences. This self-analysis led him to believe the difference between he and Abernathy wasn't a wide chasm requiring a huge leap; it was a thin line needing only a little skip to jump over. He'd come close to *raping* Ellen – at least twice– if he believed his mother – "If they say no, you stop, it's as simple as that" – Ellen had said stop and it took every ounce of his will-power . . .he'd been tempted not to stop with Kathy. . . she'd been so willing . . . but with all those people upstairs?

He'd squeezed the trigger with Abernathy. Would he have regretted it if a bullet had zoomed down the barrel and through the dark of night until it collided with Abernathy's skull? He'd never know for sure.

Kathy paid no attention to the boat on the bay. She had her own agenda. She moved Jack's hand to her inner thigh. "Mother and daddy are going to see the travel agent on Friday. I'm staying home."

With so many thoughts racing through his mind, Jack was mildly surprised he could be so easily aroused. He pressed his fingers into Kathy's V-zone and kissed her ear. "What time should I come over?"

CHAPTER FORTY-EIGHT

John opened the throttle on his outboard and steered toward the north end of the bay. The town sat up on a hill, safe from storm-driven high tides. He saw the marina. He saw two people sitting on the end of the pier at the end of the parking lot. He saw The Dock Tavern and the stores and cafes that shared the busy street.

He sped within fifty yards of Jack and Kathy. His eyes were fixed on a neon light with the word Café. It was three doors down from The Dock. He wished he were inside the café. He would order a T-bone steak and a baked potato heaped with butter. He'd eat the green beans first, then the potato, then the steak, saving the best for last. He'd go to the tavern and use his Jake Sloan ID to buy a beer.

But he knew he couldn't go ashore – and it was Terry Dodd's fault for being such a chickenshit little whiner. He decided he wouldn't tell Debbie about killing Sloan and Dodd, or about the logging camp whore, or the two women he'd overpowered to show them who the boss was. Everything that had happened before he'd met his true love would be forgotten. He was a different person now. He might tell her about Eddie and his friend, Jack Portman.

A few boats were still chugging toward the marina with their afternoon catch; but most of the boats were in their slips. That was a sign the sea was getting rough, but so what, he had a seaworthy craft with a deep keel – where in the hell were the channel markers? There was a freighter creeping toward the bar, he could follow it, but it was too slow. John saw the north jetty and figured he could run parallel with it until he spotted the markers. A fisherman on the jetty waved at him as he raced past. He gauged his speed at twenty miles per hour. How many knots was that? Sixteen or seventeen? Who cared about knots? Fast was fast, slow was slow and he was wide open. This was all his boat could do.

His back was to the town and marina. He didn't see the cruiser, a lone salmon charter boat, pulling away from the docks, a one-boat armada going against the flow of incoming traffic. He did see the Coast Guard cutter heading hell-bent toward the white-capped waves marking the exit from the bay. To Abernathy, the Coast Guard craft looked like a PT boat from a World War II movie, its American flag was flapping behind it like an aviator's scarf from an open cockpit. Were they after him? He didn't know. Had to figure they were. That was the only way to play it. The closer he got to the ocean bar, the higher the whitecaps. Double-trouble, he thought, rough water and the Coast Guard. The freighter would get through easily, he calculated. Could he use the freighter to run interference? One wrong move and he would be swamped. He cut his speed and tried to think. He could ditch the boat on the jetty and make a run for it over the dunes. No. He wasn't going to give up his boat. The boat was his ticket to Canada. To Debbie.

John steered in a wide circle, trying to get his bearings. As he arced around, he surveyed the subtly changing picture in front of him. Where was the river channel? Another freighter, one he'd seen earlier, was coming out of the river channel. The river itself looked miles wide where it merged with the bay. But half of that was a shallow, tidal flat, no more than a few feet deep at ebb and low tide. He whipped his boat to the port side of the freighter and aimed himself in the opposite direction. Where was he? The water and approaching darkness confused his sense of direction. Left was north, he told himself, hang close to the north shore, and veer east, inland. That had to be the river channel, at least it would be plenty deep for his boat. The fog was beginning to sit on the water. Where was the sun? The sun was due west. Hurry, fog, he thought. It would be dark in an hour. He'd head up the Umpqua, tuck in somewhere and wait for darkness. He looked over his shoulder; the Coast Guard must not have seen him. They weren't coming after him – so far, so good.

For the first time, John Abernathy wished he hadn't sidetracked into Reedsport, stopped at the Texaco, listened to the kid and learned about Beach Night. He wished he'd listened to Dodd and kept going to Coos Bay. But then he would never have become friends with Jack and Eddie, and he would have never met his true love, Debbie.

CHAPTER FORTY-NINE

Adams Armstrong entered The Dock tavern several minutes after Sheriff Stark, Lawyer McDonnell and Captain Norton had slipped away.

"How was the fishing today?" Adams asked any one who cared to answer.

"Good from what I hear," Greta said, motioning for Champ to stay put and let her take care of this customer.

Adams didn't need to place his order. He had an arrangement with Greta.

She served him a tall glass of fresh draft. "How you been, Adams? Haven't seen you and your friend, The Ambassador, around much lately."

Adams took a long sip, smacked his lips and said, "I've been doing some trout fishing and The Ambassador has ordered a crossbow."

"What's he going to do with that?"

Adams shrugged. "Who knows?" He joked, "Maybe try to shoot a big Chinook in the river. He's just crazy enough to try."

Greta laughed. "He does weigh in pretty heavy on the weird scale, but he has a good soul."

Adams nodded, "He's a good friend. I shouldn't make fun."

"It's okay to make fun when it's about a friend to a friend," Greta assured him.

Adams finished his beer, paid leaving a fifty cent tip, and left.

"Champ," Greta called to her bartender, "Take some quarters out of the register and feed the jukebox. I want music so loud it rattles my dishes upstairs. Let's liven things up. I expect a big crowd tonight."

What a week, she thought. It was only Wednesday and there had been a rape, a murder, the suspension of her own chastity, a heroic rescue by her son, and soon, a shootout somewhere on the bay or up the river.

Abernathy would be no match for her Henry. That much she was sure of.

The days may seem long, she thought, but years fly by faster than clouds on windy days. Her little boy was headed for college. Was it her turn? Reno? Marry Henry? Why not? She'd give the Chevy to Jack and buy the blue, '54 Mercury in Butch Thompson's showroom. They'd drive to Reno in style and stay in a nice hotel. Do it right: Flowers and champagne. Play Blackjack all day and make love all night.

Outside, Adams headed for his pick-up. As he made his way across the parking lot he saw Glenn Grafton lurking near the sheriff's car. He took a closer look. Grafton was lifting a pint bottle of liquor to his lips. He also had a small rifle balanced in the crook of his right arm.

"Hey, Geronimo! You see that no good, piece-of-shit sheriff in there?"

Adams stopped. He knew Glenn Grafton knew his name. It was Adams – after the second and sixth presidents of the United States – not Geronimo. Not a sarcastic "Chief" as the state cop had called him when he could have helped them catch the murderer.

Adams knew Glenn Grafton's brother, Wayne. He was a good customer. Wayne treated him with respect. This Grafton, however, based on everything Adams had overheard, was an awful man: An inferior human who wouldn't/couldn't address him without prefacing it with an insult. Adams turned toward Grafton. "He's not in there."

"Well, I got business with that fornicating bastard and figure, sooner or later he's going to have to come back here for his car."

Adams began walking slowly toward Grafton.

"Personal business," Grafton added.

Grafton took another pull from his bottle.

Adams slowly closed the distance.

Grafton raised his 22-rifle and pointed it at Adams. "I know what you want, Injun. You want a pull from my whisky. Too bad. I ain't never gonna let Injun lips touch where my lips touched."

With surprising quickness Adams grabbed the barrel of the gun, ripped it from Grafton's grasp and swung it roundhouse style as hard as he could. The stock smashed against Grafton's temple. *Thunk*. Rifle met flesh. Grafton dropped.

Adams looked around. No witnesses. Adams considered his situation. First, this horrible excuse for a human had been laying in wait for Henry Stark, the one and only law enforcement officer who had always treated him fairly – as a person, not as an Indian. Second, Grafton might wake up, tell a tale about the "Crazy Injun" assaulting him in the parking lot and he, Adams, would be the one to go to jail. Adams always carried a long-bladed, razor sharp, filet knife in a sheath inside his boot. He extracted the knife and slid the blade into Grafton's heart. He wiped the blood on the knife on Grafton's shirt and pushed the corpse under the pick-up parked next to the sheriff's car.

He knew about fingerprints. "White man evidence." He picked up the rifle, not knowing whether he would keep it or send it to the bottom of his lake. He was leaning toward keeping it. Then he drove home – not feeling the least bit remorseful about his unpleasant encounter with the late Mr. Glenn Grafton.

CHAPTER FIFTY

The commander on the U.S. Coast Guard patrol boat called Harry Norton on the ship to shore. "Bogey spotted along the north jetty."

The skipper relayed the information to the sheriff.

"Tell him to keep his boat between Abernathy and the open sea," Henry ordered. "Tell him we will pursue."

Skipper Harry Norton stood on the bridge, calling the play-by-play. "He's still behind that ship, Henry, he could be thinking of sucking up to the hull and piggy-backing his way over the bar."

"No," Henry said, "He'd get swamped and he knows it. He'll make a run up river."

They waited.

"Sum-bitch!" The skipper shouted as Abernathy's boat shot past the aft section of the freighter and headed up river.

"Follow him!" Henry Stark said. Norton shoved his throttle forward and aimed his boat toward the mouth of Oregon's third largest river.

James McDonnell held tight to the safety rail and watched the rooster tail behind the fleeing Abernathy.

"What are we going to do now?" he shouted over the engine noise.

"Catch the son of a bitch," the sheriff shouted. He turned to the skipper. "You have a rifle?"

"You know damn well I do. Closet in the galley!"

Henry looked into the James' eyes until James flinched. "You want the honors?"

"I've never killed a man."

"You will soon enough, whether you pull the trigger or not."

James nodded, accepting responsibility.

Henry Stark went below into the cabin and found the rifle, a 270 Winchester, lever action. He checked it: Four rounds in the magazine, none in the chamber. He flicked the lever, advancing a round into firing position. The boat was bouncing over the water at full speed. The longboat was almost as fast as the cabin cruiser. Not quite, but almost.

The river narrowed. They passed the docks and log booms in Reedsport. The cruiser slowly closed the distance. Five-hundred yards. Henry moved to the front rail of the bow and positioned himself. He looked over the gun sight. The two boats were bouncing – bouncing – it was too "bouncy" and too far to take a shot.

Four hundred yards, 300-hundred – the sheriff felt the rhythm of the boat, he timed the up-and-down motion caused by the up-down, up-down motion ... *100 yards*.

Was he really going to do this? He'd shot a Japanese officer armed only with a sword. He'd seen marines, hands tied, murdered by such a sword. End it right here and now? James was right – if the bastard got off free and clear, or was only sentenced to a few years, he'd never forgive himself. *Fifty yards.*

John Abernathy knew the cruiser was closing in on him. When he looked back he could see the man with a rifle. He turned his head from side to side, searching. He saw something on the east bank – a decaying dock with steps leading up the bank – he knew his boat couldn't out-run the cruiser. Decision time: once on dry land he should be able to outrun his pursuers.

Abernathy slammed his boat into the shoreline and scrambled up the concrete steps. The first bullet slammed into the bank inches from John's head.

The sound of a nearby rifle shot awakened The Ambassador. He'd taken a folding chair from the house down to his platform overlooking the river. He'd strung his crossbow and inserted an arrow before dozing off.

John scrambled up the stairs. A second bullet whizzed just under his right arm.

Sheriff Stark cursed the rifle's sight. Two rounds left.

John thought, maybe he should just stop and raise his hands, the man shooting must be a cop, what the hell, maybe it was time to give up, there weren't any witnesses to his crimes, *no live enemies.* What could they prove? The girl couldn't have seen his face. Dodd would tell no tales, the faggot and his feisty almost-cousin in the car could say he kidnapped them, but he could say it was a prank that went too far. He could say he knew Jack Portman from football and didn't know why Jack rammed their car. They were just having fun – maybe Jack was drinking – or better yet, he'd say he found out the Coast Guard and police were after him and panicked – who wouldn't? He hadn't done anything wrong. Yeah, sure, that would be his story. He was scared and acted a little crazy . . .

The voice confirmed his decision.

He reached the top of the steps and raised his hands high in the air. He turned slowly, now facing the river, and yelled at the top of his lungs, "I surrender!"

James McDonnell was standing behind Henry. He shouted, "Shoot, dammit, shoot!"

The sheriff believed he had no choice. He lowered the rifle.

At that moment John felt something slam into his back. He looked down and was surprised to see an arrowhead peeking out of his chest. It didn't hurt but the song-like sounds of the wind and the river intensified – then he saw a movie-like scene of Debbie, the girl who looked like his pretty, almost-cousin in Lakeside. Her image fluttered through his mind. She was pouring two cups of coffee and inviting him to sit next to her on a sofa in a lake house. He would be gentle with her.

He sank to his knees and then tumbled head first down the concrete steps, landing in a heap in his stolen boat.

Through all this, life along the river continued, disengaged from and disinterested in the drama playing out along the shoreline. Several fishermen in skiffs passed in the distance and a flock of canvasback ducks flew overhead. As far as the other boaters were concerned, some damn fool was too cheap to buy charts and had ran aground. He was lucky a cruiser/charter boat had stopped to offer help. Neither the fishermen nor the ducks changed course to bear witness to the death of John "Nasty" Abernathy.

Henry, rifle in hand, slid over the rail of the cruiser and into the longboat. He took out his handkerchief and wiped Harry Norton's "seal gun" clean of fingerprints. He then placed the rifle in Abernathy's big hands. Next, he freed the blades of the outboard motor from the shoreline muck and locked the engine into its uppermost position, rendering the boat easy to tow.

Calmly, he called to his comrades on the cruiser, "One of you throw me the tow rope."

Harry, the skipper obliged. Henry attached the rope to the stolen boat's bow.

As he climbed back into the cruiser, Henry pointed his finger at the skipper and declared, "You never owned that rifle, Harry."

Harry nodded.

"What the hell happened?" McDonnell asked, staring at the arrow poking out of Abernathy's chest.

"This is The Ambassador's place. Charley, our postmaster, gave me a heads up. Warned me that he received a crossbow in the mail the other day."

Henry took a deep breath and made eye contact with the two members of his posse. "I'm calling it self- defense. Let's make a hero out of him."

"I like it!" James said. "An elegant solution."

"So, James," the sheriff stared into the eyes of the influential lawyer, "Think you can make that judge in Roseburg smooth this whole ugly business over in a tidy way?"

"Henry, my friend, you can count on it."

"Here's our story, then," Henry said. "The suspect fired at us, ran his boat ashore and fired at an innocent citizen whom, thanks to the grace of God, was target shooting on his own property with a crossbow. Self-defense, three witnesses."

"I'll go up and handle The Ambassador," James announced. "He owns a pick-up. We'll drive back to town. Where do you want to meet up?"

"Public pier in Reedsport," Henry replied. "We'll radio the state cops on our way back."

James raised his head and looked up to the spot where Abernathy had raised his hands to surrender. He saw a gaunt figure holding an arrow-less crossbow.

James winked at Henry and couldn't resist saying, "This just might be his ticket into The Lost Tribe."

EPILOGUE

Two weeks later, The Ambassador stood at the end of the bar in The Dock and addressed a packed house. Greta was on her honeymoon so there was no one to gag him. Adams Armstrong was there but said nothing. He enjoyed his friend's speeches.

"As a newly accepted member of The Lost Tribe, I can officially announce that the evil giant, John 'Nasty' Abernathy, is no longer a threat to your wives, daughters and nieces."

The Ambassador held his glass high. "He sealed his fate when he steered his stolen boat out of Winchester Bay and into the sacred waters of the Umpqua.

"Abernathy violated the sanctity of the land of our great green river. The chiefs had no choice but to take matters into their own hands. They ordered me to execute him."

Adams Armstrong smiled. *After all was said and done, perhaps it wasn't such a bad time to be an Indian.*

Swede stood and shouted, "Three cheers for The Ambassador and the Lost Tribe!"

The crowd responded – *Hip, hip hooray! – Hip, hip hooray! – Hip, hip hooray!*

###

CPSIA information can be obtained
at www.ICGtesting.com
Printed in the USA
JSHW022048160919
1423JS00004B/3

9 781950 433155